Cadogan's Gamble

Luminari Cluster Series Book One

By: Ron Francis

Copyright © 2015 by Ron Francis
All rights reserved.
ISBN-13: 978-0996185127
ISBN-10: 0996185127

Contact

www.ronfrancisauthor.com

ronfrancis32@hotmail.com

Special Thanks

I would like to thank Laurie Incontrera and Jerry Francis for their great suggestions and continuous support. I would also like to thank Deanne Charlton for her editing help. Finally, I would like to thank God for giving me creativity and the desire to write my stories down.

Chapter one

[Bracketed] dialogue indicates an alien language.

Chase watched from the galley as a beautiful woman stepped out into the corridor. The light from his quarters reflected off her long dark hair. Her sun-kissed, pink skin all but glowed in the light, and the silhouette of her perfect body floated toward him.

He had met her at the spaceport pub last night and her name eluded him. He looked across the common room and in a whisper, asked, "What's her name again, Fixer?"

The mechanic shook his head in his usual childlike manner and replied, "Chase, her name is Selene. You always forget their names, and you know I don't like when you invite new friends to stay overnight."

"I'm sorry, buddy. I'll try to do better." He knew his actions ruined Fixer's routines and a part of him was sorry about that, but he had his own routines and the ship did not belong to Fixer.

"Remember next time, Chase. You need to do better!" Fixer repeated with a frown. Selene arrived at the galley and Chase handed her a cup of jav. She greeted him with a brief but intimate kiss. After a long moment, he pulled away.

"Sorry you have to leave so early, Selene, but I've got to run down a bounty out past Nibiru. I won't be back on Cibola for a couple weeks."

"I'll be here," she replied and kissed him again. She put her cup down and strolled toward the boarding ramp, her hips swaying, almost enticing him to change his mind. He watched her with a smile as she walked off the ship.

Kat sauntered toward the ship at the same time Selene was leaving. She greeted the woman with a frown, and aimed a disapproving shake of her head in Chase's direction. He could sense her disappointment while his eyes followed her up the boarding ramp.

She stopped at the ramp and asked, "And who was that, now?"

"Someone I met last night. No big deal."

"No big deal? Chase, you have to stop. This woman-in-every-port, routine is getting old. It's not fair to Fixer. You know he doesn't like going off routine."

"He should be used to this routine by now, Kat," he said. Then he winked at her.

"Real mature, Chase. You need to grow up!"

"I need to grow up? What about you? Where were you last night? Aren't those the same clothes you were wearing yesterday? You don't see me getting upset about it. Looks like I'm not the only one who needs to grow up." His voice had started to rise. It was too early for this type of argument.

"Just stop it, Chase, or pretty soon you'll have no crew left at all."

He was about to remind her that he would prefer it that way when Fixer saw her and lit up with excitement. "Hi, Katalla Swift!" he exclaimed.

"Hi, Fixer Faraday," she replied with a chuckle and gave him a hug. "You know you can call me Kat like everyone else does. Right, Fixer?"

"I know, Katalla," he replied. Then he started to complain about Chase. "Chase brought another new friend by, even though he said he'd try not to. Her name is Selene. Chase didn't even remember."

"Chase is an idiot, Fixer. Don't worry about him." She ruffled his hair and he smiled.

"Incidentally, Fixer, let's mark this side of the spaceport as burned for the next few months. I'd hate to run into what's-her-name, unexpectedly," Chase called into their conversation while he read over the report on his next bounty.

"Her name is Selene!" Kat yelled.

"I don't like any of your temporary friends, Chase. I only like Katalla living here. You need to stop—"

"Enough already!" Chase yelled. "Last time I checked, this was still my ship." He stood up and walked out of the landing bay. He knew it was going to be one of those days. Kat and Fixer were already ganging up on him, and they were both in a mood. *All of this could have been avoided if Kat hadn't cheated on me,* he thought, but stopped himself from saying it. Instead, he just left the room. An hour later, they were hurtling through hyperspace on their way to a fruitless hunt. When they returned to Cibola, Chase left the ship for a more personal task.

+++++

A light breeze picked up as the second sun began its slow rise over the control tower. The first sun had set several hours earlier and would not rise for several more. This section of the spaceport was all but empty at this hour save one pub that never closed. After all, it was always happy hour somewhere in the cluster.

This is the best shot I'm gonna get, Chase thought while he kept himself hidden in the shade of the control tower. It was now or never. He wiped a bead of sweat from his brow and peered in every direction. He had already disabled the security cams, so his actions would not be caught on vid. Casting a cautious glance, he hurried toward the ship. He reached the landing bay and looked over his shoulder one last time to make sure the coast was clear. Kneeling in front of the ship's hatch, he pulled the tool he would use to override the ship's entry code from his jacket.

He plugged his code breaker into the ship's hatch control panel. The hull felt cool when he leaned against it to wait for the cipher to be decrypted. The sky was overcast, but no rain was in sight. The first three digits beeped and he smiled. *I can't wait to see his smug face when he realizes it's gone,* he thought. The fourth digit beeped and he glanced around again. He was almost in and did not want the ship's owner sneaking up on him. The fifth digit beeped and he readied himself, knowing there was only one left before he would be in. Then the unthinkable occurred. He heard someone yelling his name. In haste, he backed away from the ship and started toward the pub.

"Chase. Hey, Chase. Where are you?"

He bit back a curse. It was Kat. *What is she doing here? Does she have any idea how long I've been planning this heist?* Returning his tool to his pocket, he ambled toward the pub in a nonchalant manner.

She rounded the corner and marched into the quiet stretch of the spaceport. She noticed the lights blinking on the hatch of the ship Chase had been tinkering with and looked at him. His face betrayed no emotion, but she knew something was up. "What are you doing here? The *Longshot* is docked on the other side of the spaceport."

"Nothing, let's just go."

"Why? What's the rush?"

"Kat, we can't be seen over here. Let's go," he repeated with a hint of urgency in his voice. He grabbed her arm and started pulling her away from the ship.

"Were you trying to steal that ship?" she asked with a frown.

"No, but we gotta go."

"Were you breaking in?"

"No!"

"Yes you were!" she replied. She fixed him with her harshest glare and tore her arm free of his grip. "What are you thinking, Chase?" She hit him opened palmed in the chest and said in a sharp whisper. "You run down people who do that sort of thing. You could lose your license, Chase. You could go to jail. Then what happens to Fixer? What's so important about that ship that you would risk—?"

"Stop, Kat!" he said in a rising voice. "Just stop! If you don't want to leave, fine, but I'm getting out of here." He turned away from her and picked up his pace. He rounded the corner and stepped into the pub. A moment later, Kat followed him in.

"What was that all about?" she asked. The harsh tone had abated, but he could see the curiosity in her eyes.

"It was nothing, trust me." He was in a foul mood now and Kat's nagging was the last thing he wanted to listen to.

"Then tell me what it was."

"Nothing! What did you need me for?"

She looked him up and down. He knew she was skeptical, but at the moment, he found it hard to care. She had ruined his opportunity. After a long moment of awkward silence she said, "Okay, I'll let it go for now. I came here to tell you that we have a lead on Jay Lee Hazard." She held her head just a little higher and smiled. She had his full attention. "Not only that, but it seems to be fairly credible. I think we've got him this time."

Chase put his failed heist on the backburner and replied, "That bounty can keep us going for almost a year. Let's go," he said, his demeanor changing from defensive to all business.

"Soon you're going to tell me what that was all about," she said while she pointed in the direction of the ship. Chase knew that letting things go was difficult for Kat, and he would eventually have to come clean. She continued, "But for now, let's get back to the *Longshot* and go get Hazard."

When she finished speaking, Chase took a step further into the dim light of the pub. He waited there until several men passed by the window, ambling toward the ship he had targeted. "I'm never gonna get another chance this good," he mumbled to himself as he left the pub with Kat.

"What was that?" she asked.

"Nothing. Let's go." He walked back toward the ship with his bounty hunting partner. It was now closer to an acceptable time for people to be up and out. They continued at a quick pace toward the more populated area of the port, but Chase's mind kept wandering back to his failed break in. Several men turned their heads when he and Kat walked by, but Chase knew who they were looking at. It bothered him a little, but there was nothing he could do about it; Kat was a very attractive woman. The blue highlights of her dark hair shone bright in the morning sun, and it gave her black-clad, dancer's body an almost shadowy appearance. Her light pink Elysian skin gave her the look of someone who loved spending time in the sun. He had to admit, she certainly was easy on the eyes, and for a brief moment, he thought it would be nice if they were back together.

They walked in silence back to the ship, not willing to talk about the bounty for fear of being overheard.

When they were in sight of the ship, Chase noticed Kat's lips curl upwards. His ship was as much home to her as it was for him and Fixer. The *Longshot* looked like a typical ten-year-old pleasure yacht, complete with sleek lines and flowing curves. Powerful thrusters in circular casings dominated aft. She was the type of ship a man of limited means might buy during a midlife crisis. A little old, sort of flashy, but not top of the line by any means. At least that is what it was meant to look like, until you factored in the upgrades the untrained eye would never see. In fact, the entire hull had been replaced with a military grade pentallium steel alloy. The engines, shields, everything had been upgraded. He was unsure if there was a factory-made system left on the ship.

The weapons system was his pride and joy. It had been slated for one of the fleet's newest gunships, but someone owed him a favor and it wound up in his ship. Fixer had cleared out most of the comfort upgrades a pleasure yacht might have to make room for the weapons, and it all came together to Chase's specifications. A mark would never know what they were up against.

Everything about the ship was deceptive, and that was exactly how Chase had wanted it. He wanted to be underestimated. The inside of the ship contained a small bridge that opened up into the common area and galley. A short corridor was flanked by five crew quarters and a weapons locker. Stairs from the common room led to the lower deck, which contained the landing bay, crowded with a speeder, two speeder bikes, and a holding cell made with a pentallium alloy to confine prisoners. The engine room was located further aft, and the hold, which served as the only significant storage space on the ship, was located toward the bow of the vessel. In all, she was thirty-two meters long, fourteen meters wide, and nine meters high.

As soon as they boarded the *Longshot*, Kat began to speak. "Hazard was spotted talking to a fence named Goser in the entertainment district of Agartha on Norumbega. I've already had

Fixer prep the ship for departure." She realized the breach of protocol and brought her hand up to cover her mouth. Then she harnessed her best innocent look and added, "I hope you don't mind."

"Would it stop you from doing it next time if I did?"

"Probably not." She fixed him with an impish smile and he decided it was not worth pursuing.

"I guess I don't mind, then." He knew she had Fixer wrapped around her little finger and that he would always do what she wanted regardless of any orders he had received. He was as loyal a crewman as anyone could ask for, until it came to Kat.

They walked past the galley and onto the bridge where Fixer was at his seat working on an engine part Chase failed to recognize. "Do you think he'll still be there when we get there?" Kat asked while she hailed the spaceport control center for clearance to leave.

"Probably not, but the clown he was talking to will be." Chase took his seat in the captain's chair and waited for the spaceport to reply to Kat's hail.

"I don't want to hunt a clown, Chase. You know I don't like clowns," Fixer said without looking up from his project.

"It's not a literal clown, Fixer," Kat replied. "It's a regular guy. Chase just used a figure of speech."

"Chase should say what he means, then," Fixer said with a frown and picked up a wrench from his well-organized toolkit.

"I don't think you really want me to do that, Fixer."

"Chase, be nice," Kat said in warning as she received confirmation from the control center. "We're clear to leave."

Chase hit the vertical thrusters and the *Longshot* began a slow rise out of the spaceport docking bay. An almost imperceptible rattle worked its way through the ship while it continued to ascend. He could see the sprawling Commonwealth capital unfolding before him. He watched the towering buildings and colorful spires, illuminated by the morning sun, grow smaller until he could no longer see them. Then he switched to the ship's main thrusters and took them into space. He said a silent goodbye to Quiveria. It was easily his favorite city on Cibola. He loved the idea of getting lost in the crowds of people the city always produced.

Once the *Longshot* entered hyperspace, Fixer stood up from his seat and put the engine part he was tinkering with on the floor. "I'm tired, Chase. I need to go to sleep now."

"Okay," he replied. Then he looked at the part on Fixer's chair and asked, "Hey Fixer, do we need that part in the engine?"

Fixer looked back and forth between the part and Chase and said, "No, it's not part of the engine. We will need it, but not yet. No, no. We don't need it yet." Then he turned toward Kat and said, "Goodnight, Katalla Swift."

"Good night, Fixer," she replied. Then Fixer whirled and left the bridge.

"What do you mean, "Yet?"" Chase called after him, but received no answer.

"Have you ever considered taking him to see someone? Maybe a doctor can fix whatever is wrong with him?" Kat asked.

"There's nothing wrong with him," Chase snapped. "Nothing they can fix anyway," he added a little softer. "And he's petrified of doctors."

She took no offense at his tone. She loved that he was so protective of Fixer. "What do you mean, "Nothing they can fix?""

"Fixer has a condition called Taklinsen's disorder. It's one hundred percent curable if the doctors catch it before a person turns four or five," Chase replied. He looked down the corridor Fixer had gone and balled his hands into fists before continuing. "Fixer's parents were either dead by then or just didn't care to take him for a checkup when he was that age. The older you get, the less chance there is to cure it, and by the time you reach adulthood there is no cure."

"That's terrible, Chase. How do you know all this? Fixer will never talk about it with me."

"Fixer told me." Chase saw her dubious look and added, "Then I researched it and brought a doctor on the ship. Fixer went a little bit crazy, but the doctor gave me the same diagnosis and told me some of the things I could do to help him."

"That was good of you to try." She placed her hand on his arm and said, "You never did tell me how you met him."

Chase leaned back in his seat and busied himself with diagnostic readings. "Does it matter?"

"It does to me. Come on, Chase. I know you don't like to talk about things in your past, but Fixer will never give me a straight answer when I ask him."

Chase sighed. He hated talking about this. "I don't know if he can, Kat. I found him just outside the spaceport on Kephri. Some guys were beating him up pretty good and he couldn't defend himself. They tried to rob him, but all he had was a wrench in his pocket. I broke it up and right away I could tell he was a little bit different, almost childlike. I don't know how, but I got him back to the ship, patched him up, and offered him a job cleaning up."

"Cleaning?" Kat asked with a raised eyebrow, looking around the bridge.

"I know. He's even worse at cleaning than I am, but little by little he opened up and I found out his story. At least some of it." He checked the readings again and stood up. "I need something to drink, do you want anything?"

"No I'm fine."

Chase walked to the galley and poured himself a glass of water, then made his way back to the bridge. "So, what's his story?" Kat asked before Chase sat down.

"He used to work for another bounty hunter named Mags. Mags Bishop. Apparently, Mags treated him pretty bad. Fixer completely overhauled the guy's engine, and he never even paid Fixer for his work. Even worse, he kicked Fixer off the ship because he couldn't be bothered to try and understand him. All Fixer had left was the wrench in his pocket."

"That's awful. I think I hate this man already."

"Me, too. He also kept all of Fixer's stuff. Fixer doesn't care about any of it except an antique screwdriver that he says his father gave him along with his wrench. He's always going on about his missing screwdriver."

"I've heard him mention that before," she said. "So, how did you find out he was a mechanic?"

"He fixed a broken hatch while I was out one day. Then I let him start fixing other small things around the ship and he kept going from there. Pretty soon I realized he was a mechanical genius. He was never happier than when he was tinkering, so I bought him his own tools, but he still wants that screwdriver."

"Why don't you get it back from Mags?"

"You don't think I've tried? I even offered to buy it along with Fixer's stuff, but Mags just laughed at me and slammed the hatch in my face. There's really no reason for it. He's just being a jerk."

"So, that's it? You just gave up? Fixer's our friend, Chase. We have to get his stuff back."

A flash of anger crossed Chase's face and he said, "That's what I was trying to do this morning, but you ruined it."

Kat's hand went to her mouth while a sharp inhale escaped her lips. "That's the ship you were messing with. Oh no! And then I was hassling you about it. I was so mad at you. I thought the worst and you let me." She slapped his arm and said, "You should have told me!"

"Well, now you know. I just hope I get another shot at it." Just then the sensor beeped to alert them they would be exiting hyperspace in two minutes.

"Should I wake Fixer?" Kat asked.

"Nah, he'll be fine. He probably won't wake up until after we've talked to the fence. I'm sure he still thinks the guy is a real clown. Anyway, he'll be hungry enough to go out to dinner by the time we're finished."

"Yes, his never ending search for the best jujani noodles."

"He can't get enough of the stuff." Chase's hands played over the ship's controls, the landing gear extended, and he brought the *Longshot* in for a smooth landing.

14

She paused as if she were remembering something important and said, "By the way, your mother sent you a transmission while you were out. Do you want to answer it?"

"Nah, I'll get back to her later."

+++++

Chase and Kat exited the ship into the chaos of Norumbega's busiest spaceport. The smell of lubricants and engine coolants hung heavy in the air. Kat thought the white pavement was a poor choice as she scanned the area. She imagined that this spaceport had once been pristine, gleaming white in the light of Norumbega's sun, but now, the color seemed like a mistake.

She nodded to a party of thin, furred Taquians as they walked by. The entire native population of the Luminari Cluster was human, but big cities and spaceports usually had dozens of different alien races present.

"Tons of aliens in the spaceports," Chase said without preamble. "You never see them in the small cities and towns."

They continued walking past a berth holding three boxy, mid-sized freighters. One of them was badly in need of an engine overhaul by the smell of it. "And why do we care?" Kat puzzled a look and asked while they walked.

"I was just making conversation. You're always bugging me to talk more when we're on a job."

"And this is what you choose to discuss?"

Chase began walking a little faster. "This is why I never talk to you."

"Wait, are you mad about this?" she asked while trying to hide her smile.

"No, just don't hassle me next time we're on a job and I've got nothing to say."

A high pitched whine filled the air when the mechanics working on the freighter tried to start her up. Kat covered her ears until the noise abated.

Chase turned down an alley and Kat had to jog to keep up with him. She knew he was annoyed with her and found it amusing. She took in her surroundings. To her left were three abandoned buildings. Their shells still stood, but windows and doors had been blown out and the shells were scorched. *I wonder why these buildings were never replaced. Surely there's a demand for a location this close to the spaceport.* To her right, a large metal sign that used to hang over the door of a tavern now swung freely. A couple of freighter pilots dodged it as they entered the pub. The building had been painted blue at one time, but was now an ugly mixture of rust and steel patches.

Chase looked at her and said, "Let's get this over with."

They turned into a cul-de-sac of six-and seven-story, steel buildings. Each building was a matted gray color with rust beginning to show around most of the doors and windows. Colorful signs hung out in front of each building emblazoned with slogans that read; "If You Want It, We've Got It!" and; "Anything You've Ever Wanted, For The Right Price!"

One of the buildings had a local street tough standing outside and they approached him. He eyed Kat up and down and glanced at Chase before returning his attention to the lovely woman before him.

"You wouldn't happen to know a man named Goser, would you?" she asked with a purr in her voice.

"Maybe. What's it worth to you?" He reached out to grab her hand and her reflexes took over. She twisted his arm behind his back.

"It's worth not breaking your arm," she said while Chase leaned against the wall and watched with an amused smile, his left hand hovering near his sidearm.

"Get off of me, you wh—"

"Now, now. You don't want to finish that sentence. It might make her mad," Chase said.

The man swung his free arm, just missing Kat's head. While she ducked, she put one leg in front of him and pushed forward. The man fell heavy on the dirty white pavement, and she landed on top of him with her knee in his back. She pulled up on his arm until he cried out in pain.

"Okay, okay. Across the street. The building with the green lettering."

"Now that wasn't so hard, was it?" She stood up careful to stay out of reach in case he lashed out. As of now, the only thing that had been hurt was his pride, but if he tried anything, she would make sure a lot more than that was hurting. They started to walk toward the building and stopped when they heard a growl from behind them. They turned to see the humiliated thug charging. Chase's draw was like lightning and before the man took another step, Chase shot him. The street tough convulsed and flopped to the ground with a thud, where he remained, stunned, in the middle of the street.

Chase holstered his weapon, looked at the disappointment on Kat's face, and said, "We don't have time for you to beat him up some more." Then he continued toward Goser's building. When they reached the building, he looked to Kat and said, "You go in first. Once you've got Goser's full attention I'll sneak in and we can find out where Hazard is."

"Sounds like a plan," she replied. She opened the door to the second hand store and almost laughed. She looked at the mountains of junk that lay before her. It was a challenge to her tracking skills just to navigate her way to the sales counter. *It shouldn't be very hard for Chase to sneak in*, she mused. *Though he may never find his way to the counter*. When she finally reached the desk, a beady eyed little man fixed her with a smile, straightened his sweat-stained shirt, and asked, "May I help you, gorgeous?"

"Yes, I'm looking for a man named Goser. It's very important that I speak with him," she replied, trying her best to sound innocent while twirling her hair around one of her fingers.

"What's this in reference to?"

"I'm sorry, I'm afraid that I can only speak to Goser." She set her mouth in a sultry pout, lowered her head, and peered at him out of the upper right corner of her light blue eyes.

"Well you're in luck," he replied, wiping saliva from the corner of his lip and putting on his best salesman smile. He bowed a formal bow, holding one arm to his chest and leaving one arm out. He looked up at her and said, "I'm Goser."

"Well, Goser," she said in a sugary voice. "I could use some information." She put her hand on the counter grazing his hand along the way. He looked her up and down while Chase was making his way through the heaps of "merchandise" to get into position behind him.

"What sort of information, gorgeous? I might even give it to you for free." He put his hand on top of hers and attempted to massage it. She was sure her revulsion would be mistaken for blushing as his fingers continued to fumble around her hand.

She saw Chase reach his position and said in the same sweet voice, "Would you happen to know where I can find Jay Lee Hazard?"

Goser's beady eyes widened just a bit, and his hand began a slow withdrawal across the counter. His other hand appeared above the counter with a blaster in it. "Who are you and how did you know to ask me about that name?" All pretense of flirting was gone, replaced by the now deadly serious little man.

"Whoa, there's no need for that," she said, her eyes growing wide and raising her hands while taking a step back. "I'm Jay Lee's girl friend, or at least one of them. He told me if I ever needed to get in touch with him to come here. He said you'd help me," she said, her voice quivering with just a touch of trepidation.

"Let's say I believe you," Goser replied while continuing to train his weapon on her. "What could possibly be so important that a woman like you would venture into this kind of neighborhood on the off chance that Hazard was here?"

"I found out that Chase Cadogan is after him, and I couldn't bear the thought of that vile man catching up to my Jay Lee."

"Cadogan is always after him," he replied with a sneer, seeing through her charade. "Now what are you really doing here?"

18

"Distracting you," Chase replied as he stuck his blaster into Goser's gut. Kat grabbed the blaster being pointed at her before her mark could even flinch and pointed his own weapon back at him. "Vile man? Really?" Chase asked. He noticed a smile play across Kat's face before he turned his attention back to Goser. "Now, where's Hazard?" Chase asked in a harsh voice.

"You're gonna be sorry you came here," Goser replied.

Chase hit him in the stomach, taking the wind from him. Goser fell to the floor and curled up in the fetal position. "I'm already sorry I came here. Now, where's Hazard?" Chase repeated, his volume rising.

Goser worked his way back up to a standing position, holding his stomach and pushing an unseen button while he stood. He looked at Chase and sneered, "You'll never find him, but when you least expect it, he'll find you."

"Ooh, guess what, Chase?" Kat said while she watched text scroll across her wrist unit.

"What, Kat?"

"Commonwealth Cluster Patrol has a bounty out on this guy and it's a pretty good one."

Goser's eyes grew wide and Chase smiled. "Really? How good?"

"Enough to keep us chasing Hazard for a long time."

"No, no, no, no, no, wait, wait, wait! I'm sure we can come to an arrangement," Goser stuttered.

"Yes we can," Chase agreed. "You tell me where Hazard is and you don't go to jail. This offer expires in thirty seconds." Chase exaggerated looking at his watch, almost missing Goser's mouth curl up into a brief smile. "Kat, he's got people here, let's go." Before he could stun Goser, a beam of pure light missed his head, hitting a pile of junk to his left. The blast scorched the metal, sending several smaller pieces clattering across the floor. He lost hold of his prey and Goser scurried away, knocking another pile over behind him. While the metallic ringing of falling debris was still in the air, Chase dove for cover and returned fire. Hard light from another direction burned into more of Goser's junk, and Kat hurdled the counter to return fire.

Chase could see Goser's store security cams and pointed them out to Kat. She looked at them while he fired again. She saw that Goser had three men and one of them had given him another blaster.

"You're not getting out of here alive, Cadogan," Goser shouted over the blasterfire. Kat motioned to Chase that one of the men was on the staircase behind him to his left. Chase rolled out of his cover and fired three shots in quick succession. One of his blaster bolts hit the thug square in the chest and knocked him up a couple steps before his body dropped and slid down the stairs. Another shot rang out and hit a pile of metal objects next to Chase's hand. Hot metal leapt, out burning his hand, causing him to drop one of his blasters. Chase stifled a curse and shook out his hand.

"They can see us on the monitors," Goser yelled. "Take them out." Kat dove behind a column as blasterfire erupted around the monitors. The first shot missed, the second shot hit one of the monitors, and the third shot hit the cash box. The box exploded and rained money down on Chase and Kat. Chase rolled out of his cover, pocketing several fifty-heskar chips and fired on the monitor assailant with his remaining blaster. His second shot brought the man down.

Kat could see the third thug getting into position behind Chase. She ran out of her cover and knocked a large pile of metal merchandise onto the man, then stunned him while he tried to free himself. "Goser's the only one left. He's going to be looking to get out of here," she said while she tried to wipe the grease from the metal pile off of her hand and arm. "I think I ruined this top."

"Don't worry, just pick a few heskars up off the floor to cover it." Chase replied with a laugh while he grabbed another pile of chips and put them in his coat pocket.

That's not a bad idea, she thought. *Only Chase would think to pick money up off the floor during a gun fight.* "Do you have eyes on Goser, Chase?"

"No, but I can hear his little legs moving." He picked up a chrome pipe with a release valve on the end of it and stood at the end of one of the rows of junk. He caught sight of Kat and motioned her quiet. A moment later, he heard the footsteps getting closer; then he stepped out and swung. Goser had been running and the force of the blow took him off his feet and knocked him out. His body landed in a heap, knocking over another pile of scrap. More metallic clattering and ringing assaulted his ears.

Chase looked at the pipe in his hand and realized it was part of an FTL drive coolant system. "I think Fixer has been bugging me to get him one of these," he said. He tossed the pipe to his partner and said, "Hold this and watch him. I need to go find my other blaster." He jogged off to where he had dropped it. He searched for a minute and found it at the base of a pile of kitchen appliances. After he picked it up, he scooped up some more money and plodded through the debris toward his partner. *At least this wasn't a total loss,* he thought. By the time he reached Kat, Goser was stirring.

"Ready to talk?" Kat asked.

"Okay, fine. You got me. You ruined my store and blew up my money. Isn't that enough?" He rubbed at the knot on his head and winced. He was sweating heavily from the exertion of the fight.

"Relax, Goser. Your store doesn't look any different now than it did when we arrived," Kat said with a chuckle. Chase looked around and realized to his own amusement that she was right.

"First of all, it was your guys that ruined your store and blew up your money. We only asked you a question," Chase said as he trained his blaster at Goser's face. "Now, where's Hazard?"

Goser hung his head. He knew telling the truth was his only course of action. "He's hiding in the asteroids out past Nibiru. He's stocked up and can remain there for months before he needs to come back in." He wiped his brow with his dirty hands leaving a smudge mark across his forehead.

"There, that wasn't so hard, was it? Okay Kat, let's prep him for transport."

"What? Wait, you said you'd let me go. You can't do this!" He started to squirm, greasy sweat pouring off him.

"That offer expired several minutes ago, right about the time your friends started shooting at us." He checked to make sure his blaster was still set to stun and pointed.

"Wait, I'll pay you double the bounty. Please."

"With what? Your goons blew up your money, remember?" Kat said in a teasing voice before Chase stunned him.

"You carry the pipe and I'll carry him. If it's the right size, it'll make Fixer's day." He scooped the small man up off the floor, hefting him over his shoulder.

"Uggh, you're going to have to get your coat steamed after this," she said while looking at Goser with disdain. She led the way holding the pipe as a weapon in one hand and her blaster in the other. After walking a couple blocks she stepped out in front of a cab and trained her blaster on the driver.

When the speeder stopped, she asked in her sweetest voice, "Would you be so kind as to give us a ride to the local law center?"

She tossed him a fifty-heskar chip and he replied, "Yes, ma'am."

Chase was in a good mood after collecting the bounty on Goser. *This was a pretty profitable detour,* he thought. As always, he took out the expenses and transferred a third of the bounty into an account he had set up for Fixer. He also sent a third into Kat's account. On the way back to the ship, they stopped at a noodle bar and picked up three orders of jujani noodles. Then they hailed another cab and returned to the ship.

Chapter two

Sym checked her instrument's readings and the results felt like a punch in the gut. In all of her time in the Qantaran Science Core she had never seen readings like this. *This cannot be right.* She was going to have to run the tests again, for a fourth time. If these readings were accurate, the Qantarah would soon be going to war with humans of the Luminari Cluster. Her people would invade this cluster for a tenth of what her tests showed. She prepared the tests again, but she knew in her heart that the first three were right. This planet contained the richest supply of xallodium she had ever heard of, quite possibly the richest in history. *What can I do? If I bring this information back, the Qantarah will fall upon these people like water on rocks.* She held the key to the lives of every being on five inhabited planets and three inhabited moons in her hands. She continued through the familiar motions, having performed this test thousands of times on hundreds of worlds.

The only thing she could think of was the war that would ensue to feed the needs of the Qantaran war machine if she reported her findings. She could not even manage a guess as to how long this much xallodium would last her people. It was easily enough to quadruple the fleet they already had. *What can I do? I don't really have a choice. If I withhold this information and they send someone else, my life is forfeit and my people still go to war with the Commonwealth. If only there was another way. What if I told the Commonwealth about the xallodium? It's difficult to get into this cluster, and we have no information on the military strength of these people; maybe they can defend themselves.* As she thought through her choices, the test was finished, and once again confirmed what she was afraid of, what she already knew.

Sym was now faced with a moral dilemma. *I don't want to see war destroy this beautiful cluster. Maybe I should take some time to think about it. I'll begin translating their language and see if they are indeed worthy of mercy.* She knew that just delaying her return could be dangerous, but she could always talk her way around it if necessary. Still, she felt like she should at least give these people a chance even though she wondered why she cared. She stood, stretched her arms and legs, arched her back, and walked over to the small section of her ship that served as a galley. Opening the cabinet, she looked inside and weighed her options. She had mission meals she could cook in the ship or insta-meals that required only opening the package. She took out one of the mission meals and set it in the heater. Then, while she waited, she began intercepting stray signals and communications in order to feed the translation algorithm that would help her learn the Commonwealth's trade language. The timer beeped and her meal was ready. She sat down and began eating, wondering again whether caring what happened to these people would put her life in jeopardy.

+++++

Battle Conductor Garyn read all the reports the Scientific Corps sent. There were several new xallodium sources to be mined, which would continue the construction of the Qantaran war machine. Still, one report was missing, and he did not tolerate incomplete results. The scientist was overdue and he knew there could be any number of reasons why that might happen. The most probable scenario involved her capture, and he was not willing to leave one of his scientists in the hands of humans. *If she is not back soon, we will be going to look for her.* He was on his way to his weekly briefing with the leader of the Qantarah. He strode into the meeting chamber with his usual bluster, bowed his head and said, [Primus. May you live forever.]

Primus Garyn stood from his ornate chair and replied, [Thank you, brother. What news have you to report?]

The Battle Conductor took in the meeting chamber. No decor adorned the walls. There was one illumination sphere hovering over the round meeting table. All of the chairs around the table were bare, made from the black wood of the chalange trees, found in the Dark

Forest. The only object in the entire room that showed any Qantaran craftsmanship was the chair reserved for the Primus. That chair was covered with red sarasilk and trimmed in gold.

He looked at his brother, his leader, and replied, [All of the scientists we have sent out have returned, save one.] He sat at the table, thumbed through his reports, and continued, [Scientist Sym Triot has not yet returned from the Luminari Cluster. She should have returned almost three days ago. At the very least we should have been contacted.]

[Do you think the humans of the cluster have captured her?]

[I do not know, Primus, although she should not have been testing near any of their inhabited worlds.]

[Perhaps she is just late in returning. These things sometimes happen,] the Primus said, pushing away from the table to stand.

The Battle Conductor also stood and replied, [My gut tells me something has gone wrong with her search. Either she is captured, hurt, or defecting, because she knows better than to miss her scheduled check in.]

[Brother, do we not have anyone who speaks the Commonwealth trade language?] Primus Garyn asked while he started to walk.

His brother followed a respectful two paces behind him. The Primus enjoyed the thought of his brother at the head of his fleets. Like most Qantaran leaders, he put family in as many top ranking positions as he could, so that he could be sure he had people he trusted taking care of his business. He knew his brother was gifted in the art of war, so his selection had been a fairly easy one. Upon exiting the chamber, the illumination sphere dimmed and the sphere in the hall brightened. The hall sphere followed, floating almost a meter overhead, illuminating the area around them while they proceeded down the passageway. [Take a fleet to the cluster and alert them that one of our people has gone missing. They may know what has happened.]

[What if they demand to know the reason one of our scientists was in their cluster, Primus?]

25

[That is none of their concern, and if they object, destroy their capitol,] he replied with a dismissive wave of his hand.

[I do not know if we have anyone that speaks the language of the Luminari Cluster, I shall find out right away.]

[Good! Then go and position my ships just outside the cluster. Send word to the leaders of the cluster that we demand our scientist be returned and that we will consider it an act of war if she is not.]

[It will be as you say, Primus.] Battle Conductor Garyn made a more formal bow this time and took his leave. His brother continued into another chamber of the Royal Warren.

Battle Conductor Garyn let his excitement build. He was going to take a sizable fleet group to the cluster, and he hoped the humans would defy him. It had been too long since he had tasted glorious battle. At the very least, his departure might embolden his enemies into making mistakes in his absence.

+++++

Two days later, Qantaran forces dropped out of hyperspace just outside the Luminari Cluster. Twenty-eight battle-ready warships with their gunship escorts moved into an aggressive formation around the main entrance into the cluster. Qantaran warships were flat across the back of the ship with a round body, almost like a partially deflated ball sitting on the ground. Dozens of spikes protruded almost at random in every direction except the flat rear of the ship. Each warship had two more conventional-looking gunships as escorts. It was an impressive fleet, meant to intimidate.

Upon arrival, Battle Conductor Garyn immediately had his communications officer begin broadcasting a message in the Commonwealth trade language. "Attention, Luminari Cluster Vanguard. I am Battle Conductor Garyn. I am missing one of my scientists. She entered your cluster over two weeks ago. Return her to us immediately! Failure to do so will be considered an act of war!" Garyn set the massage to play continuously.

While he waited to see if the message was heard, he went over his intelligence on the cluster. There were only three known ways in and they were all heavily defended. He knew his message was received almost thirty minutes later when several new ships arrived at the entrance of the cluster. A moment later, his communications officer told him there was an incoming message.

"Attention Qantarah. This is Vanguard Tobias, leader of the Commonwealth people. We regret to inform you that we are unaware of any of your people currently inside the cluster. If you can let us know what she was doing here and where she was supposed to be, we will immediately send someone out to find her and help get her back to you." Tobias felt the sweat beginning to form on the back of his neck. He had no idea what the Qantarah were talking about, but he knew that no good could come from interaction with them. They were one of the main reasons the cluster held to a policy of general isolation. The Qantarah had easily defeated six or seven entire civilizations that he knew about, and it seemed their main purpose for existence was expansion.

[He lies!] Garyn blurted out. He looked to his Communications Officer and yelled, [You tell him that we expect immediate compliance, and failure to do so will result in their destruction.]

[Are we sure he is lying, most magnificent Battle Conductor?] the officer replied.

[Send the message and we will find out.]

The Communications Officer sent the message and awaited a reply.

When Vanguard Tobias heard their reply, it took all the discipline he could muster to keep his face from going white. He had no idea that there was a Qantaran scientist in the cluster, but he suspected she had run into some difficulty that prevented her from returning home. He looked around the bridge of *Commonwealth One* and noticed the fear on the faces of the crew. It had been over a century since the Commonwealth had seen war. He decided then that he had to be strong for them, regardless of the consequences.

The young communications officer looked at him and asked in a voice that shook, "How would you like to respond, Sir?"

Vanguard Tobias puffed his chest out and replied. "Put me directly through to the Qantarah, full vid communication." Drawing himself up to his full height, he looked right into the vid. He poured steel into his voice, hoping the aliens could tell the difference, and began his response. "As I have said, Garyn, we know nothing of the scientist you say is in our cluster. We will begin searching for her immediately, and we will return her to you as soon as we find her. If you try to enter our cluster and search for her yourselves, we will consider it an act of war and we will defend ourselves. Am I clear?"

Garyn smiled when he heard the reply of the human leader. *It would seem these people are not without a spine*, he thought. He had his communications officer translate and send his final communication. "Very well, human, you have two weeks to return our scientist to us, or you will be forced to defend yourselves." He broke communication without awaiting a reply. Then he looked to his communications officer and said, [Open a channel to Q'Tor!]

[Yes, Battle Conductor,] the officer replied.

A moment later, the Primus' face appeared on screen and he asked, [How did the humans respond?]

[They said they knew nothing of our scientist and we have given them two weeks to present her to us. At which point, if she is not back with us, we will be invading the cluster, Oh Mighty Primus. Please send more ships to us, in case the humans attempt to defy me.]

[You shall have another battle group in two days.]

The transmission ended and the Battle Conductor busied himself continuing to study as much as he could about the known strength of the Luminari Cluster's military. He would soon have another fourteen warships with their escorts giving him a total of one hundred twenty-six ships. He sighed in contentment. *I have conquered planets with less*, he thought.

+++++

Jay Lee Hazard sat alone in is quarters, his ship, the *Hazardous*, safely nestled on the underside of a large asteroid. His thoughts drifted to his current situation. He had been lucky to last on the run as long as he had, but he knew his luck would not last forever. *Where did I go wrong?* he wondered. The answer popped into his mind the instant he asked himself the question. *Cadogan!*

He had been one of the best bounty hunters in the history of the Commonwealth, renowned for his patient and mistake-free hunts, but that all started to unravel the day he met Chase Cadogan. He lost a large bounty to him and to this day, could not figure out how the boy had beaten him to it. Maybe it was beginners luck, but the new kid's swagger grated on him. He picked several fights with Chase, but the kid could hold his own and there was never a clear winner before it was broken up. He started to make mistakes, losing several more bounties to Cadogan, and his standard of living was put in jeopardy. It only went downhill from there.

He caught his wife in bed with another man, and when she announced she was leaving him because he could no longer support her he made the first careless mistake of his adult life. He killed his wife and her lover right there in the bed in a fit of rage, and in an instant went from being the hunter to being the hunted.

An alert broke into his musing and he checked it before stepping over to the communications array.

"Hazard, it's Captain Seraphaz," the voice said.

"What's up, Captain?" he asked while wiping grease off his fingers with a rag. He held a chrome tool in the other hand and Seraphaz knew he had caught Hazard in the middle of working on his ship.

"Cadogan is on his way. He got your location from Goser. If I were you I'd prepare my EM shield. Cadogan's last three space captures have been with an EM pulse."

"I'll have to put my hyper drive back together. I took her apart for some standard maintenance." He looked at his clock and asked, "How much time do you think I have?"

"Not long, six, maybe seven hours, tops."

"That should be enough time. I appreciate the heads up."

"No problem. Anything to protect an asset and keep Chase Cadogan from collecting a bounty. Now, I have a safe house ready for you on Lemuria. The only people who know about it are me and Black, so you should be fine there."

"I'll leave as soon as possible." Hazard smiled at the thought of Chase's failure, but wondered why the captain had it in for him. "Why do you hate Cadogan so much, Captain?"

"My reasons are my own. Leave the asteroid field as soon as possible."

"Copy that," Hazard replied and then the connection died. He spent the next several hours putting his engine back together. Halfway through his repairs, he fired up the EM shielding just in case the captain's estimates were off. He wiped salty sweat from his eyes with grease stained hands, but refused to slow down. He would have plenty of time to rest if he made it to Lemuria.

+++++

Four days after the events on Norumbega, the *Longshot* was closing in on its prey. Hiding behind a mid-sized asteroid with their bounty in sight, they waited in silence for the right moment. There was no need for the silence, it just felt appropriate. When the time came, Chase said, "Fire EM pulse now, Fixer." Fixer did as instructed and moments after the invisible disabling pulse was fired, the *Longshot* drifted out of hiding and moved in to apprehend its quarry.

Chase's face went dark when the *Hazardous* fired up its hyperspace drive and jumped away. His frustration was evident as he yelled, "Dasnit!" He tried to calm himself, but the calm refused to play along. He asked, "How did we lose him, Kat? That's half a million heskars gone, just like that." He snapped his fingers for emphasis.

"Fixer's EM pulse must have malfunctioned, Chase. Hazard shouldn't have been able to get his ship back online so quickly," she replied as she continued to check the readings at her console.

Fixer looked offended as he said, "My pulse worked as specified, Katalla Swift. His ship must have abilities we are unaware of."

"It's your job to be aware of those things, Fixer," she replied while she watched Chase stalk off the bridge. *He's had a rough go of it lately. Should I go to him?*

A warning klaxon took her mind off Chase for a moment. They were being alerted to the presence of another ship approaching their location. Before she could bring up the comms, Chase was back on the bridge.

"We're being hailed, Chase," she called out, straining to keep the anxiety out of her voice. *Who knows we're out here? What do they want? Are they friendly*? Questions filled her mind, but she knew better than to ask them. No one would know what was happening until Chase answered the hail and it would annoy him if she did ask.

"On screen, Kat," Chase replied, feigning a confidence he knew was wavering. He took his seat and pushed the worry out of his eyes. The odds of someone just happening upon them were slim, and he knew that could only mean one thing. Someone had tracked them.

"Chase Cadogan, you're a hard man to find," a good-natured voice called through the speakers, unaccompanied by a video feed.

"I wouldn't be a very good bounty hunter if I wasn't. Who am I speaking with?" Chase projected a no nonsense persona. He was not an easy man to intimidate and if whoever this was thought no image would faze him, they were wrong.

"Captain Bander of the Commonwealth Cluster Patrol ship, *Legendary*. We've been looking for you for several days. Never would have found you if we didn't receive a tip as to where Hazard was going to be. We knew you'd be on his tail. My apologies that you cannot see us, there is a high amount of EM disturbance in the area."

Chase cut the feed and looked over to Kat, worry evident in his eyes. "Why is the CCP looking for me? I haven't done anything illegal lately. Should we cut and run or should I hear them out?"

She was impressed that he asked. The reality was, the ship was his, as was the decision. "Fixer and I haven't done anything illegal either, maybe we should hear them out. We can always run later."

"Good call, Kat. Let's hear what they have to say. Run a check on Captain Bander, too. Let's make sure he's in the Commonwealth database." He turned his video feed back on and forced a smile. "What can I do for you Captain?"

"First, let me assure you that you are in no trouble. We have a situation we need taken care of, and the Vanguard asked for you by name."

"How does the leader of the Commonwealth know your name, Chase?" Kat asked before he could reply to the captain.

"Long story, I'll tell you later," he whispered.

"You better." Her wry smile told him she was not going to drop it.

"What sort of situation does the Vanguard need me to address, Captain?"

"I wasn't told. I just happen to have the ship with the best tracking package, so I drew the assignment. I'm to ask you to follow us to the Capital on Cibola."

"What happens if we don't wish to follow?" Chase asked as a precaution. If this ship really was sent by the Vanguard, it might not be a "follow or go to jail" request.

"Vanguard Tobias anticipated your question and he told me to tell you that if you did not come to Cibola that he would have to pardon Hazard and give the assignment to him. He assured me you would not say no."

Chase's forced smile broke into a legitimate grin. Most of the Commonwealth knew how much he hated Hazard. "He was right, Captain, would you like to put us in tow or do you trust us to arrive there with you?" This was another test question to see just how friendly this encounter was.

"No, you may fly free with us. If what I've heard about the *Longshot* is true, you could probably beat us there anyway. Still, it might be better if we show up together, so we can escort you to the capital with no fuss."

"Sounds good, Captain Bander. *Longshot* out." When the communication ended, Chase turned to see Kat and Fixer looking at him expectantly. He sighed and asked, "What?"

"You didn't think we'd forget to ask, did you? How exactly does the ruler of our people know the name of a two-bit bounty hunter like you?" Kat asked. Then she crossed her arms and leaned against the bulkhead.

"The real question is: how did Hazard get away." Chase sat in his seat with a look of contemplation on his face. "His ship might have EM shielding, but it's a huge power drain to leave it up all the time. There's no way he would do that which means—"

"He knew we were coming," Kat finished.

"How, though? Goser couldn't have told him."

"I don't know, Chase."

"That means my pulse worked fine and it's not my fault," Fixer said.

"No one blames you, buddy," Chase replied.

"Katalla Swift blamed me," he said.

Chase raised his eyebrow and said, "Really?"

"I was just frustrated, Fixer. I didn't mean it." She hugged him, gave him a kiss on the cheek, and was rewarded by his awkward smile. Then she turned back to Chase and said, "Now spill it. How do you know the leader of the Luminari Cluster?"

"I may have saved his daughter's life once." A smile spread across his face as he watched the reactions of his two crew members.

"What? How?" Kat asked. She had never been more interested in Chase's past than she was right now.

"It happened while I was in the CCP academy."

"What happened while you were in the CCP academy?" The disbelief was evident in Kat's voice as the look of shock had still not left her face. "How have we never heard about this before? You should have one of the cushiest positions in the fleet right now. What happened?"

"Yeah, how did you screw it up, Chase?" Fixer added, and Kat stifled a laugh at his bluntness.

"Nice, Fixer," Chase replied with a frown. "What makes you so sure I screwed it up, Fixer? Maybe someone else screwed it up."

"Unlikely. Given what we know of you, there is a high probability that you did something less than honorable or we would have already heard about this before now." Chase glared at his friend in mock indignation.

"Fixer's not trying to insult you, Chase, it's just his way," Kat added, hoping Chase would continue with the story.

"I know, Kat, and he's usually right, but he's actually off the mark with this one." Chase patted his friend on the back.

"Tell us the whole story and don't you dare leave out a single detail."

"We have at least four hours for the story, Chase," Fixer said.

Chase looked at him and said, "It won't take that long." He shifted in his chair and began his tale. "Here's what happened." He sighed as he commenced recounting the beginning of his woes. "Vanguard Tobias was only a planetary governor at the time and his daughter, Delaina, found herself in some serious trouble one night."

"Serious trouble? Was she with you?" Kat asked with a sarcastic look in her eyes.

"No." He saw she was unconvinced and added, "Honestly! I just happened to be in the right place at the right time."

"Riiiight. So, what happened?"

Chase sighed again, took a deep breath and continued his story. Fixer was right. They had time to kill before reaching Cibola anyway. He let out the breath and said, "I was a Lancer, first tier, stationed at the equatorial base on Cibola. Governor Tobias had just given a speech at an awards ceremony. The base was safe enough, but the city was a different story. After the ceremony, I went into the city with two of my friends. We hit up a crowded bar in the warehouse district. A couple hours of drinking and dancing later, I had a good buzz going and then all of a sudden, Delaina walks right into the bar without her protection detail. She started dancing with these guys that I knew were no good and a wave of sobriety hit me. I knew right then I had to get her out of there."

"Are you sure it was sobriety, and not a feeling emanating from a lower region that kept you in the bar?" Kat asked.

"She means you might have been thinking with your—"

"I know what she's implying, Fixer. Thank you," he replied. "And no, while she may have been beautiful, I didn't want any part of the heat a move like that would bring down on me."

"Okay, continue," Kat said with a wave of her hand. Fixer had gone to the galley and retrieved a green fizzy. He returned with his beverage, held it up and said, "Chase always keeps green fizzys stocked in groups of ten because they're my favorite drink."

"I know, Fixer, now shh, we're getting to the good part."

"Not more than a few minutes later, I saw her leave with three of the guys and it didn't look like it was completely voluntary. I looked for my two buddies, but one had already left and the other was passed out, so I followed the men out by myself."

"Ooh, heroic. That's so unlike you," Kat said.

"I know, right?" he replied. "Anyway, when I got out into the alley, I saw one of the men punch Delaina. She fell to the ground and I just reacted. I ran up behind the third guy and rammed his head into a steel wall. He went right down, but then it was two against one. I yelled for Delaina to run, but she didn't or couldn't. I went right at the one who had hit her and landed a couple good shots before the other guy hit me from behind. I kicked out with my leg and somehow connected with his groin while the first guy hit me hard across the face a few times."

"I don't like when people touch my face."

"We know, Fixer," Kat replied.

Chase stood up, stretched, and continued. "I went with the last blow to get a bit of distance and was able to knock out the guy that I had kicked while he was trying to get up. I hit him so hard that I broke a bone in my hand." He looked at his hand and shook it.

"That's when the last guy came at me with a knife. I noticed a knife on the belt of the first guy I knocked out and dove for it. I came up with it while the last guy was stabbing me in the shoulder." He opened his shirt and pulled it to the side to reveal a scar on his shoulder. "We exchanged slashes for a while before he overcommitted, and I was able to knee him in the gut. I hit him hard across the face with the butt of my knife while he was stabbing me in the leg."

He looked at Fixer and said, "That's what I get for being nice and trying to let the guy live." Then he looked at Kat and continued. "I dropped to my knees and thrust my knife into the guy's chest as he was swinging down. His last slash cut my chest, but not bad enough to kill me." He opened his shirt further to reveal a long, mostly faded scar across his pectoral muscles.

"What happened next?" Fixer asked.

"A speeder van pulled up to the end of the alley and when the driver saw his friends on the ground, he took off."

"So, it was a kidnapping attempt," Kat said.

"I believe so. After that, Delaina ran to me to see if I was okay, and I picked up her communicator. I was able to reach the governors protection detail on their comms. I told them everything that had happened and that I suspected it was a kidnapping attempt. Then they brought her safely home. I received a medal for bravery and Governor Tobias even visited me at the med-center. My parents were never prouder. I can still remember the gleam in my father's eyes."

He paused and his eyes took on a more serious gaze when he continued, "After I was released from the med-center to recover, I was fast-tracked to enter officer school as soon as my wounds healed, but after a week or so, I was just promoted to Specialist and shipped out to Nibiru under the command of Major Tal Seraphaz. The only problem with that was he had no use for me, and he forced me to take a medical discharge because my wounds were not fully healed yet.

I couldn't figure out what I had done to deserve that kind of punishment, and it seemed like Seraphaz went out of his way to make sure my appeals didn't reach the Flag or the Governor before the discharge had taken effect." He had a rueful look on his face as he continued. "At least it was an honorable discharge. Still, my father was convinced I had done something to screw it all up, and we had a big fight about it. That's the last time I ever spoke to my father. Anyway, now you know why I generally try to mind my business and not go out of my way to help people."

"That's terrible, you saved his Daughter's life and he just shipped you off like that." Kat put her hand on his arm as she spoke. "That's a pretty big betrayal. I thought the Vanguard was a better man than that. How do you get past something like that?"

"I guess you become a bounty hunter and take it out on people even less fortunate than you," he replied.

"I still think Chase messed up somehow."

"Fixer!"

"It's okay, Kat," Chase said. "I'm not exactly what you would call a sure thing. Anyway, maybe the Vanguard had nothing to do with it, and it appears he at least still remembers that I saved his little girl's life. Maybe I'll finally get the chance to ask him what happened. Let's hope he has a quick cushy job for us that will get us back on track. We could really use the heskars. I hope this is the turning point. I really do feel like someone or something has been standing against me behind the scenes. I know it sounds crazy, but even I can't possibly be this unlucky."

Kat felt a stab of guilt for the hard time she had been giving him lately. She had almost forgotten what a difficult season it had been for him. She smiled at him and put her hand on his shoulder. "It's going to work out fine. This is where our luck turns around, and after, we'll find whoever it is that's been messing up your jobs." She nodded her head with confidence, looked back, and added, "Right, Fixer!"

"Katalla Swift is right, Chase. You won't be a loser forever."

Kat stifled a laugh and Chase shook his head and said, "Thanks, buddy, I know I can always count on you to tell it like it is."

"Fixer, put on your best clothes. We're going to meet Vanguard Tobias," Kat said. Then she left the bridge and went to her quarters to put on her favorite outfit.

Chase called after her, "I'll be on the bridge. If I fall asleep, wake me up when we're about to come out of hyperspace."

"Will do," she called back. When she finally found the right outfit, she walked back to the bridge. Chase was already asleep and it gave her some time to think. It was as close to alone time as she would ever get on the ship. Even though Fixer was on the bridge, he almost never started a conversation with her. She always had to address him first.

She watched Chase while he slept. It reminded her of when they were together. She would always wake up first and she loved watching his chest rise and fall in a rhythmic fashion. She thought his name was fitting, given his occupation.

It was far from her proudest moment when she broke it off with him. He had withdrawn from her completely, and she had trouble understanding why. She always thought he knew she had cheated on him, but he never said anything. Instead, the failure of both of them to communicate ruined what could have been a great relationship. Still, something kept drawing her back to him and that puzzled her.

It wasn't his looks, although she did find him to be somewhat attractive. His height and build were average, and his light skin tone matched his brown hair and blue eyes. His jaw was set in that immovable way that let people know he was a stubborn man.

She loved the smell of the detergent he used; it reminded her of the cool mountain air. She almost never saw him out of his work clothes, but it was a good look for him. When on the hunt, he was always in battleship gray trousers with black, knee-high boots and a black, waist length jacket. His dual holsters seemed to loop casually, halfway down each thigh, and he was a quick draw. He carried a standard military-issue blaster on his right leg and a heavy, stun cannon strapped to his left. He also had a rifle holster on his back, which, combined with the hard look in his eyes made people instinctively steer clear when he walked down a street.

For a short time, Chase was considered the best bounty hunter in the entire Luminari Cluster. None of that mattered, though; she loved him for a different reason. She only wished she knew what that reason was. She stood and checked on the FTL drive, even though she knew it would alert them if anything went wrong. As she returned to her seat she saw Fixer tinkering with some spare engine parts. Maybe that was why she loved Chase. As hard as he was, he still looked out for a person who would always be completely reliant on him. Fixer was a genius with engines and machines, but he was very much like a child in all other areas of life.

The fact that Chase took him in and treated him like a little brother was both impressive and mature. It might have been the only area in his life that his maturity was evident. He had not taken their breakup well, and the only reason they were together now was for the job. Maybe she had been wrong to dump him, but he seemed to routinely sabotage his life. Whether it was his temper or just a bad call, success always remained just out of his grasp and she wanted more out of life.

Fixer had told her that Chase always slept with women that looked like her and that infuriated her. She had broken up with him, so she really had no say about whom he saw and what he did, but she still hated that he did it. She supposed that on some level, it meant that he still loved her. Still, as much as she wanted to be with him, she would hold off until he halted his pattern of self-destructive behavior. Every problem in his life could be traced back to a poor decision and she needed him to grow out of that before she would even think about getting back with him.

The hyperdrive beeped jolting her from her contemplation. She looked over and Fixer was still tinkering with his engine parts, only now he had a green fizzy in his hand. She looked over to Chase and he was sitting in the captain's chair awaiting re-entry to real space and she wondered, *Did I fall asleep?*

They emerged from hyperspace three kilometers to the starboard flank of the *Legendary*. The *Legendary* dwarfed the *Longshot*. Almost ten times the size and bristling with weaponry, she was still considered on the small side for a capital ship. From a distance the ship looked almost flat even though it contained five decks. The visual illusion was due in part to the hull plating from the top of the ship meeting the hull plating from the bottom of the ship to almost give the vessel the look of a stingray minus the tail.

Captain Bander commed them, and this time they could see his image. He was clean cut with dark hair and dark eyes. His jaw was strong and you could tell he was tall even though he was seated. Kat practically purred as she stared intently at the screen.

"Welcome back to Cibola. I've just received a transmission. We're cleared to land at the spaceport where we will be escorted to the palace by the Vanguards personal hovercade."

"Will you be joining us, Captain?" Kat asked in a sultry voice before Chase could reply.

"Yes, of course, Miss Swift. I look forward to meeting all of you."

"Thank you, Captain," Chase replied. The transmission ended and he shot Kat an annoyed look.

"You shouldn't be upset with her; you two are not together anymore."

"Yes, I know that, thank you, Fixer," Chase replied in a clipped tone while he nodded his head and went aft to make sure the hatch was disarmed. He wanted to avoid any accidents of friendly fire. He could sense the excitement of his crew at the thought of meeting Vanguard Tobias and he was happy for them. There wasn't always a lot to look forward to, flying with him, so he was glad they would have this moment.

Chapter three

Agent Ponta Black sat just inside the sensor range of Cibola in his ship, the *Covert Enforcer*. He was sure that he was far enough out that the stealth capabilities his ship possessed would keep him virtually invisible to the sensor arrays on Cibola, but close enough to learn what he needed. He established a transmission link with Captain Seraphaz on the *Elysian Pride* and said, "Cadogan has just arrived on Cibola. His ship was escorted in by the *Legendary*."

"*Legendary*? That's Captain Bander. That's a tracking ship." Captain Seraphaz stroked his beard while he thought about what his spy had just told him. He looked into the transmission and asked, "Did it seem like it was a voluntary escort or was the *Longshot* in custody?"

"I can't be sure, but I detected no tractor beam in use and no other ships formed up on the *Longshot*. They also landed at the Capital spaceport, so I tend to think they were summoned, not arrested." Black adjusted his communications array. It was difficult to send coded transmissions from stealth mode, so he had to tinker with the alignment. "What's your interest in this kid anyway?"

"His motives and loyalties are questionable at best, so I like to know where he is and what he's doing at all times."

Black was slow to believe that excuse, but he was also hard pressed to care. Seraphaz was technically his boss, and owed him no explanations. One of Vanguard Tobias' early military initiatives was to station a special agent with each fleet group to make sure everything was aboveboard within the fleet, and to explore any possible threats to the fleet. To that end, he had been with Captain Seraphaz for several years. Only a handful of people knew who he was and what he did and he preferred it that way. This arrangement had allowed him to make a lot of money for himself while still looking out for the interests of the Commonwealth. "Well, it looks like he's being called in to a meeting with Flag Officer Victor."

"You need to find out what that's about, Agent Black," Seraphaz replied, a hint of concern evident in his voice.

"I'll do my best, sir."

"Get it done. If the Flag is sending this kid out on a mission for the Commonwealth, I'm going to shadow him and make sure it's done right."

"Yes, sir," Black replied. The connection terminated and Black set a course for Cibola.

Captain Seraphaz left the bridge of his ship with his datapad in hand. *What kind of mission could the Flag have for Cadogan, and why don't I know about it?* He walked into the mess hall and the personnel present all stood and fired off a salute. Returning their salute, he marched over to the jav station, poured himself a hot cup of a dark, Avalonian blend and sat down at an empty table. He had his own personal chef, and an officer's mess, but he still liked to be out among the crew on occasion for morale.

He called up some info on his datapad and began trying to figure out what was happening. The whole fleet was abuzz with scuttlebutt concerning the Qantarah and their missing scientist. *Why haven't I heard about this incident?* he wondered. He read the reports of the exchange, and his eyes widened. "They want him to find the scientist!" he exclaimed just loud enough to draw a couple looks. No one was foolish enough to let their gaze linger, however. He took a long draught of his jav and put the cup on the table. He stood and rushed out of the mess, not waiting for any saluting. Hurrying into his ready room, he opened a coded transmission. A moment later, a shadowy figure flared to life on the screen before him.

"What news do you have, Captain?"

"The rumors are true. There is indeed a Qantaran scientist missing somewhere in the cluster."

"You must be the one to find this scientist. We would like to interrogate her."

"I know who the Vanguard has tasked with finding the scientist, and I will put my best man on him." He paused and looked into the

42

screen. "If Chase Cadogan finds this Qantaran before I do, my man will take her from him by force."

"Cadogan?"

"Yes, I have just found out that the hunter Vanguard Tobias has put on this search is Cadogan."

"Make sure he does not return her to the Vanguard. We need to learn the secrets that make the Qantaran military so powerful, and I think this scientist is the key."

"Agent Black will find her first, and if Cadogan does get lucky, it will cost him his life."

"Do not fail us, Captain Seraphaz." The transmission ended and a lump began to form in the back of Seraphaz's throat. He suppressed a shiver and deleted the record of the transmission. He hurried from the room with a new set of instructions for Agent Black.

+++++

Captain Bander led the crew of the *Longshot* into the executive meeting chamber in the Capitol Palace. Every child in the Commonwealth learned at an early age that only the most important business took place in the chamber. Chase saw the wonder etched on Fixer and Kat's faces while they passed several priceless works of art. Chase felt naked after having gone through security. He hated being anywhere without his weapons, even when his safety was guaranteed.

Two guards opened the door to the chamber for them, and they walked into the room single file with Captain Bander leading the way and Chase bringing up the rear.

"This is amazing, Chase," Kat said in an awestruck voice. "My parents are never going to believe I met the Vanguard. Neither are my sisters."

"You have sisters?" Chase asked, eyebrow raised. "How come I never met them?"

"Because they look a lot like me."

"She doesn't want them to become your one-night friends," Fixer added.

"Yeah, got that, buddy. Thanks." Chase took in the room. Hovering globes cast soft light on the furnishings. Four cream couches sat around a blood red, glass table on one side of the room, while a large conference table with high back, chalsen leather chairs, dominated the other half of the room. The floor was made of xardac wood from the forests of Lemuria, lacquered and polished to a high gloss, and a dark, red carpet sat under the couches. Each wall showed a progression of commonwealth leadership right up to the large painting of the current vanguard behind the head of the conference table.

Captain Bander led them over to the couches and took a seat. Kat was quick to sit down next to him. Chase frowned at the display and sat down on the next couch. Fixer still stood, looking at the pictures displayed on the walls. After a long moment, Chase tugged him and he perched on the couch.

"So, Captain, how long have you been in the military?" Kat asked, pouring more seduction into her voice than Chase had ever heard.

"Fourteen years. How long have you been a bounty hunter?"

"On and off for about three and a half years."

"You look familiar, have we met?" The captain fixed his gaze on her and she could see him thinking about how he could possibly know her.

"She's just got one of those faces, Captain," Chase said into the awkward silence. He knew she hated talking about her past, and he hoped the captain would drop it.

Chase knew that was unlikely when Captain Bander's eyes lit up in recognition. "You're that dancer from Elysia. You were one of the best I've ever seen. Then one day I read that you'd lost your protected status and could no longer dance professionally. There was some sort of scandal involved, right? Is that why you became a bounty hunter?"

The air looked like it had been sucked out of Kat's lungs. The spark left her eyes and her shoulders dropped just a bit. Chase doubted anyone else would have noticed it. After a terse pause, she replied, "I don't really like to talk about my past."

Bander realized his mistake and said, "I'm so sorry. I should have had the brains to realize that before I said anything. Please, forgive me."

"No problem," she replied, and she was suddenly thankful that Fixer had kept his helpful comments to himself. She was searching for a way out of this conversation when the door to the chamber opened.

One of the guards stepped in and in a deep voice uttered, "I now present to you Vanguard Tobias and Flag Officer Victor." He stepped back into his former position and both guards saluted. A moment later, they were obscured by Vanguard Tobias striding into the room. The Flag matched him step for step, but had nowhere near the charisma of the Commonwealth Vanguard. Captain Bander and his guests stood, and the captain and Chase saluted their leader. Kat waved with a grin she failed to contain, and Fixer mumbled the formula for velocity to himself over and over.

After shaking hands with each of them, the Vanguard said, "Please, sit down." He gestured to the couches they had been sitting on and they all took their seats. "Thank you for coming, Mr. Cadogan."

"It's an honor, sir. Thank you for the invitation."

"Please, introduce me to your crew."

"Of course, sir." Chase pointed to Kat and said, "This is my hunting partner, Katalla Swift." Then he patted Fixer on the leg and added, "And this is my mechanic, Fixer Faraday."

Fixer stood up and mimicking Chase's salute, said, "I've always wanted to meet you, Vanguard, ever since you were a local mayor."

"Well, I'm glad we have this opportunity, Fixer. It is a great pleasure to meet you. I hear you are quite an exceptional mechanic."

"Chase says I'm the best one there is." Fixer beamed with pride and Chase thought this might be the first time he had ever seen his friend truly happy.

"Well Chase is a pretty smart man, so I'm going to go ahead and take that as an accurate assessment of your skills." He smiled and added, "I'd love to talk some more, but we are on a tight schedule. Flag Officer Victor is going to brief you on the situation, then I'm going to make you an offer you can't refuse." He motioned for the Flag to begin.

Flag officer Victor stood and the hovering lights dimmed. He pulled an object about the size of a heskar out of his pocket and placed it on the glass table. A holographic map of the Luminari Cluster flickered to life before them. "Four days ago we received this transmission from the Qantarah." He played back the brief conversation and Kat gasped at the threat.

"We've been searching near the coordinates of the three known entrances to the cluster. We've been focusing on the third entrance because it's the most difficult path for a capital ship to navigate." He pointed to an area on the hologram and shook his head. "The reality is, without knowing why this scientist is here, there is no way we'll be able to find her in two weeks."

Vanguard Tobias stood and the Flag took his seat. He pointed to Chase and said, "Chase, you're one of the best in the business, and I trust you. Would you be willing to help us on this hunt?"

"Of course I will, sir," he replied. "I'm honored you would even ask."

"I knew you would work with us," Vanguard Tobias replied. "I only wish you had stayed in the military. Then we could have had this conversation four days ago. Why did you ask for the discharge anyway? You seemed so excited about officer school."

Chase paused and looked around the room. His face was plastered with uncertainty, but he decided to address the Vanguard's question. "You think I asked for the discharge? I was forced to take it. I'm actually surprised you asked for me today. I thought I had done something wrong, but I couldn't figure out what." He smiled and added, "This is actually a big relief."

The Vanguard met Chase's gaze with a troubled look on his face. "You saved my daughter's life, and almost lost yours doing it. Why would you think you did something wrong?"

"Because I was forced out of the military before I was even finished healing." Chase hated to talk about this in a room full of people, but he had been searching for these answers for a long time. There was no way he could ignore these questions.

"That was not my wish for you at all. Tell me what happened, exactly as you remember it." Vanguard Tobias looked at the Flag, but he indicated he had no idea what happened.

Chase sighed and recounted his story. "When I woke up in the medical center, I was told I would be going to officer training and everything seemed great. My parents were so proud of me. A week later, I was given the rank of Specialist with no training and shipped out before I was even completely healed. I reported to my new position with a man named Major Tol Seraphaz, and it seemed like he hated me and I didn't know why. He immediately discharged me as medically unfit for duty. I sent in appeals every day until the discharge was finalized. I didn't even get the medical pension given to medical discharges. I thought I must have done something wrong."

The Vanguard's face looked even more troubled when he spoke. "No, Mister Cadogan. You did nothing wrong. Apparently, my wishes were not conveyed properly to my subordinates. None of that was supposed to happen to you. You were a hero and should have been treated better. You have my deepest apologies." He turned to the Flag and said, "Juel, will you check into how this all came about as soon as possible?" He paused and looked back at Chase before adding, "And I want his pension reinstated immediately retroactive to his release date."

"Yes, sir," Flag Officer Victor replied. "I'm anxious to see who the people were that thought it would be a good idea to sideline such a talented soldier."

"Thank you, my friend, now, back to the situation at hand." He sat down on the unoccupied cream couch opposite Chase, leaned forward, and said, "Chase, I'm going to be assigning Captain Bander and the *Legendary* to help you, but they are following your lead on this one. What are your initial feelings on the assignment?"

The apology put forth by the Vanguard had put Chase at ease, but he wanted to find out who sidelined him and why as soon as this situation was dealt with. He looked at the map and said, "There's one more route into the cluster, but it's a closely guarded secret in the criminal community. It's a smuggling route and we came across it on a hunt about a year and a half ago. It's right here." He pointed to a spot in the asteroid field. "It's an even tighter squeeze than the third entrance. No capital ships could make it through there, but a small ship like mine probably could."

The Flag pointed to the holographic map and said, "We've suspected for some time that an additional route had been discovered. I'll send a ship there right away to look for the missing scientist."

"She won't be there," Fixer said to everyone's surprise. "What is her mission?"

"We don't know, son," the Flag replied.

"What's her mission?" Fixer asked again. "We don't know. What's her mission? What's her mission?" Everyone was now looking at him.

"I think I know what Fixer is getting at," Chase said, and he then turned to his mechanic. "You're brilliant, buddy." He looked back to everyone else and said, "If we knew her mission, it would lead us to where she might be, so what's her mission? Or more precisely, what are her possible missions?"

He gave it a moment to set in. "Three possibilities come to mind right away, and none of them are good." The Vanguard nodded for him to continue, so he said, "Maybe she's here to disrupt our military before a Qantaran invasion. We should send ships to the best possible locations to prevent that."

"Already thought of and taken care of," the Flag replied.

"Option two. She's here to spy on us and gather intel about our military strength, so we should send ships to scout all of the possible locations she could gather that intel."

"We've done that as well," Vanguard Tobias added, "What's the third possibility?"

"She's here to scout our resources. The Qantarah are basically a big war machine, maybe they're scouting for resources to keep expanding."

"We've looked into that as well, Chase. Believe me; our top military minds have been on this for four days now. There's not a scenario we can think of that we haven't checked out. We have a few planets with rich oil deposits, and most of the precious metals we know about have been mined. We do have a few planets with high concentrations of basic metal ores, but we've checked those as well," the Flag said.

Chase thought for a moment before saying, "It's got to be something different. It's got to be a resource they use that isn't readily found or used by other cultures. Oil, Metal and Gold are great resources, but surely they can get them somewhere else." Chase pointed to the map hovering in front of him and said, "The cluster's natural defenses make it very difficult to invade. I'm sure the Qantarah can take us in an open war, but if they invaded the cluster, they would lose a ton of ships with no guarantee of success."

"We understand that, Chase. What's your point?" Vanguard Tobias asked.

"The point is that they would be foolish to do that for ordinary resources they could easily procure at less cost. If this scientist is here looking for resources, it's got to be something we're not aware of, but something that is precious to them." He looked down and added, "Precious enough to incur the losses they would face if they attacked. I'll begin my search near uninhabited planets with unusual make-ups."

From the look on the faces of the Vanguard, the Flag, and the captain, none of them had thought about that last idea. Vanguard Tobias stood and said, "We'll send some scout ships out to all of the uninhabited planets of the cluster. The bulk of our fleet will be stationed at the two main entry points. Thank you, Chase. Let us know the second you have something."

"Yes, sir. You can count on it."

"I know, and when this is done, we are going to sit down to a nice dinner and you are going to catch me up on your life. For now, bring in whoever you need for the job, but only people you trust. They will be well paid."

"I will, sir, and I look forward to that conversation."

"Very good." Tobias turned to leave without another word and was followed out by the Flag. Chase sat back down after they left and let out a breath.

"Chase, you did so well. I'm proud of you," Kat said. She had been so quiet during the meeting that he had almost forgotten she was there at all.

"Thanks, Kat, but it was actually Fixer's idea that got me rolling."

"Good job, Fixer," she said with a smile.

"Thank you, Katalla Swift."

"Does he always use your full name?" Captain Bander asked.

"He sometimes calls me Katalla, never Kat, though."

"Hmm." The captain stood and looked at Chase. "So, where are we off to first?"

"I'm not sure. I'll need to survey the planetary maps to get an idea. Let's get back to the ship."

+++++

Sym had amassed a working knowledge of the Commonwealth trade language over the last few days. They seemed to be a peaceful and gregarious people, and she had no wish to see them destroyed. She still had no idea what she was going to do about the xallodium, but she knew she needed to report in before her people sent someone looking for her.

She took off from the surface of the planet, and while she was in the atmosphere, a wind storm arose. The sudden nature and fury of the gale caught her completely unawares. Before the warning sensors her ship possessed started blaring, the first wave of winds buffeted the ship, sending it end over end through the sky.

Sym's fur stood straight and her eyes widened. Anything she had left unsecured now flew about the ship, slamming into the interior walls and adding to the mad symphony of sounds. Her hands tightened around the control yoke and her arms began to shake with exertion. [Gods be merciful,] she cried out.

The winds continued to push her craft along and she cut power to the thrusters. She heard a loud metallic clang on the hull of her ship and caught sight of her communications array sailing past her viewport before the ship spun again. Without warning, pain exploded in her head, adding a new dimension to the noise. She brought her hand up to her face on instinct and her hand came away covered with orange blood. She wiped her hand on her jumpsuit and brought it back to the yoke. Blood flowed down her face and clouded her vision. She knew there was little chance she could survive another hit like that. *What struck me?* she wondered. She had no time to figure it out because the ground was rushing up on her fast.

A break in the wind caused her craft to plummet even faster. Her ship was still spinning to the right, so she fired up the left maneuvering thruster to slow the spin. When her spin slowed, she used her remaining strength to force the yoke in the opposite direction. She could see the grey dirt of the planet growing closer. She fired all of her maneuvering thrusters and her vertical thrusters on full power and the ship slowed. The ground was intent on meeting her, but she finally brought the ship under control. Her vertical thrusters left a patch of scorched earth, and she left the atmosphere as fast as her ship would carry her.

Once she reached a stable orbit, she unstrapped herself from her seat and stumbled over to the cabinet containing medical supplies. She looked into the mirrored inside of the cabinet door and cleaned her wound with gauze. Crying out in pain, she sterilized her wound, and used the medical glue gun to close the gash. She applied a bandage, turned around, and slid down to the cold xallodium floor, leaving the medical cabinet door ajar. Salty sweat poured down her face and her body shook from fear and exhaustion.

Almost ten minutes later, she regained control of her breathing and found the strength to stand. She lumbered to the cockpit and noticed her sample case wedged under the console. A streak of blood near the handle told her this was the offending object and she left it where it lay. She checked the ship's systems and confirmed that communications were offline. She also discovered that sensors were offline, which, although not surprising, was disappointing. She would have to land on the nearest habitable planet to effect repairs. She checked her navigation charts and set course for a planet the humans called Nibiru.

+++++

"My sources tell me that Captain Bander and Cadogan were tasked by the Vanguard himself with finding the missing Qantaran scientist everyone has been going on about," Agent Black reported. "The Flag and Cadogan's crew were the only other people in the meeting," Agent Black added while looking at a holographic image of Captain Seraphaz.

"This is troubling," Seraphaz said, his image pacing back and forth. The site was almost amusing to Black. "Why Cadogan? He's got an army capable of looking for the Qantaran, why Chase Cadogan?"

"Why not?" Black saw the scowl that came over Seraphaz's face and expounded on his comment. "I mean, with the threat of the Qantarah looming, you would think Vanguard Tobias and the Flag would want as many of their resources available as possible. Plus, bounty hunters have resources, information avenues, and tricks of the trade not available to the military. Why not use him? I heard he saved Delaina Tobias' life once, so the Vanguard probably trusts him."

Captain Seraphaz bristled at the thought of Chase being in Vanguard Tobias' good graces. "Follow him. If he does get lucky and finds this alien, you are to take her from him, by force if necessary. Chase Cadogan will not be the hero; we will. Do you understand?"

"Yes, sir," Agent Black replied. "Do you want me to bring her in after I take her from Cadogan?"

"No, bring her to me. There is much we can learn from her before we turn her over." Seraphaz turned away from the holo-projector to speak to someone outside the range of the transmission projector. He leaned back into the comm frame and added, "And, Agent Black, Cadogan does not need to survive the encounter."

"Understood." The transmission winked out and Agent Black readied the *Covert Enforcer* to follow the *Longshot*. Questions filled his mind. *Why does my boss hate this bounty hunter so much? What's he going to do to the alien once he has her? Can I really kill someone who is doing a job the Vanguard himself asked him to do? How can I capitalize on this?* While his mind whirled, he put his ship in stealth mode and waited for his quarry to take off from Cibola.

+++++

When Chase reached the *Longshot*'s berth at the spaceport, he had trouble seeing the ship through the mountain of supplies waiting to be loaded. "Whoa, whoa, whoa, what's going on here?" he yelled to the nearest yellow-clad port employee. "What is all this stuff?" He was waving his arm to take in all of the pallets of supplies before him. "I didn't order it and I can't afford it. Take it back!"

"It's already paid for and brought here as per..." He looked at the order on his datapad and his eyes opened wide. "Flag Officer Victor?" He looked at Chase with a measure of respect, signaling two other workers to come over. "If you'll just open your ship, we'll load this and have you on your way in no time."

"And you're sure I am not going to be charged for any of this?" Chase asked.

"No, sir. I mean, yes, sir," the worker replied.

"Yes, sir, what? Am I getting charged for this stuff or not?"

The worker chuckled and said, "No, sir. It is already paid for. You will not be charged."

"Okay," Chase replied and entered the code for the landing bay. He pointed to a corridor and said, "This leads to the hold."

"Chase, make sure they have green fizzys," Fixer said while he watched the men load the ship.

"I'll check the order, buddy, but I'm not sure Flag Officer Victor knows that's your favorite." He turned to Kat and said, "I want to bring in Tev and Stone on this just in case we need some more muscle."

"I'll send a transmission to them right away." She lowered her voice and drew closer, then added, "And thanks for trying to help when the captain was about to recall my past. I was flirting with him, and you didn't have to try and help me out."

"I only wish it had worked."

"Really?" She was unsure how to take the comment.

"I just want you to be happy, Kat. I wish it was with me, but maybe we are better together as friends. I don't have to like it, but I do have to accept it."

"Maybe we should talk about this later when we're not in a public place," she replied.

"That's probably a good idea."

"I'll go make those transmissions now." She looked at Chase while he directed the flow of supplies into the ship. He almost had to hold Fixer back because the mechanic's curiosity always got the better of him. Her lips formed a slight frown, and she ducked into the ship. Her heart ached for what she had put Chase through even though his recent attitude had been a pleasant surprise. Maybe that was why she was finding it difficult. She sent the first transmission and a short, barrel-chested man came into view.

"Ah, the lovely Katalla Swift. To what do I owe this pleasure?" He bowed formally and removed his helmet in mock pageantry. "You still hanging out with Cadogan?"

"Of course I am, Tev. Where else would I be?"

"That bum couldn't even call me himself, not that I'm complaining. Who wouldn't rather look at you?" He let out a toothy grin and returned the helmet to his head.

"We have a job we could use some extra muscle on. Are you free for the next week or so?" He pressed a button and Kat heard a loud explosion in the background. A moment later, dirt showered Tev and he broke into another grin.

"Nothing going on that I can't move around for Chase, but if he wants muscle, why not call that blue Borean meathead he likes so much?"

"I'm calling Stone next," she replied with a chuckle.

"Me and Stone? Wow, this must really be a big job. Where are we meeting?" He pressed another button and another explosion could be heard.

"Hyperborea, tomorrow. What are you doing right now anyway?"

"Helping my neighbor clear his field. Why?"

"You just look like you're having way too much fun to be working, that's all." She waved at the screen and added, "Thank you, Tev. I'll see you tomorrow." The transmission winked out and she sent the next one to Stone.

"Katalla, you look even more beautiful than I remember."

"Thanks, Stone," she replied. She saw his image duck and come up firing.

"Hold on for a minute, Kat. I'll be right back." Blaster fire rang out and pockets of steam rose where hard light burned into thick ice. When he returned, there was a black scorch mark on the edge of his shoulder.

She fixed him with a look of disbelief and asked, "Did you just get shot, Stone? What are you doing?"

"I'm helping a town get rid of a violent gang of criminals, what are you doing?" He scratched around the edge of the burn mark while checking out his frozen surroundings.

"We've got a hunt and we need you. Are you free?"

"I will be in about six hours. Where's Chase?"

"He's supervising the port workers loading our supplies," she said. She heard Chase yell a curse in the background and stifled a laugh adding, "And trying to keep Fixer out of their hair."

"That sounds about right. So, when are you going to move to Hyperborea and get together with me? With your pink skin and my blue skin, our babies would be fabulous." He started laughing at the look she gave him.

"As always, Stone, I appreciate the offer, but I'm afraid we're looking at the other side of never on that one."

"You say that now, but I know I'm wearing you down." A deep laugh erupted from his stomach after his comment. "I think you're blushing, Kat."

"Or getting angry enough to kill you. I guess we'll find out which when we pick you up tomorrow. Bye Stone," He started to say goodbye and she ended the transmission. She loved teasing Chase's friends. She left the bridge and walked toward the landing bay. She arrived just as the last worker was leaving the hold.

"Kat, our hold has never been this full. I think the Flag gave us almost two years worth of supplies." His smile was almost infectious. Even Fixer was happy, which meant that his favorite beverage was amongst the supplies.

"That's great, Chase. We're picking up Tev and Stone at the usual location and time on Hyperborea tomorrow."

"Great. I hope I didn't take them away from anything fun."

"Nah, probably just a routine day for those two."

"Uh huh," he replied. "Let's load up and head out. As soon as we get into orbit, we'll contact Captain Bander and let him know that we'll check Miners' Field tonight and pick up our guys on Hyperborea tomorrow." He turned and shouted out into the port, "Fixer, Come on."

His mechanic hurried onto the ship and they prepared to leave. Then Chase said, "Kat, we have new blasters, new weapons for the ship, a whole lot of new energy modules. We probably have enough to power the ship for five or six years. The Flag really set us up."

56

"Do you think Vanguard Tobias did this because of what happened?" she asked.

"I don't know, but for the next few years, every bounty we take is straight profit for us." He ran the ship checklist and signaled the spaceport for clearance to leave. Their hail was answered in an instant and they were given the green light. "Okay, strap yourselves in, we're taking off."

"Chase, you have another message from your mother. Do you wish to send a transmission to her now?" Kat asked.

"Nah, I'll talk to her later. It's probably not important. She's probably just checking in to see if I'm still alive." The familiar vibrations of the *Longshot* taking off worked their way through the deck plating until the ship was high enough to switch from vertical thrusters to the main thrusters.

"She probably wants you to visit."

"I doubt that, Kat. She knows my father and I can't be in the same place for more than a couple minutes before things get umm... interesting."

"It can't just be because you left the military. There's gotta be more. You're going to have to tell me more about that someday."

"Don't hold your breath."

Chapter four

Agent Black drew closer to the *Legendary*. Their sensors had not picked him up yet. He stopped his ship just under a kilometer away, unwilling to further tempt fate. Holding his breath, he lined up his shot and fired a communications beacon onto the hull, beneath the communications array. After checking to see if the beacon was working he commenced with a slow withdrawal. He would now have access to every communication the *Legendary* sent or received for the next six to eight days.

Twenty minutes later his efforts were rewarded when Chase Cadogan came online.

"Captain Bander, I would like to check out Miners' Field tonight. We'll head off to Hyperborea tomorrow morning. I need to make a stop there and it's on the way to the next location I'm thinking about. Does that schedule work for you?"

"Chase, I'm here to assist you until the scientist is found. Anything you want to do and anywhere you want to go toward that end is fine with me."

"Understood. *Longshot* out."

Well that's interesting, Agent Black thought. *Seraphaz was right. They are definitely going after the missing scientist. He'll be happy to know their itinerary for the next day or so.* He retreated a little bit further away from the ships and sent a communication to Captain Seraphaz.

"You were right, Captain. The Flag tasked them with finding the missing alien. Their first stop will be Miners' Field."

"The asteroid belt? Why?" Seraphaz's tiny image asked. Black liked to keep the transmission version of his captain as small as possible just for kicks.

"Probably just a cursory check of the smugglers entrance."

"There's an entrance to the cluster through the asteroid field?" Seraphaz flashed annoyance, *That would have been useful information to have a long time ago.*

"Yes, sir. Then he's off to Hyperborea. He didn't say why."

"And how do you know this?" Seraphaz asked with a hint of suspicion in his eyes.

"Trade secret. They're on the move, I have to go." He shut off the transmission without awaiting a reply, relishing the fact that his captain did not get the last word. His therapist had told him that he was sabotaging himself with that sort of petty behavior, but what did she know?

He set course for Miners' field and engaged the hyperdrive.

+++++

The *Longshot* exited Hyperspace just outside the gravity well of Hyperborea. Chase waited for the *Legendary* to join him before going down to the surface to pick up his friends.

"Incoming transmission from the *Legendary*," Kat said.

"On screen," Chase replied.

"Chase, what's the plan?" Captain Bander asked.

"Just a quick stop to pick up some more manpower."

"Are you sure—"

"Vanguard Tobias told me to bring in anyone I need for this mission as long as I trust them. These are the only two guys in the galaxy I trust as much as my crew. This will take an hour, tops."

"We'll be here waiting."

"Actually, you can go ahead to Planet Nine if you'd rather get started. We'll make up the time in hyperspace and should be only a few minutes behind you."

"That sounds like a great idea. See you there. Bander out." His image disappeared and his ship veered to port. A moment later, a hyperspace window opened and the *Legendary* was gone.

"Let's go get Tev and Stone," Chase said. He hit the thrusters and proceeded toward the frozen planet, but he picked up a second, smaller hyperspace window opening, on the *Longshot*'s sensor readouts. He fixed the sensors in the direction of the window in time to see a small, dark ship enter the event. "Kat, I think someone is following us. See if you can sift through the sensor readouts since we emerged from hyperspace. I'll take us in."

"On it, Chase," she replied.

"Fixer, make sure the heat shielding is set to full power for reentry."

"It already is, Chase. You don't need to remind me every time," he replied while he kept his eyes on the readouts.

"It's a good habit to have, Fixer. I figured that you of all people would approve of the routine."

Chase looked out the front viewport while the ship descended through the ionosphere. A red glow covered the front of the *Longshot,* but disappeared when they reached atmosphere. The heat turned to steam in the cold Borean air. Chase set course for the smaller of Hyperborea's two spaceports. The *Longshot* landed, and the landing bay opened. Chase stepped out into the spaceport to a full-scale brouhaha. Stone, Tev and three Boreans were fighting the crew of a Lemurian freighter. The odds were two to one, but Chase's friends were making a good accounting of themselves.

"Tev, Stone," Chase shouted over the ruckus. "Stop fooling around. We're on a schedule."

"Come help us end this, then!" Tev yelled back while taking a hard right cross to the face.

"Kat, keep the engine running. We're gonna need to take off quick," Chase called into the ship internal communication system. He then stepped out of his ship and was greeted by two men charging him. He sidestepped the first and tripped the second. He spun on his heels and blocked a left hand jab by the first assailant and hit him with a solid right that rocked the man.

The second man wrapped his arms around Chase from behind and tried to ram him into the hull of the *Longshot*. Chase brought his feet up and used the momentum of his legs going upwards to free himself from the bear-hug. He flipped and wound up behind his attacker. He followed through by ramming his attacker's head into the hull. The man slid to the ground and Chase turned to square off against the first man. The man looked at Chase, then looked at his friend on the ground and thought better of it. He turned and ran from the scene. When he ran, the remaining conscious brawlers also ran.

Chase began to drag the unconscious man away from his ship when a blow to his back rocked him. He turned expecting to see more fighting, but it was only Stone with a big smile on his face.

"I wish you guys didn't have to brawl with every freighter crew that passes through this port," Chase said, letting the body he was dragging drop.

"It's just good fun," Stone replied. "Besides, they were picking on my friends. Eleven against three is not a fair fight. I had no choice." He turned and sent a wave in the direction of the other three blue-hued Boreans. They waved back and walked away.

"Tev, come on. What are you doing?" Chase called out to his other friend.

"I'm looking for my bag." He rolled over an unconscious man and yelled, "Found it." He picked it up and hurried over to the ship. "What's the big rush anyway?"

"I'll tell you on the ship. Stone, do you have all your stuff?"

"Yup," he replied, holding his backpack in the air. "Let's go."

"Good, we're already behind schedule." They stepped onto the ship and Chase closed the hatch. "Get us out of here, Kat," Chase called up to the bridge. They felt the *Longshot* lifting off while they walked toward the bridge, where they were greeted with a smile by Kat and a frown from Fixer.

"Well that looked like fun," she said and then poked a bruise on Stone's cheek. He flinched away with a grunt and she started to chuckle.

"I don't like it when you guys fight," Fixer said without looking up. "Someone's going to get hurt."

"That's the point, Fixer," Tev said, patting him on the back.

"Chase," Kat, called out while the ship was still rising. "Look, your favorite part is coming up." He looked out the viewport at the frozen white mountains. He loved taking off from Hyperborea because of the view. The sub-zero wind would whip around the mountains causing falling snow to flash freeze into natural ice sculptures. The view changed several times a day as the light of the distant sun shone through the instant ice patterns, altering their colors. It was almost like a sculpted prism. The ice patterns were usually thin and lasted no longer than an hour or so before they were gone as if they never existed. Today, there were some unusually high spires connected by a frozen net and the violet color coming through the ice made Kat pause the ship for a moment, so they could all take a look.

"Almost as breathtaking as you, Miss Swift," Tev said putting his arm around her.

"Thanks, Tev. I think you're missing one of your teeth. Should I land so you can find it?" Stone and Chase started laughing while Tev ran for the nearest reflective surface.

"Take us out, Kat. Full speed. We have to catch up to the *Legendary* and I need to tell these two what the mission is."

"Will do," she replied. Chase turned and led his friends out to the common room while the ship entered hyperspace.

After Chase had finished briefing his friends, Kat came into the common room and handed him a datapad. "I think this is what you were looking for, Chase," she said, taking a seat next to Stone. His hulking, light blue bulk dwarfed her, and anyone looking from the other direction would be hard pressed to see her there. Chase enlarged the image on the screen and recognized the Lemurian K-22 stealth fighter.

"Is that a K-22?" Tev asked while leaning to look over Chase's shoulder. Chase frowned and transferred the image to the view screen on the common room wall.

"K-22?" Stone asked.

"They're the chief information-gathering ships of the fleet, but they also have some teeth in case their mission is compromised. They're twice the size of a normal fighter," Kat replied.

"The K-22 is produced as a two seat vehicle with a space behind the cockpit just large enough for an adult to lie down, but most pilots rip out the second seat to give themselves a little extra room. Very few of the ships actually use two pilots," Tev said.

"Do we know whose ship this is, Kat?" Chase asked.

"No, sorry. We were lucky to catch it on our sensors. Seems like this one has an enhanced stealth package. If whoever that is had waited twenty seconds longer to go to hyperspace, we would have missed it entirely," she replied.

Chase stood and the others followed suit. They all walked back onto the bridge and he said, "We'll need to let Captain Bander know we have a follower as soon as we exit hyperspace, Kat."

"Good idea. I'll send the transmission as soon as we arrive."

"You just want to flirt with Captain Bander some more, Katalla Swift," Fixer said while he was still tinkering with his newest creation. He refused to tell anyone what it was yet.

"Of course I want to flirt with the captain, Fixer. You did see him, right?"

Stone and Tev glanced at Chase to see how he would respond to that comment, but before the situation could get awkward Chase called out, "Who's hungry?"

"I could eat," Stone replied.

"How about you, Tev. Should I make something soft or do you still have enough teeth left to chew?" Kat asked with a playful smile.

"Very funny. I'll have whatever you guys are having."

"I want some jujani noodles," Fixer said without looking up.

"Well, you know where they are," Chase replied.

"Chase, be nice," Kat said, and then in a sugary voice added, "I'll get them for you, Fixer."

+++++

Sym made sure every last item on her ship was secured while she orbited Niburu. She wished she still had sensors, but since the planet was inhabited, she knew she could survive. She only needed to be there long enough to fix her communications and sensors. She sat in her pilot's seat and took a deep breath. She hit the ships thrusters and flew toward the planet. Initially, her ship's reentry was smooth, but when she hit the atmosphere everything shut down. She froze for a moment before crying out, [Not again!] Nothing was coming online. Her first thought was that she had been hit by some sort of disabling weapon, but this felt different. Her eyes grew wide with panic and her fur stood on end for the second time that day. Fear threatened to paralyze her, but she shook it off and reached for the manual crank that would extend the ship's gliders.

She was unsure she was strong enough to deploy them at her current speed. She gripped the crank tight with both hands and pulled with all her might. She felt the crank move almost half a turn. She needed three full turns to deploy. Her calculations told her she had maybe a minute and a half before one of Nibiru's mountains rose up to meet her. She grunted with the effort, and sweat started to form on her brow. She managed to move the crank one full turn, but the effort was exhausting. The fear began to well up in the pit of her stomach, but she suppressed it, and with an animalistic cry moved the crank almost another full turn. She cried out again and managed a half turn, and by this point, she could see the mountains through the clouds. She exerted herself to move the crank just short of the third full rotation.

The gliders had already begun slowing the descent, but were prevented from working to capacity until they were locked in. Sym unstrapped herself and stood. She placed one of her legs up on the console for leverage and pulled as hard as she could. The gliders locked into position and she felt the steering column loosen. She now had control back. She would still crash, but the gliders would slow the ship enough that she might survive. She could also steer to an extent now, and make sure she landed far from prying eyes. By this point, sweat was pouring off her body and her jumpsuit had begun to cling to her damp fur. She wrestled with the steering yoke until she saw a canyon high in the mountains.

The gliders had slowed her ship enough that she knew if she put it down right, she would survive. She aimed for the canyon and prayed to her gods. She swung in over the tree tops and aimed for a small clearing. Her powerless ship reacted too slow and skimmed the ground for the first time at the end of the clearing. The ship bounced off the ground and the gliders hit their first set of trees. After the eighth or ninth tree, the gliders ripped off leaving gaping holes in both sides of the ship.

Wind whipped into the ship in a loud whistle. The ship bounced again and the screech of metal on rock could be heard over the rushing of the wind. The ship finally skidded sideways and stopped with a loud thud. Sym sat in her seat for a moment before trying to move. Her entire body ached with exhaustion and the fear that comes with the threat of death.

[Just breathe. Just breathe, then move,] she whispered to herself.

When she finally tried to move, she cried out in pain. Her arm refused to work properly. She could not recall hurting it, but it was broken nonetheless. She stood on shaky legs, and noticed a slow drip of blood on her chair. With her good arm, she felt her head and felt the thick texture of her blood. She stumbled over to the medical cabinet and opened the door. When she looked into the cracked mirror, she saw that her head wound had opened again. She fashioned a sling for her arm, and changed the bandage above her eye. A spark caught the corner of her eye, and she realized her ship had caught fire. She reached for her go bag, pulled out a tent, some rations and the ship's black box. She fastened a knife to her belt and looked around the cabin. It was beginning to fill with smoke, and she knew there was not much time.

She stuffed as much rations and water into her go bag as she could, then she filled her pockets with bandages, sterilizer, pain meds, and medi-glue. She swung her bag and her tent over her back, picked up the black box, and left the ship. She walked through the destroyed trees of her ship's final path and watched from a distance as her only means of getting home went up in flames. She leaned against a tree and slid to the ground. Exhaustion had finally overtaken her and she closed her eyes.

+++++

The *Longshot* exited hyperspace just outside Planet Nine's gravity well. A transmission beeped and Kat pounced on it before Chase could answer it.

"Hello Captain Bander," she said with that sultry purr in her voice.

"Hello, Miss Swift. Nice of you to join us."

Kat was slightly taken aback by the captain's less than warm greeting. She wondered if it was her, or possibly Chase's friends that caused it. "Yeah we, um, got a little held up on Hyperborea." She shrugged her shoulders and frowned.

"Really, this wouldn't happen to have anything to do with the three members of the Lemurian freighter crew that woke up in the med center, would it?"

"I wouldn't know anything about it," she replied in her flirtatious voice with a wink. "Let me get Chase for you."

"That would be greatly appreciated. Thank you."

"Captain, what we're looking for would be on the far side of the planet in the mountainous region."

"I'll send a shuttle over, thank you. What should I tell my people we're looking for?"

"Ideally a ship, but in lieu of that, evidence of mineral testing."

Captain Bander crossed his arms and asked, "So, did your extra crew members make it aboard okay?"

"Well, there was a small tussle at the spaceport." The captain's eyebrow went up and Chase added, "But it was going on before I got there. I just helped them put a stop to it. Afterward, we left immediately. What were the injuries like?"

"Nothing major, a couple broken bones and a concussion. Just try and stay out of trouble, at least until this situation is resolved." He sighed like a disappointed father addressing a teenager.

"I'll do my best." The transmission ended and Chase looked up to see Stone and Tev beaming.

"Been a long time since we got you in trouble with a captain," Tev said while a huge grin emerged from under his mustache and spread across his face.

"Feels like old times," Stone said while drinking one of Fixer's green fizzys.

"I don't remember the old times so fondly," Chase replied. "Let's just find this missing alien before the Qantarah decide to invade the cluster."

Three hours later another transmission beeped. Chase answered it this time. "Captain, did you find anything?"

"No, nothing." He looked frustrated and Chase understood the pressure he must be under to succeed in this mission.

"Not to worry, Captain. I have two more targets that are highly likely for the profile I've worked up."

"You do realize we are under a time constraint here, right?"

"It's fine. We can split up. You take Planet Four and I'll take Planet Eleven. If she isn't on one of those two planets, we'll have to hit my secondary locations. I'll send you the coordinates to focus your search and I'll send you a transmission as soon as we know anything."

"We'll do the same," Captain Bander replied. "Good hunting." The transmission ended and Chase stepped off the bridge.

Another Transmission beeped and Kat answered it. "Chase, it's your mother again."

"I'll take it in my quarters, Kat. Prepare for the next jump."

"Okay."

Chase walked into his quarters and hit the blinking button. "Hi, Mom."

"It's about time. I was beginning to think you were ignoring me." She folded her arms and tapped her foot.

"I'm really busy, Mom. Is there something you need?" He sat down on his bed and looked into the holo-projector.

* * *
67

"You're always busy with your little friends. Who are you hunting with this time?"

"Everyone. Kat, Fixer, Stone and Tev. We need to make a jump, mom, so what's up?"

"Well, I do have some news for you, but first I want to know what's so important that you need the likes of Tev and Stone on your ship."

"They're my friends, Mom." He paused for a moment trying to decide what he should tell her. "We're actually on a mission for the Vanguard. I can't discuss what it is, but it's really important and it's also time sensitive, so..." He motioned with his hand for her to tell him what she wanted.

"A mission for the Vanguard? Really? Is this what you've been reduced to now? Hanging out with thugs and lying to your mother about it?" She folded her arms again and shook her head. "I'm really disappointed in you Chase."

"Mom, it's not a lie, and like I said. It's time sensitive, so you have until Kat tells me we can jump to hyperspace to let me know what you need or we'll have to pick this up another time." A light flashed indicating Kat was ready to make the jump.

"Chase we need to talk about the decisions—"

"We'll have to do it later, mom. Bye." He cut the transmission and let Kat know he was ready to make the jump. He left his quarters frustrated that his own mother refused to believe he might be doing something worthwhile. Frustration was evident on his face when he reached the bridge.

"Chase, is everything okay?" Kat asked with a tinge of worry in her eyes.

"Kat, do me a favor. Next time my mother sends a transmission, don't answer it." He sat down in his chair and added, "I need to be in a good place to talk to her or it always goes sideways."

"Sorry, Chase." She started to walk off the bridge, but he caught her arm.

"I'm sorry. I'm not upset with you. You didn't do anything wrong."

"I know, but thanks for saying it." She lingered with her hand in his for the briefest of moments, then continued off the bridge.

"When are you going to wise up and get back together with that one?" Tev asked.

"Yeah, there's only so long I'm willing to hold off," Stone added with a grin.

"It's a little more complicated than that," he replied. He didn't want to tell them the real reason they were no longer together, because they were her friends, too.

+++++

"They didn't find what they were looking for at Miners' Field or Planet Nine. The *Longshot* and the *Legendary* have split up. *Legendary* is searching Planet Four and *Longshot* is searching Planet Eleven," Agent Black said into the transmission.

The tiny form of Captain Seraphaz pranced back and forth before speaking. "Have you figured out what his thinking is yet?" Black adjusted the pitch to make the captain's voice higher. The high-pitched miniature hologram almost made him laugh until the captain continued, "How is he deciding where to search? What makes Planet Nine a better place to search than Planet Ten?"

"I don't know, Captain. I'm only privy to what he says to Captain Bander, not why he's saying it. It is clear to me that Bander is following his lead."

"That's troubling. How could the Flag possibly put an entire ship under the command of Chase Cadogan? That's a recipe for disaster. Who have you followed this time?"

"No one yet, but I know where they're both going and approximately how long they'll be there. So, who would you like me to follow?"

"Stick with Bander. You can intercept anything Cadogan sends him."

"That's what I was thinking. I was also thinking that I'm going to need some men once it comes time to take the alien from them. I know he picked up two of his old military buddies while he was on Hyperborea, and these guys have reputations as top notch fighters."

"I'll send Hazard in an assault shuttle with a dozen men." The Tiny hologram looked at him. Black figured the captain was trying to do one of those imposing stares he seemed to love, but the effect was lost at that size.

"Hazard? Are you sure that's a good idea? He's not exactly reliable when it comes to Chase Cadogan. He's more likely to let the alien get away, just for a chance to square off with Cadogan again," Black replied. He knew it was Seraphaz's call, but he really wanted to avoid anything that meant the involvement of Jay Lee Hazard.

Seraphaz bristled at being questioned. He fixed Black with what would have been an intimidating stare had he been present or at least life-sized, and said, "My reasons are my own and not for you to question. Do you understand?"

"Yes, sir," Black replied.

Seraphaz looked right into the cam and added, "And, Agent Black. You will have everything you need to take that alien from Cadogan. Do not fail me."

"I never do." The transmission died and Black was again left to wonder what the story was between Cadogan and the captain. *It just doesn't make any sense. This mission could mean the difference between war with the Qantarah or continued peace. Why mess with that over a petty grudge?* Black shook his head and prepared to follow the *Legendary*.

+++++

Sym opened her eyes and the pain rushed back in. Her head was throbbing, her arm needed immediate medical attention, and her entire body was stiff. The smell of burning metal mixed with burning wood hung heavy in the air and through it all she caught a whiff of her own pungent odor.

[I need a shower. A shower and a week on the beach. After a week in a recovery clinic. Look at me. I'm talking to myself now. I'm losing it.] She was slow to stand and she leaned heavy against the tree. Daytime had turned to night and she decided to eat some of her rations before setting up her tent.

A half hour later, she was finding it difficult to set up her tent with only one arm. She needed both the shelter and the protection her tent would offer. The temperature was dropping rapidly and the wind had picked up. She did not have clothing rated for this kind of weather. She had a blanket in her go bag, but to survive, she would need the shelter of her tent. She was nearly three-quarters complete when she heard the first howl. [What was that?] she asked herself, and she began to work faster.

Then it was closer. "Ahooooow!"

[Don't worry about the noise, Sym. The tent will protect you. Hurry up and finish your task.] She picked up the tent hammer and swung. The clank of the metal hitting the spike reminded her how much her head hurt. Two more swings and the spike was secured. She scurried to the opposite corner and repeated the process, wincing each time the blow was struck. On her second swing of her third spike she heard the first growl. She was now colder than she had ever felt. She secured the third corner with a heavy swing of the hammer and ran to the last corner.

She hit the spike once and after the metallic clang she heard a deep growl from the trees and dropped the hammer. She suppressed a shiver, rubbed her hand on her jumpsuit, and picked the hammer back up. She hit the spike again and checked to see if she still had her knife. She looked into the trees and could see what looked like a set of glowing eyes. She hit the spike one last time. Feeling something behind her, she spun around to see a large canine with black spikes protruding from its back. The canine's front paws displayed a set of long claws, and it bared its teeth in a feral growl.

"Grrrrrr."

Sym took a step back as fear washed over her. She lifted the hammer over her head and screamed, [Get away from me, beast!] She slashed downward and the canine leapt back. She was visibly shaking as she lifted the hammer again. The beast began pacing back and forth in front of her in a deliberate fashion. It stopped off to the side and sprang at her injured arm. Sym swiped at it with the hammer again, connecting with its paw.

The beast leapt back and growled again. "Grrrrrr, grrrrrr, grrrarrr."

[Get back!] she yelled again with another swing of the hammer. She was only three steps from the opening to the tent, but eight steps from her bag. *I need both to survive. Besides, if the beast follows me into the tent before I can secure the opening, I'm as good as dead. I have to at least drive off this one, and I have to do it before more show up.*

The beast leapt at her again and sank its teeth into her injured arm. She cried out in pain and hit the beast in the eye hard with her hammer. It let out a high-pitched yelp and stumbled around for a moment.

"Grrrrrr, arrrrrr, grrrrrr." The beast leapt one more time and Sym connected with the hammer again, but the hammer flew from her hand and the beast's claws tore into her leg. Blood was now flowing freely from her arm and her leg and the beast was still coming. It latched onto her bad arm again and growled while it started shaking its head.

Sym thought she would black out from the pain, but managed to get her knife off her belt. She yelled, [Get off of me,] swung the knife up into the neck of the beast, pulled it out, and did it again. The beast let out an ear splitting cry and let go of Sym's arm. It lumbered off into the trees and she saw her chance. She hurried to pick up her bag, the black box, and her hammer, crawled inside the tent, and secured the opening. She sat in the dark and began to sob. [How am I going to get off this world? How am I going to get home to my people?] Sym took the portable illumination sphere out of her go bag, opened her hand, and the sphere rose from her palm, illuminating the inside of the tent.

Without warning, several beasts began circling her tent. She knew they would never be able to get through the material. The tent was military issue and could stop blasters, swords, and most other attacks short of an explosion. Still, the clawing on the material was unnerving. After a few moments, she heard a whimper, which turned into a cry of agony. The growling started up as the rest of the wolves vied for a piece of the injured one.

Sym sterilized her leg, glued her wound closed and wrapped it in a bandage, hoping it would remain closed. She wiped salty tears from her eyes and said, [Come on, Sym, get yourself together. You can do this.] She applied the sterilizing agent to the bite marks on her broken arm next, and as soon as the liquid touched the wound, her body shot straight up and she let out a desperate cry. The noise startled the wolves and they scattered only to return a few moments later. She started to shake, but she wrapped her wound with a shaky hand.

She drank some of her water and took a dose of pain medicine before pulling the blanket out of her bag. She hoped it was as warm as the Qantaran quartermaster's literature boasted, because she was cold. Her body was shivering and she could not stop it. She knew it was only partially because of the cold. She had lost a lot of blood and her wounds might have become infected. She wrapped herself in the blanket and tried to figure out how she was going to get out of the mess she was in. Soon, her exhaustion gave way to a dreamless sleep.

Chapter five

[What is taking these humans so long? Do they think we will spare them extinction? Do they think they are the first that will not be trampled under the mighty Qantaran war machine? I do not think they understand just what is at stake,] Battle Conductor Garyn said while he paced the bridge.

[You did give them two weeks, your greatness,] the communications officer replied. The rest of the bridge crew busied themselves at their stations.

[It has already been two weeks, and still we hear nothing from them.] He slammed his fist on the console and began pacing again. [Ready the fleet. We attack immediately.]

The bustle of activity could already be heard from the bridge crew, none of whom looked up until the communications officer spoke. [Begging your pardon, Battle Conductor, but it has not yet been two weeks in cluster time. Our days are shorter than theirs, My Lord. If we attack now, we will be breaking our word to the humans.] The officer bowed his head when he finished speaking.

[My brother would never go for that,] Garyn mumbled. [How much longer do we have to wait then?]

[According to my calculations they still have four days.]

[Well that gives us four more days to study their defenses. Then, when we attack, it will be over quickly. Then we will not be on their time schedule, they will be on ours.] He paused, looked around the bridge and added, [I will go confer with our Primus. I am not to be disturbed.]

[Yes, My Lord,] the officer replied.

[You are to instruct the captains to perform full readiness checks on each ship until I return to give further instructions.]

[It will be as you say,] the officer replied. Garyn turned on his heel and marched off the bridge. When the door slid shut, a collective exhale went up from the bridge crew.

+++++

"Chase, we've found nothing and we're running out of time." Captain Bander's holographic image said. Chase could see the worry evident in his eyes. He felt the same way.

"We still have almost three days, and I have only two possible locations left that fit our profile. If we don't find evidence of this scientist there, we're back to square one." Chase hated to be wrong, especially when the stakes were so high.

"Has anyone given any thought to the idea that this might just be a ruse?" Kat asked. "Maybe the Qantarah are going to invade anyway and they just wanted an excuse."

"Sadly, we have thought about that, but the Vanguard doesn't seem to think that's the case," Bander replied.

"I agree," Chase said. "It doesn't make any sense strategically to give us two weeks warning. Plus the Qantarah are a pretty confident people. I doubt they would even see the need for trickery against us no matter how well defended our cluster is."

"Agreed." Bander was starting to pace which was always interesting to watch on a holographic transmission. He would pass through the hologram, moving out of sight, only to pass though again a moment later.

"Okay, let's do this," Chase said while looking at his planetary maps. "You take Planet Twenty-Seven and we'll take Planet Fourteen. Let us know if you find anything."

"Will do." The transmission faded and Kat prepared the jump to hyperspace.

"I wonder why they never named the uninhabited planets?" she asked while her fingers flew over the console.

"Why bother?" Tev replied. "With thirty-one planets and forty-three moons in the cluster, that's a lot of naming to do."

"Seventy-four," Fixer said. "They would have to find seventy-four names. It's easier to remember numbers. Only planets and moons with people get names. The rest get numbers."

"There you go," Tev said. "Fixer has all the answers."

"I guess so," Kat agreed. "We'll be in hyperspace for almost seven hours, so if anyone is tired, now would be a good time to try and sleep. Chase, you've been up for two days straight. Go catch a few hours. First Mate's orders."

Chase was about to protest, but the look on Kat's face let him know this would be another argument he would lose. "Okay. You're right. I could use a little sleep." He stood up and started to walk off the bridge.

"Can you get me a green fizzy, Chase?" Fixer asked while he continued tinkering with his project. Chase was really starting to wonder what it was.

"No, Chase, get him some water. He's been drinking too many green fizzys lately. He's going to make himself sick," Kat said.

"Okay, water it is." Chase waited to hear Fixer's protest, but it never came. Kat was the only one that Fixer would ever let do that. Chase reached the galley and picked up a bottle of water. He walked back to the entrance to the bridge and tossed the bottle to Fixer. Fixer missed it and had to go retrieve it while Kat just shook her head. He turned and walked down the corridor to his quarters. *When did she become the ship mom?* he wondered as the door to his quarters slid open.

Chase woke up almost seven hours later. He sat up, draped his legs over the side of the bed, and stretched his arms while a big yawn escaped his lips. His nose wrinkled up and he decided he needed to bathe. After a hot shower, he dressed and left his quarters. He arrived on the bridge just in time to hear the computer beep to let them know they were about to exit hyperspace.

"Just in time. You look rested," Kat said with an "I told you so," look on her face.

"I never said I didn't need the rest."

"Uh huh."

"Let's hope this is it or I'm out of ideas," Chase said while he looked at a map of the planet. Real space came back into focus and

Planet Fourteen came into view in front of them. "Head starboard until a third of the way around the planet."

"Already on it, Chase," Kat replied.

"I have a good feeling about this one," Tev said.

"You've said that about every planet we've been to," Stone replied.

"Why stop being optimistic now?"

"Statistically speaking this has a good chance of being the right planet," Fixer said.

"Sooner or later Chase is bound to be right," Tev said with a laugh.

"Nice, guys. Just remember, I can drop you on the next planet if I want," Chase replied in warning. Fixer looked up to see if he was serious and saw Chase shaking his head in the affirmative. Fixer's eyes grew wide for a moment until he noticed Kat shaking her head no.

"All right, enough fooling around. Let's get to work," Chase said, moving to the sensor board to enter the specifics of their search. After an hour of searching, they received a transmission from Captain Bander. "We're going to continue the search, but so far we've found nothing. How is it looking for you?"

"We've only been at it an hour," Chase replied. "We'll let you know if we find anything significant."

"Okay, I'll leave you to it, then." The transmission ended and the bridge went silent.

"He's pretty desperate," Stone said.

"Of course he is," Tev replied. "If we fail, it could mean war with the Qantarah. No one has ever stopped the Qantarah from expanding. They've just finished absorbing the remnants of the Faydra Alliance, and the rest of the galaxy is on edge wondering who will be next."

"I'm going to miss the brandy they used to produce on Faydra," Stone said while he continued monitoring the planet's surface.

"I'm sure what's left of the Faydra are going to miss it, too," Kat said.

"I would think the Jalindi are next," Fixer said while he adjusted his search parameters. "They are the closest civilization of importance. We're much further away."

"The Jalindi are no better than the Qantarah," Tev said.

"You're right. We're lucky they're not as powerful, because they are much closer to us than the Qantarah are," Stone added.

"You all may be right, but for now we need to stop talking and keep working." Chase hated having to give orders, even though it was his ship. It was just so easy for this group to lose focus during tasks that lacked the involvement of action or violence. "Wait a second. I think I've got something here." Chase ran his fingers over the console, adjusting settings and increasing the outputs. "There's definitely evidence of recent testing here."

"I'm picking up a strange metal," Kat added. "I say we go down and have a look."

"If I'm not mistaken, it's Fourteen's windy season," Tev said.

"True, but it doesn't look like anything is building up right now. I think we can get in and out before it does," Chase said while he continued studying the readings. "Pull the communications array in, just in case."

"On it," Stone replied.

"Follow the metal Kat's sensors picked up." Chased hurried to the viewport, hoping his eyes would see something the sensors did not. The ship flew over the grey, rocky terrain for several minutes until she began to slow. They came to a stop and Chase yelled, "She definitely tested here, look." Everyone else looked out the viewport and saw the remains of the testing site. Several holes nearly a third of a meter in diameter pocked the landscape.

"Kat, would you be so kind as to take us two point six kilometers to port?" Tev asked.

"What do you see, Tev?" Chase asked while he hurried back to his sensors.

"Finished metal of unknown composition. It may be her ship!"

"No, it's too small to be her ship," Kat said.

"Maybe part of her ship," Stone said.

When they reached the coordinates, Chase spotted it. The shiny copper-like color was a stark contrast to the light grey swirling dust of the surface. "It's definitely part of a ship. Looks like an array of some sort."

"If it's her communications array, that would explain why she has yet to check in," Stone said.

"So, where's the rest of her ship?" Tev asked.

"Another planet. If my communications array fell off, I would land on another planet to repair it. She's on another planet," Fixer said without taking his eyes off the readings he was looking at.

"I agree. The closest inhabited worlds are Nibiru and the Avalon moon," Chase replied. "Kat, get us out of here, the wind is starting to build."

"So, where should we go?" Stone asked.

"Obviously we go to Avalon," Tev replied.

"Not so fast," Kat said while she took the ship out of the slight gravity well of Planet Fourteen. "If that was her communications array, chances are her sensors were damaged as well."

"Meaning?" Tev took a seat and started tapping his foot.

"Meaning, if she had no sensors she might not know Nibiru has electromagnetic problems in its atmosphere." Chase pulled up a map of Nibiru looking for a possible point of entry along their trajectory. "Nibiru is significantly closer. I think we should at least try there first. Stone, let the communications array back out. We'll send Bander a quick message and make the jump. Kat, ready the ship to jump."

A moment later, the transmission came back online and Chase saw that they had missed three. Two from Captain Bander and one from his mother. He sent a transmission to the *Legendary* and waited a moment for Bander's face to come into view.

"Hey, Captain, good news."

"We almost jumped to Planet Fourteen to find you guys. We could use some good news. Let's hear it!"

"Sorry about that. We went to the surface, so we pulled our array in just in case."

"Ah, the wind storms. Okay, I guess I'm not mad anymore, and I'm guessing you found something."

"We did, sir," Chase replied. "She was here, but we believe her ship was damaged in a wind storm because we found an array of some sort. The metallic composition was unknown to us. We're going to check out Nibiru. She needed to repair her ship and may not have known about the EM problem in the atmosphere if her sensors were damaged."

"If she went to Nibiru unaware of the EM problem, this could turn from locating to recovering pretty quick."

"I agree, sir. We'll send another transmission as soon as we leave Nibiru's atmosphere."

"The *Longshot* has EM shielding powerful enough to land on Nibiru?"

"Yeah, but it's not somewhere we can stay for the long haul."

"Understood, good luck. *Legendary* out." The transmission ended and Chase motioned for Kat to make the jump to hyperspace. A moment later, the stars elongated before them, stretching out to what seemed like forever and their ship was gone.

+++++

"Send Hazard and some men to Nibiru," Agent Black said. "I think the bet the Vanguard placed on the *Longshot* just paid off."

"Nibiru? Are you sure?" Captain Seraphaz asked.

"Not entirely, but Cadogan was able to make a pretty compelling case to Bander. It's a gamble, but I think it's worth the risk."

"Agreed. You shall have Hazard and a dozen men out to you in six hours. Let's make sure that if this alien is alive, she stays that way. Eliminate the rest if you need to."

"Six hours? They could be gone by then."

"Well than you had better make sure you know where they are going, Agent Black." Seraphaz's image paused as if something had distracted him. He looked back to Black and added, "I want that alien, do you understand?" Before Seraphaz ended the transmission, Black heard him mumble, "Cadogan will not beat me again."

What's that all about? he wondered. *I'm going to have to find out why Seraphaz hates this kid so much. It could be useful information to have should I ever need something from the good captain.* He punched up the coordinates on the ship's hyperdrive and took one last look at the *Legendary* before being drawn into hyperspace.

+++++

The *Longshot* dropped below the clouds and Chase held the yoke tight. Even with sophisticated EM shielding this would be a tricky landing. There was just something about Nibiru's atmosphere that disagreed with technology.

"You'd think that after thousands of years of space travel, the Commonwealth would have these types of problems sorted," Tev complained as he held the arms of his chair tight and gritted his teeth.

"It's just one of the cluster's many mysteries," Kat replied. "Do you need Stone to hold your hand while we land?" She smiled and looked over to Fixer. "How about you, Fixer? Are you okay?"

Fixer was strapped in, but he was still tinkering with his little project. Without looking up he said, "Chase is a good pilot, he'll land us safely." He repeated himself twice more before trailing off and becoming engrossed in his project again.

The ship hit an EM pocket and dropped a couple hundred feet, but then righted itself and Chase continued on the vector he believed the missing scientist would have used. After a few minutes had passed, he called out, "I see smoke. Can we magnify the image?"

"Not yet. There's too much interference in the atmosphere. The equipment's still a little out of whack," Stone replied.

"Is that a scientific term, Stone?" Kat asked causing an eruption of nervous laughter from Tev while Chase continued to fly toward the smoke.

Tev release his death grip on one of the armrests and pointed out the viewport. "There! A trail of downed trees," he said.

"That has to be our missing alien," Kat replied.

"Let's just hope she's still alive," Chase said. He flew over the area and swung back around to a small clearing right before the tree damage began. He set the *Longshot* down and said, "Fixer, you stay here and keep the EM shielding running at as close to one hundred percent as possible. Looks like we've got a little over a kilometer of forest to get through."

"We shouldn't stay on this planet more than a couple hours, Chase. It's bad for the ship," Fixer replied while walking toward the galley.

"I know, buddy, we'll have to get in and out. Everyone gear up. Weapons only, there are a lot of jocawolves up here."

"I don't like jocawolves, Chase. Katalla Swift is scared of jocawolves, too."

"I know, buddy, that's why you're staying on the ship. Don't worry, they can't get in."

"I don't like them because they perceive anyone as a threat. They're more than happy to eat each other if they run out of food, but as long as any humans are roaming around, they'll all be after us," Kat said.

Chase turned to the rest of the crew and said, "Okay everyone, let's go. From the looks of the area, this is probably a recovery mission." They left the safety of the ship and headed out toward the smoke. Not much tracking would be involved because there was a trail of downed trees for them to follow.

Ten minutes into their trek they began to hear growling all around them. "I don't like the sound of that," Kat said.

"What's the matter, Kat, afraid of a few cuddly puppies," Tev said in teasing. Kat was usually pretty confident and loved to dish it out, and Tev relished the opportunity to finally tease her back.

"That's ironic isn't it? Our little kitty Kat afraid of a few nice doggies," Stone added with a laugh.

"That's not really ironic, Stone," Chase said, "And it sounds like more than a few." He looked at his team and said, "Kat, up here on my left. Stone behind me and Tev behind Kat. You guys cover our six. I don't think these wolves are going to let us through without a fight." They continued making their way through the damaged trees. Over broken trunks, under burnt leaves, they followed the path of destruction while the smoke hung heavy in the humid air.

Not more than a minute later, Chase's prediction came to pass. The growling intensified and the wolves started appearing at the edge of the trees.

"I hate the way their eyes glow. They look so evil," Kat said while keeping her blaster trained on the trees to her left. Without warning one of the wolves jumped out at Chase and was met with a blaster bolt to the neck. A high pitched yelp died out, and the scent of charred flesh filled the air. Then the growling reached a crescendo.

"I don't like this," she said while she inched closer to Chase.

"Calm yourself, Kat, they can sense your fear," Tev said. Several wolves appeared through the trees. Their hungry mouths were dripping saliva. Their feral snarls grew louder and their eyes glowed a burnt orange through the smoke. Their collective growl turned to bass-filled barking before the lead jocawolf charged.

Chase now had a blaster in each hand and the rest of his crew followed suit. Jocawolves surrounded them and charged. Barking and growling rang out through the canyon. Chase's team stood back to back and began firing at will. Wolves went down with high pitched yelps, but more took their place.

"We need to keep moving," Chase yelled over the sound of blasterfire. "If we stay here, eventually they'll get the upper hand."

"How many do you think there are?" Kat asked, her voice shaky. Chase could see the sweat forming on her brow and neck, and he could see the wide-eyed look on her face. He had never seen her like this before. He fired again, taking down another wolf. He heard an explosion and looked over to see Tev with a smile on his face as he loosed another grenade.

The second explosion was enough to give the wolves pause and Chase yelled, "Now, let's move." They stayed in formation while they jogged through the once quiet forest. "I see a tent of some sort, she may still be alive." He noticed the wolves that were scratching at the tent and mused that there may end up being too many wolves for them to get out of the forest alive.

+++++

Sym knew she was dead. She was saying prayers to the gods of the Qantarah. She knew she would see them in the afterlife soon. Her injuries needed more attention than she could give, and after clawing away at her tent all night, the creatures were beginning to scratch through. She had either underestimated the strength of their claws, or overestimated the military strength fabric of her tent.

She could think of nothing more horrible than being eaten alive, so she planned to take her own life. She only hoped her gods could forgive her. The pungent smell of her own sweat, blood, and fear filled the tent and drove the creatures outside into a frenzy. Watching the blood seep through the bandages on her leg and her arm, she began to cry. [I am not ready for my life to end,] she whispered.

She drew her knife and paused for a moment, dropping her knife when she heard the sounds of blasterfire followed by two explosions. The growling and barking still filled her ears, but now she could hear the yelps and the agonizing cries of death as someone had engaged the beasts in combat. The blasterfire was getting closer now, and she wondered if that was good or bad. The sound of the energy was unlike Qantaran weapons, she only hoped the people fighting the creatures outside the tent would help her.

"We have them on the run," she heard a deep male voice say.

"They won't be gone for long. We've got to get back to the ship quickly," another male voice said.

"My grenades seem to be keeping them at bay, but I've only got a few left," a third voice added.

"Let's just find her and go," a frightened female voice yelled. Some more blasterfire rang out and there was a knock at the tent.

"My name is Chase Cadogan and I've been sent to rescue you."

[How do I know I can trust you?] Sym replied.

"I'm sorry; I don't understand your language."

"She probably doesn't understand ours either," the female said.

Sym did understand their language, but had never spoken it out loud. She decided that these people were a better option than the wolves or her knife, so she opened the flap of the tent and limped out, knife in hand. The exertion of standing caused her to stumble, but a steady hand kept her from falling.

"Easy there, Ma'am. Looks like you've had quite the ordeal." She pointed to her black box and her go bag and the man helping her stand said, "I think she needs her bag and that piece of equipment." He noticed her shaking her head and asked, "Can you understand us?" Her nod was affirmative and she saw the female go into the tent to grab her gear.

"We're gonna need to move pretty fast. Do you think our friend here is up to it?" the big blue one asked.

"The jocawolves are gonna come back, can you move quickly?" the man holding her up asked.

"Do you think she understands us, Chase?" the female asked the man holding onto her.

"I think so, can you?" he asked again. Sym shook her head and pointed to her injured leg.

"Okay, I'll carry her, Stone, you take point, Tev, Kat, you cover our six." He pressed one of his blasters into her hand and asked, "Do you know how to shoot?" Sym shook her head yes and he added, "You point it at the wolves and press here." He pressed the trigger and the blaster fired. She shook her head again and the one holding her, she thought he was called Chase said, "Okay, let's move."

+++++

They had made it just over half a kilometer back toward the ship before they heard the first growls of the jocawolves. "That's not good," Kat said.

"Don't worry, Kat, I shall save you from the wolves," Tev replied, with a laugh.

"You're really enjoying this, aren't you, Tev?"

His big white teeth shone out from under his bushy mustache and she could have sworn his helmet strap tightened as he grinned. "Of course. It's a very rare day indeed when I get to tease Katalla Swift and she has nothing to say in return."

"I'll think of something," she mumbled.

"I don't think they're going to let us pass," Stone said pointing at a long line of the wolves. The ship was now in sight, but over a hundred wolves stood between them and their means of escape. Jocawolves, being extremely intelligent, often acted in ways that could be considered strategic. Unfortunately, this seemed to be one of those times. The howling and barking started up again and the wolves readied for a charge. Just then, the rear thrusters of the ship fired a short burst, burning nearly half the wolves. High pitched howling could be heard and the smell of burning fur was in the air. The wolves that weren't killed instantly rolled on the ground in agony.

"Way to go, Fixer," Tev yelled in triumph while he threw a grenade into the midst of several confused canines.

"Let's get to the ship," Chase yelled while he shot one of the wolves. His eyebrow rose in surprise when his alien charge dropped one as well. "Great shot," he said, and she managed a weak smile.

Stone was working his way through the jocawolves as if he were taking target practice. Kat stayed close to Tev and they were eliminating their share, but some were getting pretty close. Three broke through and Tev shot one while Sym shot one. The last jumped at Chase and locked onto his arm. He cried out in pain and dropped Sym as gently as he could. He punched the wolf in the face twice and grabbed the knife off his belt and stabbed it through the neck. The wolf slouched with a high pitched yelp and Chase retrieved his blaster and shot the next one.

Stone picked Sym up and made a break for the ship while Tev and Kat cleared a path. A wolf leapt for Kat's back only to be shot in mid-air by Chase. The wolf's dead body still hit Kat with a good deal of force, knocking her over, but her quick reflexes and dancer's grace had her back on her feet in what seemed like one fluid motion. She was lucky to be wearing protective gear or the spikes on the wolf's back would have impaled her when the dead wolf hit.

"That was too close," she yelled when she and Tev made it to the ship. They laid down cover fire for Chase to sprint the last twenty meters. Chase dove into the ship and could hear the wolves slamming into the hatch as it slid closed.

"I'd prefer to never do that again. Now, let's get out of here," Chase said while he marched toward the bridge. Tev was already in his seat prepping for takeoff.

"I've got this one, Chase. You need to rest and let Kat see to that arm," Stone said.

Chase nodded at him and asked, "Where's our guest?"

"She's on one of the couches in the common room," Kat said while she led Chase off the bridge. "C'mon. Tev, Stone, and Fixer should be able to get us out of here."

Chase agreed that he needed to take some pain meds and lay down. On the way out he stopped and called to Fixer, "Nice move, Fixer. You really saved our butts out there."

"Tev told me to say I was aiming for you, but I don't know why. I would never aim for you."

"He was just trying to be funny, Fixer. He would never hurt Chase either," Kat said with the usual kind smile she reserved for Fixer.

"He should try harder to be funny," Fixer replied.

"Yes he should," Chase said before leaving the bridge. He saw the scientist sitting on the couch and she still had a panic-stricken look in her eyes. "Hello. My name is Chase. Can you tell me your name?"

"I... I am... called Sym," she stuttered.

"Sym, that's a nice name," Kat said. "So, you can speak our language."

"Understand... nev... never spoke."

"So, you understand us, but don't have any practice speaking our language. We can work with that," Chase said.

"Chase, we need to look at your arm," Kat said.

"Her first, I'll just keep pressure on the wound," he replied.

Sym looked at them and said, "Tha... thanks... you?"

"You are very welcome," Kat replied. She looked at the wounds and mumbled, "What a mess." She removed the blood soaked bandages from Sym's leg, arm and head. Sym cried out in pain when Kat touched her arm. "I'm so sorry, Sym. This is probably going to hurt a bit." She looked over to Chase and added, "I'm pretty sure she broke her arm."

"Just do the best you can," he replied.

Kat cleaned her lacerations and closed her open wounds with medical glue. She put fresh bandages on Sym's head, arm, and leg. She also fashioned a much more useful sling for her broken arm. "I'd like to give you some pain medicine and something to prevent infection, but I'm not sure what is safe for you to have."

Sym pointed to her bag and Kat handed it to her. She took out some medication and nodded her thanks. Kat brought her a glass of water and moved to help Chase.

She took a look at the ugly bite marks on his arm and winced. "That must really hurt," she said. She opened up an anti-infection liquid and prepared to pour some on the wound. "This is really going to hurt." She poured the liquid over the wound and watched Chase's face skewer up into a grimace, but he only grunted. She then applied the medi-glue and covered the wound with a bandage. She handed him a painkiller and said, "That wasn't so bad now, was it?"

"No, it was fine," Chase replied. "How come we're not off this rock yet?" As if in answer to his query the ship began a low rumble. The *Longshot*'s deck plating began to shake while she rose into the atmosphere. A few moments later, they were in orbit around the planet.

"Chase, we should have Bander meet us on Avalon. I'm not sure Commonwealth doctors will know how to treat Sym. The priestesses there can get her into the healing waters and she'll be doing a whole lot better by the time we meet up with Bander."

"Sounds like a plan, can you call it in? I'm starting to feel the effects of the pain meds. How long until we can jump?"

"Fixer said it would be a little while until the system is okay again. He thinks we were on the planet a few minutes too long." Kat turned and left for the bridge. Chase watched her the whole way.

A moment later, she was on the comms. "Chase, I've got your mom on transmission. I'm transferring it to the common room."

Chase bit back a curse. He was in no mood to speak to his mother again. Still, he put on a smile and hit the transmission button. "Hey, mom, what's up?"

"You cut me off before I could even tell you why I was contacting you. What kind of son does that?"

"Mom, I'm still on the mission you don't believe I'm on, and we are jumping to hyperspace in a few minutes. How about you save how disappointed you are in me until after you actually tell me what you need to say. This way if I have to leave again—"

"Chase Cadogan! I thought I raised you better than that."

"Look, mom, I love you, but I'm on a very important, time sensitive mission, whether you believe it or not. I just got bit by a jocawolf and I'm not in a good mood, now please," he broke off because his voice had started to rise. He composed himself and continued, "Please, mom, what's up?"

"It's your father. He's contracted Dizer's syndrome. He doesn't have long to live. I'd like you to see him before he's too far gone."

"Dizer's? How?" Even though he had not been on speaking terms with his father for a while, the news hit him like a punch in the gut.

"I don't know, Chase," she replied in a voice that quivered.

"Mom, I'm so sorry. How are you doing?" Chase had forgotten his impatience with his mother and now he felt awful about it.

"I'm holding up. Your sister and Sol are on their way in from Norumbega to spend a couple weeks with him. It will be good for him to have them here. How about you? Are you coming home?"

"It would be great to see Laney and Sol, but are you sure Dad even wants to see me? We haven't spoken in a long time." His father's last words to him flashed through his mind. "You are the biggest disappointment of my life." Chase had decided at that point that he would never go back home. "If he's got as little time as you say, are you sure he wants to spend any of it with his greatest disappointment?"

"Chase," his mother's voice softened. "He's regretted saying that from the moment it left his lips. He's proud of you. We both are. He wanted to apologize, it's just that the two of you are both so stubborn. Please come home. I need you here."

"Okay, Mom. I should be done with all of this in a day or two. Then I'll drop off Tev and Stone and swing by for a couple days."

"Thank you. Now, what's this about being bitten by a jocawolf?"

"Just another day with us ruffians and thugs, Mom."

An alert beeped and Chase knew they were ready to go. "I really do have to go now, but I'll see you soon." He ended the transmission and looked out the common room viewport. He thought he saw the K-22 again, but before he could confirm, the stars began to elongate until the *Longshot* was pulled into hyperspace.

"Tev," he called up to the bridge. "I thought I saw that K-22 again. I think we're being followed."

"Copy that. What do you want us to do about it?"

"I'm not sure. Bander's going to meet us on Avalon, so it might not matter. Just keep an eye out would ya?"

"No problem. Fixer is already adjusting the sensors to look for a K-22 with an enhanced stealth package."

"Sounds good." He turned off the comms and looked to his guest. During the conversation with his mother he had forgotten she was there. "Sorry you had to hear all of that," he said. She just nodded and laid her head back.

Chapter six

"Cadogan came through for us, Flag Officer Victor. We're on our way to rendezvous with him on Avalon," Captain Bander said into the transmission. He was beaming with pride.

"That's fantastic news, but why go to Avalon?" the Flag asked, motioning one of his men to go find the Vanguard.

"The scientist crash landed on Nibiru and sustained heavy injuries. She was also attacked by jocawolves. Cadogan and his people had to fight their way through the wolves to retrieve her. The crew of the *Longshot* figured the priestesses and their magic pools of water could heal her better and faster than our doctors could."

"They were probably right. Last thing we want to do is give the Qantarah their scientist back looking like we tortured her for information." The Vanguard walked in the room and the Flag acknowledged him with a crisp salute. "Is there anything else we should know about?"

"Cadogan believes he is being followed by a K-22 with an enhanced stealth package. Do you have anyone else on this?"

"No we don't," Vanguard Tobias replied. "I have faith in you and Cadogan. If anyone is following him, they are not getting their orders from here."

"But the K-22's are our ships. We haven't sold any in the private sector, have we?" Captain Bander hated to think there was someone else out there with one of their stealth fighters, but he had to know what he was up against.

"We have not," Flag Officer Victor replied. "If a K-22 is following them, it is one of ours, but it is acting without authority."

"Does Cadogan have permission to defend himself if the K-22 becomes aggressive?"

"He not only has the authority, but he'll have our complete backing," Vanguard Tobias said.

Flag officer Victor added, "I'm going to query all of our fleet groups right now and tell them to recall all K-22's. No one should be out there following you or impeding your progress. This mission is too important."

"It's probably some overachiever ready to help if necessary." Even as he said it, Bander knew it wasn't true.

"That is likely," the Vanguard replied. "Let us know as soon as you have her. Then we can begin to make our preparations to turn her over to the Qantarah."

"Yes, sir," Bander replied with a crisp salute. He still felt a thrill every time he spoke to the Vanguard. He supposed he had Cadogan to thank for that.

After the transmission ended, the Vanguard looked at the Flag and said, "If we avoid this war, Victor, I'm going to make Cadogan a wealthy man."

"I'm still trying to find out what happened concerning his discharge, Tobias. It's troubling to me that one of my soldiers, especially one so heroic, could be cast aside so easily without my knowledge."

"Don't beat yourself up, Juel. You weren't the Flag yet. This isn't your fault. I should have followed up more closely, but all of that is in the past."

"And like a good soldier, Cadogan came through for us again. Now, if you'll excuse me, I have to go find out which fleet group has a missing stealth fighter." He stood up and saluted, spun on his heel with practiced precision, and marched out of the room leaving the Vanguard alone with his thoughts.

+++++

"You were spotted, Black!" Seraphaz yelled through the transmission.

"That's impossible, Captain. No one spots me!"

"Well Cadogan did, or I wouldn't have just gotten a transmission from the Flag asking after the whereabouts of all of my K-22's."

"I guess the kid is as good as advertised," Black mumbled. He hated making mistakes and he hated giving anyone his respect even more, but Cadogan was earning it right now. "Cadogan was gone when I arrived at Nibiru. I believe he is on his way to Avalon. So, what happens now?"

"I'll send Hazard to Avalon. You have to double time it back here. I'll have to put Sergeant Tendissa in charge of the operation."

Black felt his blood pressure rising. "Are you sure that's a good Idea? Sending Hazard in with a bunch of mercs smells like failure to me. I'm the only one that can reign in Hazard once he gets going."

"No, it's not a good idea!" Seraphaz yelled. "But you had to go and get spotted, so it's all we've got."

Black knew his face was starting to redden. "You can't take me off this. It's my assignment!" he said, enunciating each word for effect.

"I can and I am!" Captain Seraphaz replied. "I need you back here ASAP! Do you understand?"

"You're going to regret this! Mark my words, Hazard will mess this up over his stupid vendetta!"

"Let's hope not."

Agent Black could see that he was not going to win this argument, so he relented and asked, "Where are you now?"

"I'm leading a flotilla stationed at the third entrance to the cluster. In case the Qantarah try to send something small through."

"Once Hazard gets to Avalon, I'll be able to reach you in seven hours."

"I hope you get here before the Flag discovers you're gone, or we'll both have some explaining to do."

"Do you really think he's going to waste his time tracking down a K-22 that he can't even prove was following his bounty hunter when he's got a possible invasion coming?"

"I'd rather not find out. The Flag has already passed me over for a fleet captain position once. I don't want to give him any reason to do so again."

Now Black understood what this was really about and his anger began to abate. "Ah, so you're angling to be one step away from the Flag. Copy that. I'll make sure I'm back as soon as possible." Black had to take a parting shot, and he enjoyed the look of indignation that crossed the captain's face. It was even funnier in the miniature setting he had the hologram programmed to. He almost had to stifle a smirk.

"Glad you see my dilemma," Seraphaz replied in a dry tone before cutting the transmission. Black took note that the captain made sure to get the last word in this time.

+++++

"How are you feeling, Sym?" Chase asked while he rested on the couch opposite his guest. She was humanoid in appearance, with light brown fur almost a quarter of an inch long covering her lithe body. She had a pleasant face with big, brown orbs for eyes. Her nose and mouth almost reminded him of a bear's muzzle, but not nearly as pronounced. Her fingers ended in nails that looked like they could become claws if she were less civilized, and she had long brown hair. Kat had given her some clothes because her jumpsuit was ruined, and she wore them well.

"I am... still in... hurt, is it?" she replied, cradling her broken arm.

"Pain. The word you're looking for is pain. I'm sorry to hear that. You are picking up our language very quickly. Are all of your people as smart as you?"

"My ship... took your sounds... and made... my sounds." She hated searching for words. She was one of the most renowned scientists on her world, but she knew that right now she must have sounded like a child.

"Oh, you had a translation program. That's how you understand us. That's fantastic." Chase smiled to try and put her at ease.

"Yes, translation program," she repeated.

"Good. If I start speaking too fast and you don't understand me, tell me to slow down."

"Slow down," she repeated again.

"Great. We're taking you to a place where your injuries can be healed or at least mostly healed. Then we are going to pass you off to one of our military leaders, and he is going to return you to your people. They sent a whole bunch of ships looking for you. You must be very important." Chase paused and adjusted his bandage. "What were you looking for, anyway?"

He asked politely, and he was pleasant, but she knew that he knew it was a less than honorable reason. "I was... searching for xallodium."

"Xallodium? Never heard of it."

"It is the...important... metal for Qantaran ships and... battle."

"It's important for Qantaran ships and weapons? Did you find any?" Chase was really interested now. This could be huge for the Commonwealth.

"I did. I found... abundance... more than enough... for war."

"You think your people would invade us to get this xallodium?"

"I know... they destroy for... much smaller."

"Why are you telling me this?"

"Trust you... not to hurt... Sym."

"I would never hurt you. You're right," He looked her in the eyes and added, "But others might not treat you as kindly."

"I will not tell... Garyn... what my... finding is."

"Why? Why would you help us?"

"I do not want... cluster... destr—"

"You don't want to see us destroyed." He looked her over again and added, "I believe you."

Sym felt she could really open up to this human and it left her wondering why. "Garyn... killed my... papa... teach my... town... learning."

"Your military leader killed your father just to teach your city a lesson? I think I hate this guy already. I'm really sorry, Sym."

"Your papa... not well?"

"No, I guess you heard that, huh?" She nodded and he continued, "I haven't gotten along with my dad for a long time, and now I may never have the chance." He thought he saw compassion in her eyes, or it could have just been the pain of recalling her own father's death.

She was about to reply when Kat called over the comms. "We'll be exiting hyperspace in two minutes. Then I'll put a call in to my cousin and she should get us right in."

"Cousin?" Sym asked.

"It's a relative. Not a sibling, a cousin is the offspring of your Mother or Father's sibling. Kat's cousin is one of the priestesses of Avalon and will hopefully be the one to help you." He stood up and added, "I need to be on the bridge, would you like to come? I'll make Stone sit in the jump seat." She nodded and he helped her up. She leaned on him while they walked onto the bridge.

As soon as they entered the bridge, he brought her over to Stone's seat. He stood and let her take it. Fixer stopped what he was doing the moment he laid eyes on Sym and became transfixed.

"Say hello to Sym, Fixer," Kat said while she continued to watch his reaction. She stood and let Chase have his own seat and Chase thought it was funny that both Stone and Tev had deferred to her while he was resting. *She really is a force to be reckoned with*, he thought.

"Hello, Sym. My name is Fixer. I have never met a Qantaran before."

"Fixer?"

"It's a name my dad gave me when I was younger because I like to fix things."

"She doesn't know a lot of our words yet, Fixer, but she does understand us and she's happy to meet you," Kat said.

"Yes," Sym said and noticed that Fixer was still staring.

"Buckle up, Fixer. We're heading down to Avalon," Chase said in a voice loud enough to shake Fixer out of his fascination with Sym.

"When we get there I have to change out the energy modules, Chase. You made us stay on Nibiru too long and now we need to change out the modules," Fixer said with a frown.

"Okay, buddy, no problem."

"Next time don't stay as long, Chase."

"It's not like we stopped for zarack burgers. We were fighting for our lives."

"This is my favorite moon," Kat said before Fixer could carry the discussion any further. "It's so beautiful here. Almost all of the people here worship Avalon, the goddess of nature. Very few defile the planet in any way."

Sym nodded her understanding and asked, "Avalon is the name of the moon and the goddess?"

"Yeah, the people here named their home after the goddess they worship," Tev answered from behind her.

Chase brought the *Longshot* in low, so they could see the flowing rivers and rolling hills. The sky almost had a light green hue while the brown, unnamed planet that Avalon orbited could be seen heavy in the sky like a parent afraid to leave her child's side. The light blue grass swayed as their ship flew by, and Chase brought the *Longshot* down next to a patch of trees. The priests and priestesses had constructed their abbey using the trees as corner and centerpieces. They damaged as little as possible while keeping the organic feel of the trees. The craftsmanship was remarkable and Chase sent Kat an approving nod.

The party of six exited the ship to see a woman who looked a lot like Kat, wearing a flowing white robe, waiting to greet them. Kat ran ahead of them and wrapped her cousin in a fierce embrace. "I've missed you so much, Felicia."

"I have missed you as well, Katalla. Please, introduce me to your friends." She gestured to take in the remaining crew members and bowed slightly.

Kat began pointing. "This is my ship's captain, Chase Cadogan, and that's my good friend, Fixer Faraday." She pointed to Fixer who was busying himself tinkering with the project he wouldn't say anything about. "That's just Tev and Stone," she said with a smile and a wink in their direction. She pointed to Sym and added, "And she is our injured friend, Sym."

"I see she is of the Qantarah. What brings her so far from home?"

"Her ship crashed on Nibiru," Chase said. "Then she was attacked by jocawolves. Can you help her? We need to get her back to her people in two days or there might be... problems."

A light of understanding filled her eyes. The news of the possible Qantaran invasion had reached the abbey almost two days ago. "I understand, Chase. Please, come this way." She stopped and looked at their weapons and added, "There's no need for those, I assure you, we are quite safe here."

"Thanks, but if it's all the same to you, we'd rather be ready just in case."

"Suit yourselves. Please follow me." She led them to a cave, hidden at the base of a sprawling mountain. Picking up a torch that had been left by the entrance and igniting it, she then led them to a pool of water, where four other priestesses were standing ankle deep, offering prayers to Avalon.

"Can I wait outside?" Stone asked. "This isn't really my type of scene."

"Yeah, sure. We should probably have someone keeping an eye out anyway," Chase replied while looking around the cave. Stalactites hung overhead, but not in a menacing way. Torchlight cast shadows on the smooth walls and the reflection of the light on the water cast a warm, orange glow that lit up the cave.

"This cave is stunning," Kat said to her cousin.

"Avalon has indeed blessed it. Come, let us submerge your friend in the healing waters."

+++++

"Have you found out anything about the K-22 that was following Cadogan?" Tobias asked when the Flag walked back into the conference room.

"In fact I have, sir. Captain Seraphaz began acting a bit strange when I asked about his K-22's, so I followed up with an officer I had personally placed on one of his ships. I found out that a K-22 had been deployed off book."

Tobias craned his neck to look up at his loyal military commander and asked, "Seraphaz? Why do I know that name?"

"Because he's the man that threw Chase Cadogan out of the military after he had saved your daughter's life, and now, he's the one dogging Cadogan's steps." Flag Officer Victor sat down next to his leader and long-time friend. He pressed a button and the windows tinted dark, the door slid closed and a short burst of static followed. He leaned over and in a conspiratorial tone added, "We're off record now."

It was almost unheard of to go off record in the conference room. During his entire tenure as Vanguard, this constituted his first off record meeting. "What is it you would like to discuss, Juel?"

"Captain Seraphaz, sir. My source also told me he warned Jay Lee Hazard of his impending capture, and that it wasn't the first time he ruined a bounty for Chase Cadogan." He stopped talking when a servant entered with a cart containing drinks. The servant hurried out and Juel swept the cart for listening devices.

"What could he possibly have against Cadogan? He met the man once and summarily dismissed him. Do you think there's more to Chase's story than he let on?" Tobias was searching for an answer, but one did not seem readily available.

"There are always three sides to a story, sir."

"Three sides?"

"Your side, my side and the truth. I believe Cadogan was being honest to the best of his knowledge of the situation, but there were things going on behind the scenes that he had no knowledge of." Victor shifted in his seat waiting for the inevitable question.

"Things? What things?"

Victor let out a heavy sigh before he replied, "I found out that your daughter had taken an interest in the boy after his heroics. Your former campaign manager found out about it and reasoned that you couldn't win the election for Vanguard if your daughter were to get together with Cadogan, so he's the one who sent him to Seraphaz."

"That man had no honor," Tobias spat. "That is one more of the many reasons he is my former campaign manager. Still, what's all of this got to do with Seraphaz?"

"Seraphaz had his sights set on fleet captain at the time, even though he was only a Commander. Maybe he thought Cadogan was damaged goods and didn't want him ruining any chance he may have had at reaching his goal." Victor stood up and began pacing on the dark red carpet.

"Okay, fine. I can almost see that being a reason, but why continue to sabotage the boy's life?"

"It is possible that once he was passed over for the position, he blamed it on his dismissal of Cadogan."

Tobias stood and walked past the conference table over to the serving cart. He began to pour himself a glass of water, but stopped mid-pour. "I still don't understand why he would continue to blame Chase for that," he said while still holding the pitcher and glass.

"From what I know of Seraphaz, it doesn't need to make sense," Victor replied. Tobias held the glass out to him, but Flag Officer Victor declined and sat back down. "I inherited him, and I've never really known how to use him. He was already a captain with three ships under his command when I became the Flag Officer. After passing on him for the fleet captain position, I gave him command of another two ships. He is now at the maximum amount of ships he can command without taking the next step."

"So, he's successful. He may not be a fleet captain, but why worry about someone like Cadogan?" Tobias asked while he sat down. He took a long swig of water, savoring the cool sensation on the back of his throat before placing the glass on the blood red table before him and looking to his friend.

"I really believe that Seraphaz thinks that Cadogan cost him his shot at fleet captain." He paused before continuing. "He's wrong, obviously. He doesn't have the leadership skills to command the five vessels he has now. I would never promote him, but I think he believes it's his divine right to eventually become the Flag."

"We'll have to have a talk with him. Chase Cadogan is out there risking his life for the Commonwealth, just like he risked his life for my daughter. I'll not have some two-bit captain with delusions of grandeur making life difficult for a real hero over some imagined grudge."

"And what about his harboring of Jay Lee Hazard?" Victor asked.

"He had better have a good explanation for that or he may find himself in prison." Vanguard Tobias stood and began walking toward the door. Before he reached it he turned and added, "Do nothing until after this Qantaran crisis is over. Once they're gone, if they go, we'll have a sit down with the good captain."

"Yes, sir." Flag Officer Victor fired off a crisp salute to the Vanguard, standing at attention until he was gone. He would follow his orders to wait until the current crisis was over, but he would to get to the bottom of Seraphaz's behavior.

+++++

Agent Black strode across the bridge of the *Elysian Pride* with a look on his face that kept anyone from approaching him. He was still annoyed at having been called back to the ship, but this was his standard demeanor when onboard. The fewer people that approached him the fewer he would actually have to speak to. He stopped a few feet from the captain's chair and waited for Seraphaz to address him.

"Did Hazard and his team arrive on Avalon?"

"I jumped to hyperspace while they were landing. Hazard said they were landing ten klicks southwest of Cadogan's position. They planned to take speeders the rest of the way."

"More stealthy that way; good choice." Seraphaz stood and began walking toward the exit to the bridge. Agent Black walked by his side. The bridge of the *Elysian Pride* consisted of several stations almost three meters apart and was bustling with activity. Each crew station was located three steps below the main thoroughfare of the bridge with the captain's chair and console alone overlooking each station. While Captain Seraphaz and Agent Black walked toward the exit of the bridge, Black could see the first officer stepping up to the captain's seat.

"I still think I should have stayed," Black said as the door to the bridge slid open.

"No, I don't think the Flag is going to drop this. It's better for you to be here if he arrives, or sends someone to check."

"Why do you think the Flag would be checking up on you out of everyone?" Black asked. They reached the door to the bridge and it automatically slid open for them. They continued walking without slowing.

"I'm next in line for fleet captain. There are no other captains in the entire fleet with more experience than I have. I am already commanding the maximum of five ships. The next logical step is the promotion. I have to be at my best, so he has no reason to pass me over for the promotion again, should one of the fleet captains retire."

"Or should they be lost in the upcoming war?" Black asked with a telling nod.

"We shall see," Seraphaz replied with a look that suggested that was his hope.

+++++

When Sym emerged from the water, she looked like a new woman. All of her cuts and bruises were gone, although there was scarring where the worst lacerations had been. She still cradled her arm, but Chase noticed the pain was gone from her expression.

"Your turn, Chase," Felicia said while she walked to the water's edge. Her wet robe now clung to her honed body and droplets of sacred water rolled down her dark hair and spattered in the pool.

"No thanks, I'll be fine."

Felicia took two quick steps and snagged his arm. "This is not fine. Avalon feels your pain. Now, get undressed and come into the water."

Chase felt his face flush, Kat and Tev grinned at him, while Fixer still prodded away at the machine he was building.

"You may cover yourself with one of the towels on the rocks if you must," Felicia said while she continued walking through the water back to her sisters. Her white robe trailed, causing ripples in the water. The light reflecting off the water's surface began to shift in the ripples and the effect was a soothing rhythm to the movement of the light. The priestesses offered prayers while Chase undressed and after a few moments, he joined them in the water.

"So how does this work?" he asked.

"Just kneel and be still," Felicia replied. "We will do the rest, and Avalon will heal your arm."

Chase knelt and the water came up to his neck. One of the priestesses knelt in front of him and held his submerged arm in her soft hands. She had yet to look at him, but his eyes were glued to her. All of the priestesses were beautiful, but he felt no attraction to them. The other priestesses laid their hands on his head and shoulders and Felicia began to offer up supplications to Avalon in a whisper, "Enna acti salannabbi zectri Ave Lon drissia, drissia ploctannia bintallab!"

The holy women circled him and the water stirred. The priestess holding his arm began her supplications as well. After a few moments, the stirring grew more intense and the water began heating up. The other priestesses joined in and they were all chanting in a language Chase had thought dead. "Enna acti salannabbi zectri Ave Lon drissia, drissia ploctannia bintallab!"

The chanting reached a crescendo and stopped. The ending's abruptness surprised Chase. The water also stopped stirring and returned to its previous temperature.

When the priestess let go of his arm, he stood and looked. His arm had been completely healed. A scar remained, but the wound was closed and there was no pain. "I don't know what to say," Chase said into the silence. "Thank you," he added in a reverent whisper.

"Thank Avalon," Felicia replied. "She has seen fit to heal you."

"Thank you, Avalon," he said more out of respect for the priestesses than belief in their god. Still, he knew that something in that water had healed his arm. He ducked behind a boulder to towel dry and get dressed, and when he finished he rejoined his crew.

"Please do not wait so long to visit again, cousin," Felicia said while she held Kat's embrace. Chase saw that her robe had already dried and wondered if it was because the fabric was so thin.

"I'll do my best to come back for a proper visit soon, Felicia," Kat replied. She kissed her cousin's cheek and held her embrace.

"We need to go, Kat," Chase said and looked at Felicia. "Thank you, and please, thank the other priestesses for us. We'd love to stay, but it's important we get Sym back to her people."

"I understand. May Avalon bless your journey." She waved one last time and Kat returned the gesture. The soft orange glow of the cave made the scene seem somber. Chase turned to lead his crew out of the cave when Stone came in with a concerned look in his eye.

"We can't go that way, Chase," he said. "Hazard's outside with a dozen guys and they look like military. Probably mercenaries"

"Mercs? Are you sure?" Chase asked, brushing past Stone to get a look from the mouth of the cave. Stone and Tev joined him and he asked Stone, "Did they see you out here?"

"I don't think so."

"They seem to be in a standard military search pattern," Tev whispered.

"Okay, let's go see if there's another way out of this cave," Chase said leading the crew back into the cave. When they arrived he looked to Felicia and said, "I'm sorry, but it appears as though trouble has followed us to your peaceful abbey. Is there another exit to the cave that we could use? I'd rather not have to shoot anyone while I'm on Avalon."

"Avalon appreciates your respect for her holy grounds. I shall lead you out of the cave through a passage to the other side of the mountain, but how will you get back to your ship?"

"I'm not sure, we may just have to wait for Captain Bander to land some forces to help us," Chase replied.

"Unless he's the one that dispatched Hazard and those soldiers," Tev said.

"No, he wouldn't. He's a good man," Kat said. Felicia took her by the arm and led the group to one of the smooth walls. She recited an incantation and a doorway appeared with a tunnel behind it.

"They shall never find this entrance," Felicia said. "Quickly, we must go. My sisters will seek to confuse them if they enter the cave."

"No, I think they should come with us. I'd hate for anything to happen to them," Chase replied.

"Avalon will protect them, now come." They entered the tunnel and Felicia recited the incantation again.

The doorway disappeared behind them and they were left in darkness. Fixer started to whine and squirm, but Kat took hold of his hand and said in a soft, reassuring voice, "It's going to be all right, Fixer. Don't worry."

"I don't like the dark, Katalla Swift. I don't like the dark."

"I know, sweetie, but my cousin shall light the way, just give her a little time."

A moment later, torchlight illuminated the tunnel with the same soft orange glow that had lit the cave. Fixer still stood close to Kat and Tev picked up the previous conversation. "Even if we can trust Bander, that doesn't do us any good now. How are we going to get to the ship?"

"I don't know," Chase replied as they continued walking through the tunnel.

"We can just use this," Fixer replied and held up the little machine he had been working on. "Chase will have to climb forty meters up the mountain for the signal to get through, but then he can call the ship to us."

"Wait a minute, Fixer. Are you telling me that you built a remote for the ship?"

"Yes Chase, weren't you listening?"

"Yes, buddy, I was just surprised. Good job," he replied while Kat smiled at Fixer. "Hey, can this thing fire weapons and shield the ship, too? Or is it just flight control?"

"It can raise shields and fire weapons as well, but those systems are not fully integrated yet because I didn't have time, so, yes, but probably not yet."

"That's okay, Fixer. Chase wouldn't want to fire the ship's weapons while we are on Avalon anyway," Kat said, giving Chase a disapproving nod.

"Of course not. I was just wondering." He frowned when a different thought occurred to him. "I can't believe I'm this close to Hazard and I can't bring him in."

"I know, but our current assignment is so much more important," Tev replied.

"I knew there was a brain under that helmet and all that hair," Kat said and then chuckled.

"Everyone has a brain, Katalla Swift."

"That's right, Fixer, but not all of us use our brains, do we Tev?"

"There's the Kat I love so much. I see you are no longer frightened. Remind me to get a pet jocawolf before the next time we meet up," Tev replied and Stone started laughing.

Felicia smiled at the banter. She knew all of these men would do anything to protect her cousin. "We are almost through the mountain," she said.

"Great, we need to get out of here, fast," Chase said. A few moments later, they could see daylight peek through the dark of the tunnel. Felicia extinguished her torch and left it near the tunnel entrance. They stood on a trail that led to a field easily big enough to land the *Longshot*. On the other side of the field they could see a deep ravine with a flowing river at the bottom.

"I'll climb up and send for the ship, you guys all go hide in the trees until she lands." He looked at Fixer and asked, "How does this thing work?"

"Red line is vertical thrusters, blue line is main thrusters. Push the line for ignition and slide your finger in either direction to steer. The white switch extends the landing gear." He paused and added, "I made it simple, so that you could use it."

Kat laughed and said, "Well, Chase certainly likes simple."

"So, green is shields and orange is weapons?" Chase asked.

"Yes, but they might not work yet, Chase. We already said that."

"I know, Fixer. I was asking for future reference. Now go hide." He waved them toward the trees and started climbing up the steep slope. He could see that he would have to free climb the last fifteen meters, so he put the machine in his pocket.

Chase saw his crew crouching behind a patch of bushes and he saw Felicia go back into the tunnel. He hoped Fixer's gadget worked because there was no other safe way for them to get to their ship. He climbed up as far as he could without gear and took out the homemade remote. Sweat began to trickle down his back and he wiped his brow with his free hand. He balanced himself on two rocks jutting out just enough past the others for his feet to rest on, hoping they would support his weight. The sun beat down on his head, causing him to sweat even more. He pressed the red line and heard the roar of *Longshot*'s vertical thrusters. He motioned the gadget forward, and a few moments later, he could hear the ship getting closer.

"I think it's working, guys," he yelled down toward the trees and he could see Fixer nodding his head, no doubt confirming that the remote worked. Just as the ship appeared overhead, a blaster bolt hit the rocks beneath him and he lost his footing. He started to slide down to the base of the mountain and he could see his ship diving toward the ground. He was at a loss for what to do. The *Longshot* was meters from the trees and more blasterfire filled the air around him. He managed to level off the ship when his descent was momentarily halted by a larger boulder.

The boulder did not stop his progress, however, it only managed to cause him to flip over and he began tumbling down the steep slope. The ship bounced in the air, shedding tree tops, while his crew returned fire at his assailants. The *Longshot* hit a couple trees and bucked like an undomesticated zarack in heat. The ship threatened to plummet into a ravine when Chase finally slid to a stop. He barely had time to take a breath before he was running for cover. He dove for a boulder and came up firing. At least now he had better control of the ship.

"Are you all right, Chase?" Kat called into the noise.

"Yeah, just a little bruised." More hard light charred the ozone, whizzing by his ear, too close for comfort. Stray bolts sent patches of burnt grass and dirt into the air and loose dirt rained down on him. Chase managed to stop the *Longshot* above the field. "I don't know how we're all going to be able to get to the ship," Chase yelled over the sound of the ship.

"We'll just have to make a break for it," Tev yelled back."

"Okay, I'll put down as close as I can and you guys go for it."

"I don't think Fixer can run that fast," Kat yelled.

"I don't know what else to do," Chase replied.

Hazard and his men were creeping closer. The heavy weapons they carried were starting to damage the beautiful landscape. "There's nowhere to run, Cadogan. Give the alien to us and I may let you live," he said.

"You have no idea what you're interfering with, Hazard," Chase replied. The sky had gone dark, it looked like it was about to start raining. Chase silently wondered if it was Avalon disapproving of their actions.

"You have three seconds to make a decision, Cadogan. Then I kill you and your merry band of misfits. Either way, I still wind up with the alien!" He punctuated his statement by firing off another volley that came too close.

+++++

[What news from Q'Tor?] Battle Conductor Garyn asked the officer entering his ready room.

The officer stopped a respectful distance away and replied, [Our sources have picked up a large fleet being assembled by the Jalindi. We believe they are about to fall into our trap.]

[Very good, then we only need to retrieve scientist Sym Triot and make sure she has not divulged any sensitive information to the Commonwealth leaders.]

[Primus Garyn believes it may be necessary to attack the Commonwealth flotilla to convince the Jalindi of our actions.]

Battle Conductor Garyn smiled and replied, [I agree. It will also provide us the opportunity to see how their ships fare against our armada. If we finish the Jalindi quickly, I would like to come back to this cluster and destroy these humans.]

[Let us hope the Jalindi take the bait, then. If we can rid the galaxy of them and the humans, there will be no one left with enough power to oppose us,] the officer replied.

[I would hardly say these humans have the power to oppose us, if not for the Luminari Cluster's natural defenses, they would be easy prey. Now go, report back to Primus Garyn that we are ready to lure the Jalindi into a war they cannot win.] He turned to look out the viewport, indicating the conversation was over.

[It will be as you say, mighty Battle Conductor,] the officer replied and scurried from the room.

+++++

The *Longshot* was hovering above the field and Chase decided this little battle needed to come to an end. He engaged the shield button that Fixer indicated might not work, and he saw the energy field flicker for a moment before solidifying.

"Everybody, get down," he yelled. He hit the thrusters and the ship swooped toward Hazard's men and crashed into their speeders, sending them and seven or eight men flying into the ravine. The shield gave out, but it had done what Chase needed. He swung the ship around and it wobbled to a landing twenty meters from their position.

"Everybody, run to the ship." He laid down cover fire while his team ran. Then Tev and Stone laid down some cover for him to come aboard while Kat and Fixer hurried to the bridge to take the controls.

Chase dodged several blaster bolts before arriving at the landing bay. Tev yelled through the intercom, "Go, go, go!" The ship was in the air before the hatch finished closing.

Stone looked at Chase and started laughing. "You look like zarack crap, Chase."

Chase queried him a look and then saw his reflection. He had a whole new set of scratches and bruises and he was covered with dirt. "Thanks, Stone," he said and walked up to the bridge. He was met by the concerned looks of Sym and Kat, but before either could speak, he said, "I'm fine." He saw Kat's dubious look and added, "It looks worse than it is. Now, we need to get Captain Bander on the line and let him know what just happened."

"I'd love to," Kat replied while she punched in the buttons to send the transmission.

Chapter seven

Hazard watched with a look of pure hatred as the *Longshot* raced toward space. He had allowed Cadogan to get away. *I'm gonna kill that kid if it's the last thing I do*. He had a long walk back to the shuttle to think about what he was going to tell Captain Seraphaz. When he finally arrived, there were several messages waiting for him. He wished he could put off the inevitable transmission, but he knew better. He swallowed hard and hit the transmission button.

"Hazard, I've been trying to reach you for hours. What happened?" Seraphaz demanded.

"Cadogan got away. He killed eight of my men and destroyed the speeders before he left. I had to walk almost eleven kilometers to get back to the ship."

Seraphaz wanted to scream. Cadogan was going to return the alien to the Vanguard and now he needed a new plan for becoming fleet captain. Black had been right, Hazard screwed it up. "Just get what's left of your team back here immediately."

"But I have an idea—"

"Now!" he yelled and ended the transmission. He pounded his fist on the console, startling several members of the bridge crew who busied themselves to avoid his gaze. He turned away from his station and left the bridge without a word.

"I'm going back to the abbey," Hazard said to Sergeant Tendissa.

"But the Captain said—"

"I don't care what Seraphaz said. I'm not one of his soldiers and he doesn't get to order me around." He turned and began walking back to the abbey. He turned back and asked, "You coming?" He waited while she thought about it, and for the first time, he took note of her appearance. She hailed from Hyperborea and her light blue hue gave her attractive features a ghostly appearance. Her shoulder length royal blue hair framed her face and her military fatigues were cut to show off her physique. It was apparent that even as a mercenary that she trained regularly, and he found himself thinking about inviting her back to his ship when this assignment was over.

"What's the plan?" she asked.

"Cadogan had to know one of the priestesses to be seen so quickly. I'm going to find the one he knows and take her hostage."

"I'm not sure that's a great idea, Hazard. These are priests we're talking about here."

"Trust me. I know Cadogan. Once I have the hostage, he'll be forced to meet me and turn over the alien. We can still accomplish the objective." Hazard continued walking through the forest, toward the abbey, with his four remaining mercenaries in tow.

A soft breeze whistled through the trees and the light green sky turned a shade darker as the sun began its descent. "If Cadogan has already met up with the *Legendary*, it might already be too late," Tendissa said.

Hazard fixed the mercenary with a hard stare and said, "I don't even want to think about that."

They reached the abbey forty minutes later. Hazard and his four mercenaries took cover behind some bushes and watched the priests and priestesses milling about, performing the mundane chores required of the Order of Avalon. He watched for almost fifteen minutes before he saw who he was looking for. He turned to the sergeant and said, "There! The Elysian woman. That has to be Cadogan's contact."

"How do you know that?" she asked.

"His hunting partner is Elysian and is rumored to have a sister or cousin in the order." He turned his head to face her and added, "And if she is not their contact, she will know who is." Hazard broke cover and Tendissa followed suit. They proceeded to where Felicia was hanging some robes on a thin line. A gentle breeze swayed the robes, giving the mountains in the distance a shimmering effect in the light of the setting sun.

"You," Hazard called out while pointing his blaster at Felicia. The other members of the order stopped what they were doing and looked up at the armed men and women in their presence.

Felicia looked at Hazard and replied, "You have no need of weapons here. Avalon will protect you." She lifted another robe out of the basket next to her and hung it on the line with the other robes.

Hazard pointed his blaster at her and said, "I don't need Avalon's protection. You do. Now, what is your name?"

"Felicia."

"How do you know Chase Cadogan?"

"I do not know, Chase Cadogan, I only just met him today."

One of the priests moved to stand in between Felicia and Hazard. He raised his voice and exclaimed, "What is the meaning of this? You cannot just come to our abbey waving blasters and threatening my people,"

Hazard hit the priest in the face with the butt end of his blaster. The priest fell to the light blue grass, blood dripping from a gash above his eye.

"Anyone else moves, and they'll get the other end of this blaster." He waved it in the air and added, "Are we clear?"

"There is no need for violence," Felicia said, her tone neutral while she continued her task.

"If you don't know Cadogan, how is it he received such quick treatment when he arrived?"

"Avalon wished to heal his alien friend."

Hazard grabbed her arm, pressed the blaster to her face and said, "Enough of this runaround. Are you related to Katalla Swift? And if you are not, who here is?"

Felicia started to tremble, but she held her composure. "I am Katalla's cousin," she replied.

"Why didn't you just say that, then?"

"Because that is not what you asked," she replied, her chin held high in defiance.

Hazard backhanded her to the ground and kicked her. She let out a painful grunt as the air left her lungs. "You knew what I was really asking. Don't you play those games with me. Now, get up." He turned to the mercenaries and said, "We're taking her with us. If any members of the order get in the way, kill them."

Sergeant Tendissa took hold of Felicia's arm and started to lead her away when a priest and two priestesses moved to block their path. Hazard shot the priest, leaving a smoking hole in his chest. The light left his eyes in an instant. Tendissa stunned each of the two priestesses, not wanting to kill them. They fell to the ground and Hazard looked disappointed.

"You didn't need to murder the priest," she hissed, "This is not what we signed on for," she said.

"Well, you're in it now. Let's go," Hazard replied. They began the walk back to the shuttle with their hostage in tow.

Felicia looked at Hazard and with as even a voice as she could muster, said, "Avalon will repay you for the disrespect you have shown here today."

"Really? I'm so scared," he replied in a mocking tone. "Oh, Great Avalon. Please don't strike me dead." He paused theatrically and cringed while looking at the sky. After a moment, he started to laugh and continued walking. "Looks like Avalon is taking a nap right now. She'll probably wake up once we're gone. Goddesses are convenient that way." He looked at Felicia and a wicked scowl crossed his face. Then he said, "Now, no more talk about your little god repaying my disrespect." He shoved her and she stumbled, but did not lose her footing.

"You don't have to be such a jerk, Hazard," Tendissa said while she walked alongside Felicia. "You have your hostage; now let's get on with your plan." She glared at the ex bounty hunter and hefted her rifle a little higher.

Hazard looked at her glare and chuckled. They continued to the ship without another word.

+++++

"Captain Bander wants us to meet him at Cibola. He doesn't want to take any chances that someone else will confront us while we are waiting on him," Kat said.

"Did you tell him it was Hazard on our trail?" Chase asked.

"Yeah, he's going to let Vanguard Tobias and the Flag know," she replied.

"Chase, we haven't changed the modules yet?" Fixer complained.

"Can it wait until we get to Cibola?"

"Yes, but I don't like to wait, Chase"

"We're good to make the jump to hyperspace," Stone called out.

"Okay, let's do it," Chase replied. Stone's fingers worked the buttons and a moment later, the elongated white streaks of hyperspace were flying by the viewport.

"Do you think we'll get to meet the Vanguard again?" Kat asked.

"Probably," Chase replied.

"We've already met him, Kat," Tev said, flashing another toothy smile and pointing to Stone.

"No you didn't," she replied with a laugh. "As if the Vanguard would sit down with the two of you for a chat."

"Actually, he was Governor Tobias at the time and we happened to be keeping Chase company in the med-center when Tobias arrived to thank him for saving his daughter. We even took vid of the momentous occasion." He held up a portable screen and played it, laughing at Kat's reaction.

"Well I met him after he was Vanguard," she replied with a look that said she was the winner. Then she stood up to leave the bridge.

"Where are you going, Kat?" Chase asked. "Don't let these guys get to you."

"I'm not. I'm just going to make sure Fixer isn't bothering Sym too much."

"He certainly seems fixated," Tev replied.

"Good one," Kat said in a sarcastic voice as the door to the bridge slid shut behind her. She saw Sym and Fixer sitting at the table in the galley and Sym was writing notes; a lot of them. "Hey, Fixer. What's going on?"

"Hello, Katalla Swift. Sym is writing the directions for mining xallodium and we are feeding them into a translation algorithm I created. Then she's going to teach me the formula for transforming the xallodium into an alloy more indestructible than anything the

Commonwealth has." Fixer looked up at her with the same gleam in his eye he always had when working on an engine.

"We will also learn... transform xallodium... wiring that can handle, far greater... energy."

"She means that the xallodium can also be used as a conduit that can handle far more amounts of energy than what the Commonwealth has, Katalla Swift. It would make our weapons stronger." He flashed her an awkward smile.

"That's great news. We should tell Chase."

"No," Sym replied, a tinge of urgency in her voice. "Qantarah have people that... know truth. They will ask me if I give any knowledge to... cluster leaders, and they will ask leaders... if I gave them knowledge. They will... know truth. They will also ask to meet Chase, but not ask for any of you."

"So, Chase can't know or they'll know that he knows. Got it," Kat replied. She sat down at the table with them and noticed they both had empty green fizzy bottles in front of them. "That means that Fixer is not allowed to give this information to anyone until after the Qantarah have gone."

"Kat is right, Fixer. Please... very important," Sym replied while she continued writing.

"Okay, I won't tell anyone until Katalla Swift tells me I'm allowed," he replied.

"Will cluster leaders hurt Sym?" she asked with what Kat assumed was worry on her face.

"No, Sym. Our leader is a good man. I think He is already planning to fly straight to the mouth of the cluster to hand you over to your people as soon as we arrive. Are you going to be okay?"

"Sym will be... good."

"Your leaders won't punish you for being late and causing this big fuss?" Kat asked.

"Sym has nothing to fear," she replied. "Sym has box, they will see Sym was in... crash."

"I'm sorry, I just get the feeling that they are not the forgiving type and I don't want to see anything bad happen to you."

"Sym appreciates Katalla's concern."

"I'm going to get a green fizzy, Sym. Do you want one?" Fixer asked while he walked to the refrigeration unit in the galley.

"Please, it is a... good taste."

"So, Fixer got you hooked on his favorite beverage," Kat said with a chuckle. "Hey, Fixer. Could you get me some water while you're up?" she asked in a sugary voice.

"I will, Katalla Swift. I will get two green fizzys and a water."

"Thank you, Fixer." Kat called up to the bridge on her comm and asked, "How much longer do we have in hyperspace?"

"About seven hours, Kat," Tev replied. "Is there anything you'd like to do to kill some time?"

"Yeah, Tev. Come on back, we could go to my quarters, get comfortable, dim the lights and turn on some music."

"I like the sound of that, Katalla," he replied.

"Then I can slip into something a little more comfortable." She paused just long enough to pique everyone's interest and added, "And then we can shave that forest above your lip." She started laughing and winked at Fixer, who had returned with the drinks. She could hear Chase and Stone laughing over the comms. "What do you say, Tev?"

"As tempting as that sounds, Miss Swift, I'll have to decline."

"We should be hearing from the Vanguard as soon as we exit hyperspace, Kat. Go get some rest," Chase said.

+++++

[I grow weary of this waiting,] Garyn said to his first officer.

The officer looked at the leader of the Qantaran fleet and said, [They have only two days to comply, then the Primus has given us the latitude to do whatever we see fit to these humans.]

[I think I will not wait that long. Send six of our gunships to go through the third entrance to the cluster. I want to see what kind of defenses they have. I am also interested in seeing if their weapons can penetrate our xallodium hulls.]

[It will be as you say, mighty Battle Conductor!] The officer sent the orders and six gunships broke off from the fleet without delay.

Two hours later one of the ships sent a transmission, [We are entering the cluster now. We will send our next communiqué after we destroy the pitiful human defenses.] Garyn allowed himself a smile. There was something about this Luminari Cluster that appealed to him.

[I want this cluster,] Garyn said to his officer. [I am going to ask my brother to give it to me.]

[Our Primus may wish to conquer the Jalindi first, so we will be able to maintain a proper supply chain. This cluster is too far away otherwise.]

[Maybe or maybe we take this cluster first and attack the Jalindi from two sides.] He paused and looked at the tactical display of his fleet. [I suppose we will have our answer soon enough.]

+++++

Captain Seraphaz paced the bridge of the *Elysian Pride*. He had just received a troubling transmission from the Flag. It would seem Hazard's failure could be connected back to him. He had to figure out his next move or he might be dishonorably discharged. Black had been spotted and Hazard had failed to obtain the alien. Cadogan was still alive, and this was all being traced back to him by the Flag. "Why is the Flag even involved?" he mumbled. "Why are they gunning for me?"

Agent Black approached him and asked, "Any word from Hazard?"

Seraphaz straightened up and put his questions on hold. "He failed. Cadogan killed eight of his men and got away with the prize. This could wind up having some serious consequences for us." He paced back and forth and Black could see he was agitated.

"Us?" he replied.

"Yes us! You were the one following Cadogan, weren't you?" Seraphaz continued his pacing, hoping to find a way out of this situation.

"If the Flag finds out you sent Hazard after Cadogan, you can kiss your fleet captain position goodbye," Black said.

"Yes, thank you, Agent Black. I am well aware of the situation."

An alert from the first officer broke into their conversation. "Captain Seraphaz to the bridge. We have incoming Qantaran vessels." A moment later, he added, "We're being hailed."

"On screen," Seraphaz replied.

The transmission flared to life and the imposing figure of the Qantaran hailing them could be seen. [Humans,] a deep voice bellowed. [I am Captain Prataa of the Qantarah. Stand down or we will destroy your pitiful vessels.] The translation came through a moment later.

"Captain Prataa, I am Captain Seraphaz of the Commonwealth Cluster Patrol. You are in violation of sovereign cluster space. Turn around and leave now or we will be forced to open fire." He turned to Black and said, "Call for reinforcements, but call the press first."

"Press? Why?"

"If I stop this incursion, the Flag will be hard pressed to demote me even if he can prove Hazard is connected to me. Oh, don't forget to scrub the call to the press. Wouldn't want anyone thinking we were seeking this glory."

Black looked at him for a moment and suddenly realized he loathed this man. "I'm on my way," he replied in a clipped tone. While he was hurrying to another transmission terminal, he thought, *We are about to be invaded by the Qantarah and all he can think about is covering his own butt. I might be a little shady, but Seraphaz is downright traitorous and there's nothing I can do about it. If he goes down, I go down with him.* He reached the terminal and made his two transmissions, making sure to call reinforcements first.

[Captain Seraphaz! You stand in violation of the will of the Qantarah. You will be destroyed,] Prataa said. A moment later, the translation came through and the Qantaran gunships began firing lightning-type energy. All six gunships fired on the cluster ship *Paragon*, overwhelming the shields and disabling the ship. The brazen nature of the move, and the sheer power of the weapons gave the commonwealth forces pause. Paragon listed while smoking from several of its bays.

After a moment of shocked silence, Seraphaz yelled, "Open Fire!"

Hard light shot out across space and connected with the Qantaran vessels. A smile played across Captain Seraphaz's face as the solid orange light connected with the enemy, but his smile faded as quick as it had come. Their main weapons had splashed uselessly off the hulls of the alien vessels. The cluster patrol ships began evasive maneuvers after seeing their weapons have little effect on their enemy. "All ships, coordinate fire on the lead enemy vessel. Officer Tisdale, arm our tactical missiles and fire on my command." He watched as the combined firepower of four ships damaged the lead Qantaran vessel, but nowhere near enough. The enemy vessels might have been smaller, but he knew he was outnumbered and outgunned.

[Their weapons are of no use. Press our advantage. I wish to kill the one called Captain Seraphaz for his defiance,] Captain Prataa said to his first officer.

"Sir, the *Paragon* is in trouble. Should we move to protect it?" Officer Tisdale yelled above the battle klaxons.

"No, their weapons are too powerful. We'd only lose more ships. If they can't retreat, tell them to evacuate," Seraphaz replied. While Tisdale was relaying the order, the *Elysian Pride* took two hits. The ship rocked and alarms blared.

"Shields holding at forty-six percent," a crewman who looked too young to be in battle yelled.

"Forty-six percent? We've only been hit twice!" Agent Black said, disbelief creeping into his voice.

"Fire missiles," Captain Seraphaz yelled. Eight Commonwealth missiles streaked out toward the enemy ships, the fuel burn leaving brief trails of smoke across the divide. Five missiles were intercepted by the strange Qantaran weapons before they reached their target.

The other three found their mark and after a brilliant flash the Qantaran vessel still remained.

"That's not possible. We hit it with three missiles!" Seraphaz yelled.

"Captain, we have confirmation on enemy damage. Our missiles damaged their engines and one of their main weapons batteries."

"Launch all fighters; let's give these animals more targets to shoot at." Each ship launched their full complement of two dozen fighters. The fighters raced toward the Qantaran gunships, dodging the lightning-like weapons of the enemy.

"All fighters are away, Captain."

Skilled Commonwealth pilots flew towards their enemies, the first enemy they had ever faced, and opened fire. Their weapons had little effect, and they swung around for another pass.

"Our weapons have no effect. Please advise," a nervous lieutenant called. He juked around another barrage of the strange enemy lightning.

"Tell the pilots, missiles only until the enemy ships show damage. Continue firing main weapons and prepare the next round of missiles to be fired." While the captain was speaking, another blast from the Qantarah hit the *Elysian Pride*, rocking the ship. Sparks and smoke filled the bridge, and several people were launched from their seats, but the crew remained diligent. The injured were replaced with a quickness born of discipline while damage control teams arrived on the bridge.

The *Elysian Pride* continued evasive maneuvers and loosed another round of missiles. Several found their mark, and Seraphaz allowed himself a moment's satisfaction as smoke rose from one of his enemies. The fighters began scoring hits with their strafing runs, and the tide looked as if it might turn.

Planet Thirty-Four hung heavy in the background as the struggle progressed. Another round of lightning fired from the enemies and caught the *Elysian Pride* with a glancing blow. The already damaged ship reeled.

"Shields holding at twenty- three percent," a crewman yelled over the symphony of sound.

"Hull breach; decks eight and nine," another crewman yelled.

A bright explosion caught Captain Serephaz's eye off to the starboard side of the ship, followed by more of the Qantaran energy striking another ship.

"Sir, the *Paragon* has been destroyed," Officer Tisdale said, fear creeping into his voice. "And the *Reliant* has taken serious damage."

We're not going to win this, Seraphaz thought. "Fire next round of missiles!" Seraphaz commanded. Eight more missiles streamed toward the lead enemy ship. This time, five connected and the ship split open. He saw another enemy ship flash bright white and now the battle was almost even. The fighters were scoring direct hits on their missile runs, but the Qantaran lightning was taking them out at a pretty good clip.

A coordinated strafing run by the remaining fighters left another enemy ship severely damaged, but the capital ships were out of position to finish it off. The enemy had caught them off guard, and they had never been able to get into any sort of formation after that. This entire battle had been a free-for-all. Another flash of light told Seraphaz the news was not good.

"We've lost the *Reliant*," Officer Tisdale, yelled.

"What's the status of our reinforcements, Agent Black?" Captain Seraphaz asked.

"Our nearest support is still almost forty minutes away," Black replied.

"Then I guess it's up to us."

"So it would seem," Black said. His words lacked conviction, but he stood by his captain. At this point, it looked as though the battle was not going to go their way. The Qantaran ships began to grow more aggressive. Two of them flew towards the Trident and opened fire. The shields didn't last long under the enemy barrage.

"Sir, the *Trident* has lost shields, main weapons, and decks four through eleven are venting atmosphere. Captain Cheston has issued an abandon ship order," Officer Tisdale reported.

"That leaves it at four to two. We need to turn this tide quickly or the Qantarah will have a foothold in our cluster!"

The *Borean Spear* broke loose and fired on the damaged Qantaran ship. A dazzling flash lit up space for a moment, then the *Borean Spear* came about, firing on another Qantaran vessel. A dozen fighters soared past for another strafing run while the enemy let loose on the *Elysian Pride* once again.

Another lightning strike rocked the ship, setting off a new wave of alarms. Several bridge crew members were thrown from their stations, emergency techs scurried to put out fires and a crewman yelled, "Shields have failed."

"Receiving transmission from the *Trident*," Officer Tisdale called out.

"We have no help to offer!" Captain Seraphaz yelled.

An image of the captain of the Trident flickered to life on the bridge. He was by himself, and his bridge was damaged and smoke-filled. Blood poured from a gash on his forehead, and he looked into the transmission for a moment before speaking. The look in his eyes was the sad resignation of a man that knew he was about to die, but wasn't ready to go.

After another moment, he started speaking, "Tol, my ship is evacuated, but the Qantarah are firing on the escape shuttles. I have a plan that might turn the tide of battle. I only need you and the *Borean Spear* to cover me until I'm in position. Can you do that?"

Captain Seraphaz knew what he was planning and said, "We can sure try." The transmission ended and Captain Seraphaz let the *Borean Spear* know the plan. All remaining fighters flew escort while the *Trident* armed all of her missiles and set the hyperdrive to overload. She raced toward the enemy while Captain Seraphaz's remaining two ships provided cover. Another shot blasted the *Elysian Pride*, taking main thrusters offline.

"Captain, we've lost main thrusters," Officer Tisdale yelled.

"Keep firing on the enemy. The *Trident* has to get through," he replied.

The *Trident* collided with one of the Qantaran ships and detonated its Hyperdrive along with all of its remaining ordinance. Two of the enemy vessels were engulfed in the explosion and the remaining ship was severely damaged.

"Captain, we're receiving a hail from the enemy."

"On screen," he replied.

The image flared to life and Captain Prataa's bewildered face appeared. [We offer our surrender, Captain.] The translation came though a moment later.

"I don't think so. All ships, open fire," he replied. The *Elysian Pride*, *Borean Spear* and all of the remaining fighters opened fire and the last Qantaran vessel flashed for an instant and was no more.

"Captain, they were surrendering," Officer Tisdale said. "We are not allowed to fire on surrendering ships, sir."

"What would you have me do, Officer Tisdale, spare him so the Qantarah can demand him back? Spare him so he can tell his leaders that our primary weapons are all but ineffective against their ships? How long do you think it would be before the Commonwealth was overrun if they had that information?" He paused and looked around his battered bridge, the once pristine gray stations scorched and cast in dim light. Red alarm lights cast deep shadows over the bridge while medical personnel removed fallen comrades. He raised his voice, so he could be heard over all of the commotion and said, "This is battle. The loser doesn't get to go home; this was survival. Until we have weapons that are effective against their ships' armor, this is the only course of action."

Twenty minutes later, seven ships exited hyperspace, along with several media vessels and medical frigates. Activity buzzed around the severely damaged *Elysian Pride* and the less damaged *Borean Spear*.

Captain Seraphaz received a transmission. When he took it, the *Cibola's* bridge materialized on screen. "Damage assessment, Captain," Fleet Captain Gordon asked.

"The *Paragon*, the *Reliant*, and the *Trident* have been destroyed along with several shuttles trying to escape, and sixty-seven of the one hundred twenty fighters that were launched were also eliminated. The *Borean Spear* and *Elysian Pride* have sustained severe damage and will need to be put down for repairs."

"How many casualties?"

"I don't have a final count at the moment, sir. We have over eleven hundred confirmed dead and just under five hundred still unaccounted for."

"The price of this victory was high indeed," Fleet Captain Gordon replied.

+++++

Vanguard Tobias was incensed when he heard the news. "They what, Fleet Captain Gordon?"

"Six Qantaran gunships attacked the cluster's third entrance. Three of our ships have been destroyed and over fourteen hundred men and women have been confirmed dead. Reports indicate that our main weapons were completely ineffective against their ship's armor, but missiles had more of an impact. Still, the battle would have been lost if the captain of the *Trident* didn't ram the enemy vessels while overloading his hyperdrive."

"What are you saying, Gordon?" the Vanguard asked.

"Sir, I'm saying the enemy's weapons are far more powerful than ours and I can't see us surviving if they attack en masse."

"Thank you, Fleet Captain," The Flag said before cutting the transmission. "Vanguard Tobias, we need to address this with the Qantarah now. We need to make it seem like it was an easy victory and challenge their honor."

"Why would we do that?"

"These people despise weakness. If we come off as the least bit weak or scared, it will be over for us. I believe bluster to be the only course of action. It may give them pause until we can develop more powerful weapons."

"I will send the message now." He gave the order and the screen flared to life. He held his head high and puffed out his chest. "What is the meaning of this, Garyn?" Vanguard Tobias yelled into the transmission. He made no attempt to hide the contempt he felt.

[The meaning of what?] the Qantaran replied. His communications officer translated the reply into the Commonwealth trade language.

"You send ships into our cluster to attack out people. We still have two full days! You have no honor!"

A moment later, the reply came. [Careful, human. Challenge my honor again and I promise it will be your people that suffer. Now, where are my ships?] Garyn allowed the transmission to go out in the Qantaran language and followed with the translation because he wanted the human to hear the strength of his anger.

"Your ships were destroyed by the vessels they attacked."

[Impossible! Human ships are no match for us,] Battle Conductor Garyn replied. The translation followed.

"Apparently, they are. We've found your scientist and she will reach Cibola in three hours. When she arrives, we will put her aboard a ship and we will deliver her to you as planned. Any more incursions into our cluster before then will result in the destruction of more of your ships and the imprisonment of your scientist. Do you understand?"

Battle conductor Garyn flew into a rage. [Who does this human think he is? Does he believe he will be spared? Prepare to attack at once.]

[Sir, the Primus has ordered us not to attack if they keep their word and return scientist Sym Triot, to us,] his bridge officer said.

[We will not attack, but we will prepare. I want these human dogs to cower in fear.] The next transmission the communications officer sent said, [Be careful that you do not threaten us, humans.]

"I would never dream of threatening you, Garyn. I am only stating what will happen if you break your word again," Vanguard Tobias said. He cut the transmission before Garyn could reply and hoped his bluff worked. He knew the Qantaran ships were much more powerful than his, but they had no way of knowing for sure. All they knew was that six ships went in and none came back out. If this turned into a war, they would need to upgrade their weapons fast. He already had supplies of extra missiles being delivered throughout the fleet, but they were going to need a lot more.

"Do you think he bought it?" Flag Officer Victor asked.

"I hope so. We don't really have a plan B at this point."

"I guess it's going to be difficult to go after Seraphaz now. The press is all over the battle of Planet Thirty-Four, and they are hailing him a hero."

"I have no doubt it was he who alerted the press for just such a reason," Vanguard Tobias replied drily. "He thinks it will erase all he has done."

"It just may, at least for a little while," the Flag said, shaking his head. "How do we demote the only officer in our entire Fleet with battle experience while war looms?"

"Hence the press. It's like he's taunting us," the Vanguard replied in disgust. He looked back to the Flag and asked, "Are we ready for Cadogan's return?"

"Yes, Bander has just exited hyperspace in the *Legendary*. He estimates the *Longshot* to be about an hour behind. It's just a shame we won't have long to question the alien. Maybe she can tell us how we can level the playing field against her people's weapons."

"She would have no incentive to do that and if we try to force it out of her, we risk open war."

"Do you really think we will avoid war at this point?"

The Vanguard shook his head and his sad eyes grew heavy. He brought his hand up to his face and pinched the bridge of his nose. He looked at his friend and whispered, "I don't think so, Juel, and it's going to take a miracle for us to survive."

Chapter eight

"Whoa, Chase, are you seeing this?" Tev asked in awe.

"It's sitting right in front of me, Tev."

"I've never seen the fleet mustered before," Stone said.

"Enjoy it while you can, guys," Chase replied while they continued to look out the viewport. Arrayed above Cibola, sat fifty ships, ready for battle. In the middle of the fleet sat *Commonwealth One*. Chase counted twenty destroyers, ten heavy cruisers, ten frigates, and ten gunships. Several support craft and cargo vessels buzzed around the fleet delivering supplies and personnel to each vessel. Fighter squadrons raced past the fleet, banked on a long arc, and zipped past again.

"Something must have happened while we were in hyperspace," Chase said.

"Something big," Stone agreed.

Tev looked out the viewport before saying, "Bander told us that the entrances were already fortified. This seems like overkill."

"Incoming transmission," Stone said.

"On screen," Chase replied. The image of the Vanguard flared to life and greeted them with a smile. "You have no idea how good it is to see you, Chase," Vanguard Tobias said. "We are on the brink of war and the alien you have found may be the only means of preventing further hostilities."

"Further, sir?"

"Yes. A short time ago, six Qantaran gunships entered the cluster through the third entrance. They attacked a fleet group consisting of four heavy cruisers and a destroyer. Three of the cruisers were lost and the other two ships took heavy damage. Our primary weapons are all but useless against their vessels. If not for the *Trident* sacrificing itself, the enemy would already have a foothold. Our missiles seemed to be a little more effective, but we are not going to win a war against the Qantarah using just missiles."

"Sir, their hulls are made of a metal called xallodium, and their weapons are powered somehow by this xallodium as well. That's what Sym was doing here, she was checking for deposits of the metal."

"Why?"

"She told me the Qantarah live to feed their war machine. She also told me that Planet Fourteen has the richest supply she's ever seen and that if her people knew about it, they would invade us for it. She also assured me she wouldn't tell them about it."

"And you believe her?"

"Yes, sir. I do."

"You are cleared to come aboard. Use Landing Bay Three."

"Thank you, sir." Chase weaved the *Longshot* through the fleet on one tenth thrusters. He knew every ship's captain would be on edge and didn't want to give anyone the wrong idea while he headed toward the Commonwealth Flagship.

He lined up his approach to *Commonwealth One* and was taken aback by the sheer size of it. Containing fifty-three decks, she stood almost two hundred meters tall. She was almost twelve hundred meters long and four hundred wide. The main body looked like a triangular tube balancing on its point. The top contained the landing bays and curved out on each side to form what appeared to be back-to-back semicircles. The bridge stood several decks higher than the body of the ship and sloped downward in the front. Near the middle of the ship stood four towers and the rear of the ship contained the secondary bridge, sloped downward toward the back of the ship. The entire back of the ship contained the engine which emitted a soft blue glow through the grated engine plates. Forty weapon batteries protruded from various points on the ship while several missile tube openings could also be seen.

Chase entered through Landing Bay Three near the top of the ship. An escort was waiting to take him and Sym right to the Vanguard. As soon as his ship landed on the deck, he could feel the rumble of the deck plate indicating the destroyer was powering up her hyperdrive.

"Looks like they're wasting no time. Kat, you have the bridge until I get back. Keep everyone aboard the *Longshot*. We probably don't want to be wandering around while everyone is on high alert."

"I will, Chase. Don't worry about us." She stood by the open landing bay hatch and said goodbye to Sym. The rest of the crew also said their goodbyes and Fixer gave her an awkward hug.

"Okay, Sym, let's go," Chase said. He waited for her to turn and then they walked toward their escort. She had decided to wear a normal jumpsuit instead of the clothes Kat had given her. Chase carried her ship's black box and the detail led them to a speeder. "This ship is so big you need a speeder to get around," he said, once again in awe.

Sym smiled and replied. "This is about the same size as Qantaran warships. Our gunships are... smaller."

After Chase and Sym left the ship, Fixer walked toward the engine room with his tool kit.

"Where are you going, Fixer?" Kat asked.

"I have to change the modules before Chase forgets and we have to leave again."

"Fixer, you should give Chase a break about those modules. Things got a little crazy and it's not his fault."

"Okay, Katalla Swift. I'll give Chase a break this time." He kept walking, entering the engine room a few moments later. A cooling conduit was bolted to the floor and stood almost a half-meter high. Fixer stepped over the conduit, needing only another step to reach the energy modules. They were covered by a protective cap that needed to come off before the modules could be switched out. Two minutes and four bolts later, the cover was leaning against the conduit and Fixer was taking out the first module. He pulled a small red lever back and pressed a green button next to the housing and the module began to rise. When it stopped, he took it out and replaced it. He repeated the process, bolted the cap back in place, and left the engine room.

Chase and Sym arrived at the bridge and were greeted by suspicious glares from most of the crew. Vanguard Tobias and Flag

Officer Victor met them half way across the bridge. The crewmen that had brought them to the bridge saluted and said, "Chase Cadogan and Sym Triot as ordered, sir."

"Very good, Crewman. Dismissed," The Flag replied. The man saluted again, turned on his heel, and marched off the bridge.

"So, this is the missing scientist," Vanguard Tobias said. "There's been a lot of fuss about you, young lady."

Sym cast a nervous glance at Chase and he put a calming hand on her shoulder. He motioned toward her with his other hand and said, "Vanguard Tobias, Flag Officer Victor, this is Sym Triot of the Qantarah."

"Hello," she said.

Vanguard Tobias raised his eyebrow and said, "Oh, she speaks our language."

"Mostly, sir," Chase replied. "Her ship ran a translation program and she studied it. She can understand us very well and she can speak pretty well, too, but she doesn't quite have all of the nuances down yet."

"Still, that's something. Sym, Chase tells me that you were testing Planet Fourteen for something called xallodium. Can you tell me more about that?"

"No," she replied, worry etched on her face.

"No?" Flag Officer Victor replied.

"She means no disrespect. The Qantarah have people capable of detecting the truth when speaking to others. If she tells us anything of strategic value, they'll know and consider it an act of war," Chase interjected

"We're already at war," Vanguard Tobias said.

"Pardon Sym, but six gunships... not war. They will not... make decision until Sym is back."

"Okay, so after they get you back they are going to test you to make sure you have not given us any Qantaran secrets and if you haven't, they'll leave?" Vanguard Tobias asked with a confused look on his face. "Why send so many ships, then? Why not just send a diplomatic envoy?"

"Qantarah like to intimidate, judge strength," Sym said.

"So, they're basically sizing us up, sir," Chase said.

"Yeah, I got that," he replied, annoyed that the aliens would cause so many problems just for an opportunity to intimidate them. "Let's hope they don't like what they see."

"Entering hyperspace," a crewman called out. Chase watched from the viewport of the bridge as the stars became elongated white lines before them. The entry into hyperspace seemed to be smoother and he wondered if that was due to the size of the ship. Six hours later, *Commonwealth One* emerged near the edge of the cluster.

The fifty vessels that escorted *Commonwealth One* brought the cluster flotilla up to one hundred eighty ships, which represented just under a third of their six hundred ship fleet. He knew the Qantarah had at least ten times as many ships, but Commonwealth spies were convinced the Qantaran empire was too spread out to send more than four or five hundred to the cluster. He knew that as it stood now, they would lose, so he had to pray they would avoid war without looking weak.

"I've never seen this many ships in one place," Chase said as his eyes scanned both fleets.

"This isn't all the enemy has waiting for them should they try to enter our cluster," Flag Officer Victor replied. "If these people think we are going to run and hide just because they are the Qantarah, they are mistaken. We will fight and we will give them a reason to never come back."

Chase knew this was bluster for the sake of the crew. Part of being a bounty hunter was learning how to read people, and he could see the fear in the Flag's eyes.

+++++

The director of the Jalindi information gathering services rushed to give the king the news. He stopped at the door of the royal chamber and waited to be motioned in. He bowed before his king and looked up at him, waiting to be given permission to speak. The king sat on an elevated throne mounted on a platform. There were four wide steps, carpeted in royal blue sarasilk, leading up to the throne. The entire fixture was laden with rare jewels and inlaid with gold. The king enjoyed the height of his throne because he preferred to look down on all who entered the chamber.

The chamber was dark and a little damp, just how the king liked it. Sconces, mounted to walls, cast enough illumination for the Jalindi to see well, but other species would consider the room dim. Etched on the otherwise smooth wall behind the throne was a depiction of a great battle the Jalindi had won several centuries earlier. The other side of the chamber held treasures of untold value. Every item in the room held significant financial or personal importance to one culture or another. The chamber served as a trophy room of sorts; a reminder of vanquished foes.

While waiting to be addressed, the information gatherer looked up at his king. His magnificent grey scales shimmered in the shadowy light of the room. His eyes glowed yellow and his razor teeth shone white. His sleeveless, black military tunic was accented by a blood red cape. He looked down on the one he had summoned and nodded, giving him permission to speak.

[My Lord, the Qantarah have sent over one hundred twenty ships to the Luminari Cluster. My source inside the cluster has confirmed this. There are also indications that they are readying more ships to join them.]

The king stood and fixed his chief spy with a look that pinned him in place. He began a slow descent, pausing at each stair until he stood face to face with his trusted advisor. [What do you suggest we do with this information?]

Even though the king had come down from the throne, the advisor still found himself looking up at him. The king stood almost two and a half meters tall, head and shoulders above the rest of his clan. He was powerfully built and blessed with a glare that could melt ice. [I suggest we attack Q'Tor as soon as those additional ships leave for the cluster, My Lord.]

[Should we not wait to see if all of the posturing outside the Luminari Cluster actually leads to war before we commit our forces?]

The advisor lowered his head and replied, [Once the additional ships are in hyperspace the Qantarah will not be able to recall them until they reenter real space, which will take almost two days. If their homeworld is under attack, the Qantarah will recall their forces from the Luminari Cluster, so we have to decide if we wish them to have one large fleet to reinforce them, or two smaller fleets.]

[Ready the fleet, we shall make the decision when the time comes,] the king replied. [What of the scientist?]

[My sources have no new information on the missing scientist, My Lord. The entire cluster is on alert after six Qantaran gunships attacked a small cluster patrol group. The six gunships were destroyed.]

[I did not think the humans had weapons that could pierce their xallodium hulls. Tell your source to find out how that was accomplished.] Without further discussion, the king turned and strode from the royal chamber.

+++++

"I need to speak to Cadogan," Hazard said with a growl.

"Why would he ever want to talk to the likes of you, Hazard," Kat sneered.

"Because I hold something of great interest to him," he said and paused for effect, "And to you."

"There's nothing you could say that would interest either of us."

"Go find Cadogan and we'll find out." Hazard scowled at the screen while he waited for Kat to reply. He looked forward to seeing the shock on her smug face when he held up her battered cousin in front of the screen.

"Chase isn't even on board right now. He left me in charge, so what do you want?"

"I want to make a deal. The alien for her!" He hefted Felicia up off the ground. One eye was swollen shut and her lip was split. Blood dripped down her face and spattered on the floor. It was clear that she was in pain, but she still managed to look dignified. She held her head up high, in defiance of her captor.

When Kat saw her cousin she let out a gasp and her hand was quick to cover her mouth. Concern filled her eyes, followed by rage. She leapt out of the captain's chair, pointed right into the screen, and said, "Listen to me you worthless son of a jocawolf. If anything more happens to her, I will find you and kill you in the most painful way imaginable. Do you understand me?"

Hazard looked at her and laughed. His laughter was almost eerie. With a malicious smirk he replied, "You and Chase have never even been able to find me. You'll do nothing to me. Now, stow your impotent rage and find Cadogan for me!" His smirk was gone, replaced by a menacing look.

"Do nothing this man asks, Katalla," Felicia said. "Avalon will repay him for what he has done."

"Shut up!" Hazard yelled and backhanded her hard across the face. She tumbled to the deck and out of the transmission. "If I don't get the alien, the priestess dies."

Kat shot daggers from her eyes and said, "I am going to make you pay, Hazard." By this time, Tev, Stone, and Fixer were all in the transmission with her.

"And if she doesn't, I will," Tev added.

Stone stood silent, a scowl fixed into position and anger radiating from him.

Hazard just looked at the motley crew of the *Longshot* and laughed. Then he said, "Find Cadogan and bring the alien to me, I grow weary of this conversation."

"Chase is on *Commonwealth One* with the Vanguard. He already took Sym and they are on their way to make the exchange with the Qantarah. We no longer have access to the alien," Kat said, her tone harsh and her body stiff with anger.

"Well, I guess that's too bad for the priestess!" Hazard replied and ended the transmission.

"Fixer, get him back. That can't be the end of it. Get him back!" Kat yelled.

"Katalla Swift, I cannot trace the transmission. It was encrypted," Fixer replied.

"Just get him back, Fixer!" she yelled. "Do whatever it is you do and get him back!"

"Katalla—"

"Kat, Fixer would do it if he could. You know he would," Tev said. He turned her to face him and took hold of both her shoulders. He looked her in the eyes and said, "We will all do whatever it takes to bring Felicia back safely to the abbey. We will find your cousin."

"And then we make Hazard pay!" Kat hissed.

"Then we make Hazard pay," Tev repeated.

She melted into his arms and sobbed on his shoulder. When she was finished, she sent a transmission to the bridge of *Commonwealth One*.

"Sir, we're receiving a transmission from Landing Bay Three for a Chase Cadogan?" a confused technician said.

Vanguard Tobias looked at Chase and asked, "What's this about, son?"

"I honestly have no idea, sir, but it must be important for them to call me now."

"Take it over there," Vanguard Tobias replied, pointing to the communications station.

Chase hurried over to communications, aware that all eyes were on him. He looked into the transmission and immediately knew something was wrong. He saw the dried tears on Kat's cheeks and asked, "What's wrong, Kat?"

"I'm sorry to bother you, Chase—"

"No, don't worry about it. What happened?"

"Hazard took Felicia." She started to tear up again, but kept herself composed. "Chase, he's going to kill her if we don't turn over Sym to him."

"What? Why? What could he possibly need with Sym?"

"I don't know. I only know he has Felicia and he's already beat her up!"

Chase thought about the kind priestess and he grew angry. "I'm gonna kill him, Kat. If he hurts her, there will be nowhere in this galaxy he can hide!" Chase's voice had risen, and there were now several people including Vanguard Tobias and Flag Officer Victor staring at him.

"Chase, what are we going to do?"

"Did you tell him we were already on *Commonwealth One* and that Sym was no longer in our possession?"

"Yeah, then he threatened us and ended the transmission."

"He's trying to come up with a new plan. As soon as he's figured it out, he'll call again."

"What do you think he's going to ask for next?"

"Me, and we will make the trade if he asks."

"Chase, we can't do that. He'll kill you." By this point, several members of the bridge crew were listening intently to the conversation.

Vanguard Tobias walked over to the communications station and asked, "What's going on, Cadogan?"

"Sir, when we took Sym to Avalon to be healed, Jay Lee Hazard showed up and tried to kill us and take Sym captive. He failed and lost several of his mercs in the process."

"Yes, you've told me all of that when you briefed me."

"What we didn't know at the time was, after we escaped, he took one of the priestesses, Kat's cousin, captive. He wants to trade her for Sym."

The Vanguard looked confused as he replied, "What could he possibly want with her?"

"I don't know, sir. I think he was hoping to get to us before we turned her over. He knows now that she is already in your custody, so he'll likely call with an alternate demand."

"What do you think he'll ask for?" Flag Officer Victor asked.

"Me."

"You?" Vanguard Tobias repeated. "Why you?"

"His op is blown, and I'm the one he blames. Plus, he already hates me. If he can't get to Sym, I'm his second choice."

"I do no... wish to see you or priestess hurt... for me," Sym said. Everyone looked at her when she spoke, because no one had even heard her walk over.

"That is a nice sentiment, young lady, but we have to return you to your people."

Chase put his hand on Sym's shoulder and said, "He's right, Sym. Getting you home is our top priority. We all knew it would involve risks."

"Fighting beasts was risk. Priestess... not ask for this."

"That's why I'm going to rescue her," Chase said. He turned to face Vanguard Tobias and asked, "Permission to leave and find Kat's cousin?"

"Not yet, Chase. The Qantarah have made it clear they want you to be at the exchange that will happen in a few minutes, after which you have my permission to leave."

"Thank you, sir." Chase looked back to the screen and said, "I'll be back to the ship as soon as I can. Have her prepped and ready. If Hazard calls back, agree to meet him at any pub in the cluster, any time he wants, to make the exchange."

"Chase, we're not going to give you to him," Kat replied.

"Don't worry about me, I'll be fine. I'm going to get Felicia back and I'll live to tell the tale."

"How can you be so sure?"

"Hazard's never beaten me yet. Just have the ship ready to go." The transmission ended and Chase sighed. *Now all I have to do is come up with a plan to match my bluster*, he thought.

"Do not worry, Chase. I am sending six of my men with you."

"You don't have to do that, sir."

"If this was solely because of his vendetta toward you, I would agree, but this is because he wants Sym and he's working for someone. My men will want to find out who that is; not to mention that the Commonwealth is now in your debt. I would also like for you to survive until our dinner. We have much to discuss."

"Thank you, sir." Chase felt his face start to flush. He had never felt comfortable with any sort of accolades.

"I'm not kidding. And, if there is anything I can ever do for you, just ask," Vanguard Tobias said.

"Sir, the Qantarah are hailing us. Their Battle Conductor wishes to come aboard to speak to you and retrieve his scientist," the communications officer said.

Vanguard Tobias turned to face the transmission and said, "Battle Conductor Garyn, You have permission to come aboard. Please set down in Landing Bay Three. We reserve it for only our most honored guests."

[That is acceptable,] Garyn replied and cut the transmission.

After the translation, Vanguard Tobias turned and strode off the bridge. He was followed by the Flag, Chase, Sym, and an honor guard. "Juel, please station some soldiers on the catwalk of Landing Bay Three. Just in case this Garyn gets it in his head to try some more intimidation."

"Yes, sir."

They took speeders through the ship and arrived at the landing bay. Artificial light gleamed off the light grey deck and when Chase saw Sym squinting her eyes, he said, "It's awfully bright in here."

"Yes, it is," Flag Officer Victor replied and Chase wondered if the light was a ploy to make the Qantarah uncomfortable. Before Chase could comment further, the shuttle arrived. The Commonwealth envoy watched the rectangular Qantaran shuttle alight on the deck. A moment later, the hatch lifted, a ramp descended from the side of the cobalt colored ship, and seven Qantarah disembarked, all males.

The first Qantarah off the shuttle was a large being. Standing just over two meters, his short fur was significantly darker than Sym's and the muzzle-like features of his face were more pronounced. He was humanoid, but looked less human and less friendly than Sym. He wore a jade cape that almost reached the floor over the shoulders of his black jumpsuit. His black boots were studded with precious stones and he wore a silver gauntlet on his right arm with matching stones. A blaster hung in an easy manner from his right side and he had an irritated look on his face as he paraded toward the Vanguard. There were two smaller Qantarah carrying equipment that looked to be scientific in nature, followed by four larger aliens marching like disciplined warriors. All of the Qantarah wore similar black jumpsuits.

Vanguard Tobias held out his hand and said, "Welcome to *Commonwealth One*. We have found your scientist and rescued her after her ship crash landed in the mountains of Nibiru."

Battle Conductor Garyn did not take the Vanguard's hand in a gesture of welcome. He sneered at the Commonwealth leader and looked at Sym. He spoke in the harsh, guttural Qantaran language. A moment later, the Commonwealth translator said, "Crash landed? How is this possible?"

Sym replied in Qantaran, but when she spoke, it sounded far less severe. She told him about the windstorm on Planet Fourteen, suppressing a shiver when she recalled Niburu. She showed Garyn her healed wounds, even as she still cradled her arm.

One of the Commonwealth techs was translating the conversation as the Qantarah were speaking. His voice was just loud enough for the Vanguard, the Flag, and Chase to hear. After questioning Sym, Garyn turned to Vanguard Tobias and growled something. The translation immediately followed. "What did scientist Sym Triot tell you she was doing in the Luminari Cluster?"

"I didn't ask her," Tobias replied while holding eye contact with the large alien.

Garyn turned to Flag Officer Victor and asked the same question. The Flag replied, "I didn't ask either. None of my men did."

Garyn turned back to his scientists and they spoke for a moment. The translator started deciphering what they were talking about. A few moments later, he said, "It would seem as if their scientists believe you to be telling the truth."

Vanguard Tobias rolled his eyes and said, "Of course we're telling the truth."

With a scowl that Chase knew was a permanent fixture on his face, the alien faced him and asked, [How did you find scientist Triot?]

Chase waited for the translation, a stern look fixed to his face. When the translator was finished, Chase said, "We found evidence of testing on Planet Fourteen. We also found a sensor array made of a metal we had never encountered. We figured that if she lost her sensors, she would put down on the nearest planet for repairs. We knew that Nibiru was closest, so we went there. Nibiru has significant EM disturbance in the atmosphere, which Sym wouldn't have been able to detect with no sensors, so we looked for a crash site. We were lucky to get to her when we did because the jocawolves were almost through her tent."

A moment later, the translator said, "He believes you."

Garyn then asked, [Did you discuss Sym's mission while she was onboard your ship?]

After the translation, Chase replied, "Yes. I asked her what she was doing in the cluster and she told me she was testing for resources."

[What kind of resources?] Garyn said and his man repeated, "What kind of resources?"

"She said it was a metal precious to you, so I figured it was gold or silver. I didn't give much thought to it after that." It wasn't technically a lie, but Chase hoped he didn't raise any Qantaran red flags.

"It would seem they believe you, Chase," the crewman said after more of the guttural speaking.

"Well, gee. I guess I'm all warm inside now," Chase replied in a mocking tone.

Satisfied that Sym had not divulged anything useful, Garyn said, [I've had enough of these humans. Let us take our leave.] He grabbed Sym with a massive hand by the nape of the neck and shoved her forward. Then he turned and sauntered toward his ship, his entourage turning to follow.

"That's it? They're leaving just like that?" Vanguard Tobias asked. He yelled to be sure the Qantarah heard. "Next time you'd like to do your testing on one of our worlds, you speak to me first. If I allow it, your people will be under our supervision, so we can make sure nothing like this ever happens again. And, if you ever send a fleet to the mouth of our cluster without an invitation again, you will not find us as welcoming. Do you understand?"

When the Vanguard said that last line, Garyn stopped and turned. He growled something and ran toward the Vanguard. His bodyguards ran behind him and it looked as if blasters would be drawn. Chase stepped in front of the Vanguard, and before the Qantaran could lift a finger, he had his blaster pointed inches from the alien's face. "I don't know where you think you are, but you better turn around and go home."

By this time, all of the soldiers in the bay had their weapons drawn. More Qantarah had exited the shuttle. Even Kat, Tev and Stone had run out of the *Longshot*. Garyn stared down the barrel of Chase's blaster, but didn't look concerned. Instead, he puffed out his chest and stood up straight.

[You would start a war, human?] The translation followed the question.

"No, but I would protect my leader, no matter the cost." His blaster was still pointed at the alien and neither one of them were flinching.

[Make sure your leader knows that no human speaks to me in such a way if he wishes to live.]

After the translation, Chase replied, "He gets the picture. Next move is yours."

A tense silence filled the expansive landing bay. They were all aware that they were sitting on a powder keg. One misstep would lead to all out war. Garyn growled, his honor guard trained their rifles on Chase, but no one moved. Chase held his blaster inches from the Battle Conductor's face. Every muscle in his body tensed, but his arm held completely still. A casual eye would have wondered if he was a statue. The look on Chase's face told the massive Qantarah that he meant business. The standoff threatened to stretch out to eternity when Chase broke the silence. "I don't care who you are. If you ever threaten the leader of my people again, we're gonna have problems."

Garyn laughed, turned, and marched back toward his craft. He turned to Sym and said, [This is all on you, scientist. As soon as we have emptied you of information useful to us, you will be put to death for your failure.] The translation came in from the crewman next to Vanguard Tobias.

"They're gonna kill her, sir," Chase whispered with a note of urgency in his voice.

"There's nothing we can do about that, son," He replied.

The Qantarah boarded their ship without looking back, and when the ramp went up, a collective exhale filled the landing bay.

"Well, that was exciting," Vanguard Tobias said, followed by a nervous chuckle. "How did you get your blaster up so fast? I never even saw you move."

"I don't know, sir. I just hope I didn't screw things up for you." The Qantaran vessel cleared the landing bay shield and flew toward their fleet.

"No, what you did was keep us from looking weak and intimidated. Well done, son."

"You didn't do too bad yourself, sir. You didn't even flinch with that guy bearing down on you," Chase replied, respect for his leader etched on his face.

Kat called out from across the bay, "Vanguard, sir. We have some information about the Qantaran ships that you might find valuable."

Vanguard Tobias looked at Chase and asked, "What is she talking about, Chase?"

"I have no idea, sir, but Sym did spend a lot of time with Fixer while we were in transit. I didn't ask what they talked about because

Sym had already told me they can tell if we are lying. I figured if I didn't know, they wouldn't know."

"Well, let's go find out, then. Juel, you'll want to hear this, too." He waved Kat over and waited for her and Fixer to arrive.

Kat hurried along the landing bay with Fixer in tow. He was holding an arm full of papers and a data transfer device. When they arrived, Kat said, "Chase, Sym gave us everything. She didn't want us to tell you until she was gone."

"What do you mean, "Everything?"' Chase asked. He knew how big this could be, and he could feel the excitement starting to build in the military brass behind him.

Kat smiled wide and replied, "I mean everything! She gave us the process to mine the xallodium. She gave us the process to build our ships or coat current ships' hulls with it. She even gave us the process to turn it into conductive wiring that would enhance our weapon strength."

"That's incredible!" Flag Officer Victor said. Chase could already see the scenarios playing out in his mind.

"That's not all, sir," Kat continued. "She also gave us the weak spots of the Qantaran ships. She wrote it all in Qantaran, and Fixer designed a translation program for the math."

"It's an algorithm, Katalla Swift."

"That's right, a translation algorithm. My mistake." She flashed the same kind smile she always reserved for Fixer and he sent back his usual awkward grin.

Chase looked at Vanguard Tobias and Flag Officer Victor and added, "Sym told us that Planet Fourteen contained the richest supply of xallodium she had ever heard of. She also told us the Qantarah would invade the cluster and destroy us for a tenth of what she believed was there."

"We need to begin mining that rock as soon as these aliens leave our doorstep," the Flag said. He called for one of the Commonwealth scientists to meet them in the landing bay. "Fixer, do you mind if I give all of this information to our scientists? I'd like them to get familiar with it right away."

Fixer fired off a less than crisp salute and said, "Yes, sir." He started to hand the information to Flag Officer Victor, but then pulled it back. "When they need help, you should call me and Chase. Me and Chase will help. They'll need our help. Actually they'll only need my help, but Chase has to bring me because I live on the *Longshot*." He looked around and when he saw Kat nod at him, he handed the information to the Flag.

The scientist arrived and the information was passed over to him. He started to pore over the papers. He stopped and asked, "What is all of this, sir?"

Flag Officer Victor beamed and said in a theatrical voice, "*This* is everything you need to know about a metal called xallodium. It is the source of Qantaran power and we now have the secrets. We know where it's located, how to mine it, and the different ways to process it. Study up on it. If you need help understanding any of it, contact Fixer Faraday."

Fixer smiled, but the scientist gave him a dubious look.

"Don't let him fool you. Fixer here is as brilliant as they come," Vanguard Tobias said with a smile.

+++++

The *Longshot* departed *Commonwealth One* to await the next transmission Hazard would send. A shuttle carrying six commandos left with them to provide assistance in retrieving Felicia from the criminal. The transmission beeped and Chase took his time answering. He regretted that decision when he saw that it was Vanguard Tobias.

"Chase, as soon as you retrieve your friend, come back to Cibola. We still have much to discuss."

"Yes, sir. I will."

"Excellent. For now, we take our leave. We begin mining the xallodium the moment the Qantaran fleet departs."

"Are you sure they're leaving? They don't look like they're in much of a hurry."

"Yes, I've noticed that as well, and it's troubling."

"At least your people know where to aim now, sir." Another string of beeping let Chase know he had a new transmission waiting. "Looks like Hazard is trying to get through, sir. I'll contact you when the exchange is over."

"Thank you, Chase. Be safe out there."

Chase ended the transmission with the Vanguard and eyed the button to answer the next one. He plastered a stoic expression to his face and pushed the button. "What do you want, Hazard?"

"Is that any way to answer a transmission, Chase? And are you still trying to find that murderer, Jay Lee Hazard?" Upon hearing that, the crew of the *Longshot* had to stifle their laughter.

"Sorry, mom. I thought it was Hazard calling. What's up? Is everything okay with Dad?"

"There's been no change in your father's condition. I just wanted to see when you'll be dropping by. Your sister is really excited to see you."

He let out a deep sigh and said, "I'll be there as soon as I'm finished with this mission."

"Right, the top secret mission for the Vanguard," she said in a tone that said she refused to believe him.

He ignored the implied insult and in a patronizing tone of his own, said, "That mission is over. Now we're going to rescue Kat's cousin, Felicia. She was kidnapped by Hazard, during the mission you don't believe we were on. I'll be by to see you as soon as that's done."

"How do you plan on rescuing Felicia?"

"Don't worry about it, mom."

"Chase Cadogan! Don't you dare do anything stupid! Do you understand me?"

"I won't, mom. This will be a simple grab." The transmission beeped again and Chase added, "Okay, this has to be him. I'll see you soon." He returned the stoic look to his face and switched over before his mom could reply.

"Cadogan. So nice to see you finally care enough about your friend to answer my transmission," Hazard said in a voice dripping sarcasm. His glare could have melted ice.

"What do you want, murderer?" Chase replied.

"I have your friend, the poor little priestess. Her goddess has yet to rescue her, so the task will fall to you."

"What is it you are suggesting?"

"A trade."

"We've already turned over the alien to the Flag, and she's back with her people. I watched the exchange myself."

"I already know that. I want to trade her for you."

"What makes you think I care enough about her to put my life on the line? Her cousin and I broke up a long time ago." He could see Kat looking at him with a tentative expression and he winked at her out of transmission view to reassure her.

"I think you're still closer to the lovely Miss Swift than you would have me believe. In fact," he said with a smug grin. "I believe she is the one person in your pathetic little world you would do this for. Now enough posturing. As soon as I think this exchange is no longer worth it, she dies like the priest that tried to save her."

Chase burned with anger. This monster just casually admitted that he murdered a priest to get Felicia off of Avalon. "Fine! When and where? I'm looking forward to finally killing you."

"And I, you. We will meet on Kephri. There's an old pub about fifteen kilometers due south of the spaceport just outside Zona. It's called the Thirsty Varker."

"Are you sure you want to do this near the planet's capital? You're a wanted man. That's a lot of extra heat you might wind up with."

Hazard's face grew red and he replied, "No one will know I'm near Zona. Got that? If I even smell a tail. I cut and run. Then you'll have to explain to your precious Katalla why her beloved cousin is dead."

When Hazard made that last remark, Kat jumped in front of the transmission and yelled. "If anything happens to Felicia, I will find you and I will kill you in the slowest, most painful way imaginable! Do you understand?"

"Cadogan, keep control of your dancing whore. I grow weary of her threats."

With fire in his eyes, Chase growled a reply, "So when are we gonna do this, Hazard?"

"It should take you no longer than twelve hours to get here from the mouth of the cluster. I'll see you then." He cut the transmission and Chase was left glaring into the empty view screen.

Stone broke the silence first. "Chase, remember my buddies from the brawl? They're already in Zona. I can have them to the pub in about an hour and Hazard will never suspect they are with us."

"That's a great idea, Stone. Kat, send our shuttle full of friends the coordinates. Tell them to ditch their uniforms and to try to look like civilians. Let them know the three Boreans are on our side, but not to make any contact with them. I'll let the soldiers get there an hour or two before us." Kat sent the transmission and a moment later, the shuttle entered hyperspace.

"Fixer, prepare the ship to make a jump to Cibola. I need to pick up something I think will be helpful." Fixer began the preparations, but the entire crew was distracted when what looked like lightning raced across space and struck *Commonwealth One*.

"The Qantarah are attacking our fleet!" Tev yelled.

"Do you think the Flag has relayed the Qantaran weakness to the rest of the fleet yet?" Stone asked while he was strapping himself in.

"I don't know," Chase replied. "Battle stations!" Now everyone was fastening their restraints. Kat had sensors, Stone had weapons, Fixer was monitoring power, and Tev was standing ready with shields. Chase had the helm and he raced toward the Qantaran Flagship. "I guess we're about to find out how good Sym's intel was," he said. "Stone, ready missiles, all four tubes."

"On it!"

When the *Longshot* reached firing range, the crew looked to Chase for the order, but he remained silent. They drew closer and Kat said, "Shouldn't we be shooting at them?"

"Not yet," Chase replied. "They obviously think we're no threat, and it looks like their weapons intercept a lot of missiles before they reach their mark. I'd rather conserve what we have until I know it will do the job." Solid beams of light streaked across space and found their mark, doing little damage to the superior Qantaran vessels. Missiles trailing fuel burns were able to damage several enemy ships, and when the first warship blew, Chase knew the Flag had gotten the word out.

The *Longshot* was now only a few kilometers away from what Chase thought was the enemy Flagship and he yelled, "Fire all missiles." Four missiles flew the short distance without being intercepted and three of them found their mark. The missiles hit the casing attaching the engines to the back of the ship, which started a chain reaction, destroying the ship and causing a wave of energy. Chase leaned hard on the helm, willing his ship to go faster. He peered around the bridge to see the worried, but focused faced of his friends. They managed to outrun the energy released from the warship, but other enemy ships had seen them take out the vessel and began to open fire on them.

"Hold on. This is going to get bumpy," Chase yelled while he wove the ship in and out of other Commonwealth vessels. Still, the unpredictable lightning-like energy of the Qantarah came at them. They were struck by a blast that rained sparks down on the bridge, but before the enemy could take advantage, its ship was destroyed by *Commonwealth One*. The *Longshot* made it safely to the back of the Commonwealth formation and Chase turned his ship for another run.

"Status report," Chase bellowed.

"Shields holding at fifty-three percent. We can only take one more hit, Chase," Tev said.

Chase slowed the *Longshot* and glanced at his crew members and asked "What do you think?"

"I think we take a minute to see how the battle is playing out before we charge in for no reason," Kat replied.

"I agree with Katalla Sift," Fixer added.

"Big surprise there," Chase replied. "What about you, Stone?"

"Just tell me who to shoot."

Chase watched the battle. Aside from the Qantarah's six-ship foray through the third cluster entrance, this was the first full-scale battle the Commonwealth had been a part of in well over a century. The Qantaran lightning energy weapons were lighting up space. The energy was splashing off Commonwealth shields, but if the first battle was any indication, the Commonwealth ships could only take a few hits before being destroyed. The red and orange beams the cluster forces shot back at the superior alien vessels were doing little damage. Still, enough missiles were finding their targets to keep this battle relatively even.

A transmission alert beeped and Chase took it without picture to keep focused on the battlefield.

"Good shooting, Cadogan," Flag Officer Victor's voice called over the comms. "Now, go save your friend. That's an order!" The transmission ended and Chase looked at his crew, still not wanting to leave the battle.

"We were ordered, Chase," Tev said.

"Chase, we're not going to affect the outcome of this battle. Please, we need to go get Felicia," Kat said with a plea in her voice.

He knew she was right, but he wanted to stay and fight. "Send a message to *Commonwealth One*. Let them know we will be taking our leave."

"That's the right choice, Chase," Tev said while Kat made the transmission.

"The Flag said, 'Good hunting!'" Kat said, continuing to watch the battle unfold through the viewport. She had never seen anything like it. She had seen an occasional explosion in space, but nothing that could rival the size and scope of the battle unfolding before her. Hundreds of ships were fighting, and the survival of their people hinged on the outcome.

"Fixer, get us into hyperspace before I change my mind."

"Okay, Chase. Don't change your mind. We have to save Katalla Swift's cousin." His hands flew over the controls while he spoke. Chase turned the ship toward Kephri and said, "Forget Cibola. Jump us to Kephri, Fixer." The mechanic pressed the button, the stars stretched out before them, and they were pulled into hyperspace. "Kat, I need you to find out how the battle is going the moment we exit hyperspace, okay?"

"Will do, Chase."

Chapter nine

"Crewman, Get Vanguard Tobias and his honor guard to a shuttle and get them out of here," Flag Officer Victor said, his voice not quite a yell, but loud enough to be heard over the battle klaxons.

"Launch all fighters, except the honor guard," Fleet Captain Johan shouted.

"Juel, I will not run from battle," Vanguard Tobias replied.

"Fighters away, sir," a crewman called out. They glanced out the viewport and saw thousands of fighters launching from hundreds of ships, streaking towards the enemy. Lightning leapt from Qantaran ships, but the nimble fighters weaved around it and began strafing runs on the intimidating enemy vessels. The Qantarah followed suit, launching their fighters into the chaos. Commonwealth gunships fired into the Qantaran bays as they tried to launch fighters, destroying many of them before they could ever get into the battle, and causing secondary explosions that damaged several of the warships. The tactic had the desired effect, leaving the Commonwealth fighters with a significant numerical advantage over their enemies.

The Flag returned his gaze to the Vanguard and continued, "Sir, it makes no strategic sense for both of the Commonwealth leaders to be on the same ship. You don't see the Qantaran Primus on the Battle Conductor's bridge, do you?"

"Fine! I'll relocate to another destroyer."

The Flag sighed and said, "Sir, I wish you'd reconsider. If we lose this battle, we'll need you on Cibola calling the shots."

"All ships have launched fighters. Qantarah have launched their remaining fighters as well," a crewman announced.

Vanguard Tobias gaze slipped a fraction and he replied, "You're right, Juel. I need to be where I can do the most good." He turned to the crewman and added, "Lead the way." The ship rocked after being hit by the powerful Qantaran energy weapons and the crewman made haste to the shuttle bay with Vanguard Tobias behind him.

The lighting in the corridor had gone dim. Bright strobes accompanied the warning sirens. The deck plates thrummed with exertion and, even from the center of the ship, the Vanguard could tell *Commonwealth One* was in trouble. The corridors were crowded with people leaving affected sections and damage control teams hustling to where they were needed. Still, everyone made way for the Vanguard to get to the landing bay. Another blow struck the ship, and the blaring alarms grew more insistent.

On the bridge, Flag Officer Victor commed the landing bay and yelled, "I haven't seen any shuttles departing, what's the hold up?"

"Vanguard Tobias has yet to arrive, sir," a voice responded.

"Get him out the second he arrives, crewman. Do you understand me?"

"Yes, sir. The shuttle is ready to go the moment the Vanguard steps through the hatch."

"Very good." He ended the transmission and looked at the controlled chaos on the bridge. A sensor station exploded, sending bodies and debris flying in all directions, and leaving the ship blind. Damage control teams arrived and put the fire out, but dark smoke hung think in the air. Three bodies had been nearly incinerated by the brunt of the blast, and the Vanguard looked away as they were removed by young med-techs. The smell of charred metal and flesh filled his nostrils and sent him into a coughing fit. Emergency teams were on the way with oxygen filters for the remaining bridge crew. Announcements were coming rapidly and none of them were good.

"Warning, decompression on decks ten through twelve, port side, mid-ship."

"Shields holding at eighteen percent."

"Missiles away, loading next round."

"We've lost port side maneuvering thrust."

"The *Renaissance* has been destroyed."

"The *Zona* has been destroyed."

"*Argatha* has lost shields."

Outside, the battle raged. The Qantarah were focusing their attack on the center of the Commonwealth formation in an attempt to break their line, but the line held. The Commonwealth fighters were doing much better against their counterparts than the capital ships were, but smaller explosions still lit up space. The cluster of Stars that gave the Commonwealth their natural defenses had become the backdrop to the largest battle in the recorded history of the Luminari Cluster.

"Send the ships at the left edge of the formation to flank the Qantarah. Have a flight of fighters lead them in. We can exploit their overzealous attack at our center!" The Flag yelled. A young crewman was quick to relay the orders, and a moment later the left edge of the formation could be seen streaking toward the enemy. The move had been unexpected, and the enemy broke ranks to stop the Commonwealth advance. The lightning weapon strikes aimed at the center of the Commonwealth formation slowed considerably.

Fleet Captain Johan used the temporary reprieve to look at the Flag and say, "It's time for you to get out of here, sir!"

"Like hell it is."

"Sir, we need you as much as we need the Vanguard and this ship is going down." He pointed to a crewman that looked young and scared. "Crewman Thomes, get the Flag to the landing bay."

"I will not—"

"Subdue him if need be," Fleet Captain Johan barked. Thomes was joined by two more and they escorted the reluctant Flag from the hazy bridge. "Where is my next missile barrage?" Johan yelled, no longer looking to see if the Flag was resisting. He knew getting the Flag to safety was the right thing to do. *Commonwealth One* was going down. The Qantarah had targeted them in their cowardly first strike and they had never recovered. Several ships had been destroyed while giving them the opportunity to get their leaders to safety and he was resigned to holding on until the Flag was clear.

"Vanguard's shuttle is away!" A triumphant voice called. The bridge crew cheered. A moment later, the voice added, "Vanguard's shuttle has entered hyperspace." Another cheer rose up on the doomed bridge.

"Fire missiles at will," Fleet Captain Johan said.

"Sir, we have no sensors," the weapons officer replied.

"Set them to engage the closest enemy vessels. If we go down, I don't want to leave any missiles unfired." He looked around the once proud bridge of the Commonwealth Flagship and added, "Full power to forward shields. Maybe we can take one more hit."

Commonwealth One listed to its port side causing the next barrage to miss. Fleet Captain Johan gave the word and another round of missiles fired, racing toward the enemy like a courier with an urgent message. Qantaran fighters broke off their engagements in an attempt to intercept, but several missiles found their target even as dozens of fighters were reduced to superheated particles. The Commonwealth fighters freed up by their counterpart's sacrifices used the opportunity to strafe the closest enemy vessels. A shockwave pulsed outward as two of the enemy vessels were destroyed in the attack. The flash of light, and the spreading debris field, chased retreating fighters trying to ride the shockwave to safety, and the battle raged on.

+++++

On Jalindi, the chief advisor to the king ran toward the throne room. He stopped at the threshold out of respect and waited for the King to motion him in to the damp room. The signal came and the advisor bowed before the throne.

[Rise, my friend. What news have you?]

[My King, the Qantarah have attacked the Commonwealth. They have sent a second fleet to the cluster. They now have over two hundred fifty ships committed to the operation.]

[How certain are you of this information?] The king rose from his ornate throne and descended the stairs. He stood in front of his advisor, arms crossed, waiting to hear that his plan was finally going to come to fruition.

The advisor looked at his king and smiled as he said, [One hundred percent. My sources in the Luminari Cluster have told me a fierce battle has erupted. The Qantarah attacked even after their scientist was returned, and they focused their attack on the Commonwealth Flagship. I know the Vanguard escaped, but the fate of their military leader is still unknown. My source on Q'Tor has just contacted me to let me know that reinforcements have entered hyperspace. One of our stealth vessels confirmed this to be the case. The Qantarah will not have enough ships available to repel our fleet.]

[Very good. Deploy the fleet. The mighty Qantarah will be on their knees before us within the week.] The king savored the thought of finally defeating the ancient enemy of the Jalindi. He relished the idea of being forever remembered as the king to make that happen.

[It will be as you say, my King.] The advisor hurried from the throne room to the nearest transmission terminal. He commed the Fleet Commander and waited for the reply.

[What news?] the gruff voice on the other end of the comm asked.

[The King has ordered the fleet deployed!] he replied, satisfaction rolling off him.

The gravelly voice of the Fleet Commander sounded pleased when he replied, [Very good.] The transmission ended and the advisor hurried to the war room to watch the fleet depart.

Ten minutes later, the Fleet Commander's image flared to life in the middle of the war room. All eyes looked in his direction. He pressed his elbow against his tunic and touched his fist to his shoulder. Then, in a deep voice that was almost a growl, he said, [For Jalindi!]

[For Jalindi!] the entire war room roared as one. The hologram disappeared and a moment later, the fleet was gone.

+++++

The Flag finally stopped resisting and hurried through the corridors with his escort. They were three turns from the landing bay when a crowd of people turned the corner and ran their way. A lancer yelled, "That way's blocked off due to decompression. We just made it past the automated lockdown."

"We've got the Flag here and he has to get off the ship. What's the quickest way available to a landing bay?" Crewman Thomes asked.

"Quickest way was through there," the Lancer replied, pointing toward the sealed off corridor.

"Quickest way AVAILABLE," Thomes shouted, impatience filling his ash smudged face.

"Back down this corridor. Pass the first junction, then take the emergency stairwell up two levels. That level is clear for now. Then come back the way you were going. You will wind up on the main catwalk of the landing bay. Then you can find your way down to the deck from there. "

Crewman Thomes turned to the Flag and said, "Let's move. We have to hurry."

"Agreed," the Flag replied.

They raced down the busy corridor and passed the bulkhead at the first junction. When they arrived at the emergency stairwell, two crewmen began to turn the lever. They strained, but the lever stayed put. "It's dogged down really well," Thomes grunted while they tried to turn it again. Two more crewmen joined them in their efforts and the lever finally gave way. When they opened the hatch, smoke billowed out into the passageway. "Fire's below us, a crewman said."

"Good thing we're going up," the Flag replied. They started their climb and when they had reached the level, they struggled to open the hatch again. Smoke followed them into the corridor while two crewmen hurried to close the hatch and dog it down. "How much further?" Flag Officer Victor asked.

"If there are no more detours, we should be there in a minute or two." They made it to the Landing bay catwalk just as the ship was rocked again.

"Warning, shields holding at three percent," the announcement blared.

"Next shot is going to destroy us, sir. We need to move."

"There's no way we can get down there quick enough," The Flag replied.

"There is one way," Thomes said. He ran ten feet down the catwalk and busted through an emergency glass panel holding a hose. He rolled off a dozen meters and tied it off on the protective railing of the catwalk. He threw the rest of the hose over the railing, and the metallic clink of the hose nozzle hitting the deck could be heard through the warning klaxons. "After you, sir."

Flag Officer Victor looked over the edge, looked at Thomes and the other two crewman and said, "Well, desperate times." He climbed over the rail and started to climb down. A crewman in the landing bay saw what was happening and ran over and steadied the hose.

"You're coming, too, Thomes," he yelled up to the young crewman.

"I'm right behind you, sir."

Halfway to the deck, the ship was rocked and the Flag lost his grip. He fell to the deck and landed badly. He heard a loud crack and writhed on the floor, clutching at his lower leg.

The crewman that had been steadying the hose ran to the Flag's side. "Sir, are you all right?"

"I think I've broke my ankle, Crewman."

"Let's get you into the shuttle." He helped the Flag up, and another deck hand ran over to help carry him to the shuttle while Thomes slid down the hose, burning his palms in haste. They made it to the shuttle while smoke started to fill the landing bay. The crewman put him in his seat and the hatch closed.

"We need to wait for Crewman Thomes," Flag Officer Victor shouted, but the shuttle was already off the deck. "We can't just leave him. Put back down. That's an order."

The shuttle returned to the deck and a ramp slid down. Crewman Thomes and the other men escorting him ran aboard. Several other deck hands began running for the shuttle, but one of the hatches to the landing bay exploded and flew across the bay. Fire shot into the bay, engulfing the crewmen that had been trying to reach the shuttle.

158

A steady stream of fire prevented them from seeing out of the landing bay, while the last screams of the men caught in the fire were dying out. "We need to go now," the pilot yelled and lifted off while Thomes closed the hatch. A large beam fell in front of the shuttle with a mighty crash. The pilot jerked the yoke up to avoid it. The beam, which the pilot recognized as part of the main bulkhead, blocked the exit "We're blocked in, sir. Nowhere to go."

"So, this is it, then. It's been an honor, men," Flag Officer Victor said.

"For us as well," Thomes replied. A Commonwealth fighter pilot saw their dilemma and fired a missile into the beam. The explosion threw the shuttle back, but cleared the path. The pilot hit the thrusters and the shuttle shot through the flames and out of the landing bay. A moment later, *Commonwealth One* exploded.

The shuttle raced to get ahead of the explosion, but the flames began to swallow it whole. "I don't think we're going to make it," the pilot yelled.

+++++

Chase sauntered into the Thirsty Varker flanked by Kat and Tev with Stone behind them. They were in battle gear and fully armed. Chase supposed it made for an imposing entrance, but after glancing at the clientele, decided it was probably normal. He could see Stone's friends huddled at a table in the corner, drinking and carrying on. The soldiers he had sent ahead had split into two groups in position to lay down cover fire if needed.

The pub was a dive. Shady characters leaned against the old chalange wood bar, not caring about the brewing showdown. Secret deals were being made in dim corners, and it looked as if the place had probably not been painted since it opened decades earlier. Cards were being dealt, money changed hands, and thugs drank. Chase wrinkled his nose when the scent of the place hit him. The smell of alcohol mixed with the unwashed dregs of humanity left a pungent odor that would not soon be forgotten.

Chase spotted Hazard, holding Felicia's arm. The first thing he noticed was that she had been beaten bloody. Hazard stood and was immediately surrounded by four mercenaries. "Right on time, Cadogan," he said in greeting. "Now, drop your weapons and walk toward me."

"Not so fast, Hazard," Chase spit the name out as if it were a curse. "You send the priestess to my people while I walk to you."

"That doesn't work for me. I guess I'll just kill her now."

Chase could see the worry in Kat's eyes, but he held his ground. "If she dies, my first shot goes right between your eyes. Your choice, you can make the trade or you can die."

"Fine, but the first sign of betrayal and I shoot her in the back, do you understand?"

"Let's do this." Chase un-holstered both of his blasters and gave them to Tev. He slid the rifle out of the holster on his back and handed it to Kat.

"Keep going, Cadogan," Hazard sneered.

Chase glared at his enemy, then bent over and removed a large knife from a sheath on his right leg. Finally, he reached down and removed the holdout blaster his left boot contained. He straightened up and began a slow spin with his jacket open and hefted above the waistline. "Satisfied?"

"Not yet, Cadogan, but I will be." Hazard let loose an evil grin and motioned Cadogan forward. He shoved Felicia out in front of him, laughing when she stumbled into an empty table.

Almost ten meters separated the two groups. Dozens of patrons filled several tables, but the path between them had cleared out. Chase wondered how many of these patrons were with Hazard while he began a casual stroll toward his nemesis. Felicia limped toward him and his face reddened when he saw how much pain it caused her just to walk. *Hazard will pay as soon as she's safe.*

When they reached the halfway point, Chase stopped. He Looked at Felicia and said, "You're going to be all right. My people will get you out of here and back to Avalon where you can be healed."

"What about you? He means to kill you."

"I'll be okay. I've been after this guy for a long time, and now the idiot just invites me in. I couldn't have planned it better if I tried."

She saw through his bluster to the uncertainty in his eyes. "Avalon will repay him for what he has done," she said.

"I'm happy to be the avatar of your goddess to accomplish her will," he replied. He smiled and stepped around her to continue moving toward Hazard.

"So, face to face at last, Cadogan," Hazard bellowed. "I'm going to enjoy killing you."

Chase stopped and said, "Good luck with that." Without warning, four tables were flipped onto their side and all of Chase's people had their blasters out. Tev Hurried Felicia behind one of the tables as blasterfire erupted in their direction. When they had reached cover, Kat began to fuss over her cousin.

"I am fine, Katalla. Keep your focus on your friend."

"You're right. I was just so worried about you."

Return fire caused Hazard to duck behind a table before he could fire on Chase. The Thirsty Varker had descended into chaos and the bartender disappeared behind the bar. The patrons that were not part of the festivities ran for the door and, in the confusion, Chase dove for an empty table.

Hazard yelled from his position, "Looks like I have more men here than you, Cadogan. I guess I'm glad you have so few friends." He peered out from behind his cover and fired. Chase just managed to get his heavy table over in time. He reached up into the back of his jacket and pulled out a small blaster.

"I have all the friends I need, Hazard and I didn't have to pay mine to be here," he replied. He stood and fired. He estimated almost thirty men on Hazard's side. Several shots burned into the table near where Chase had been. Two of Hazard's men went down to fire from the Boreans, then another one was hit by Kat.

Chase rolled out of his cover and fired off three quick shots, hitting one of the mercenaries in the head. He dove behind the next table when they returned fire. The six Commonwealth soldiers the Vanguard had sent were advancing in a military formation from table to table. They took out three of Hazard's men before one of them was hit in the side. He went down in pain, but his teammates kept him covered.

Tev tossed Chase one of his blasters and his rifle, and Chase started pouring on the blasterfire.

"There's too many of them," one of the Boreans yelled.

"We have to pull back," a soldier added.

"It's no good, we've got nowhere to go," Kat replied. "Keep firing!"

"That's right, Cadogan. You've got nowhere to go. You've led your people right into a trap," Hazard yelled over the sounds of battle. The smell of burnt wood filled the air and burnt flesh added to it when another soldier went down.

Chase popped up from behind his table and took down two more soldiers, but he was too slow taking cover. He took a blast to the shoulder that sent him flying backwards. He landed hard on a couple chairs and cried out in pain.

"Chase," Kat yelled, her eyes big and her voice high.

"I'll live," he grunted while he crawled toward another table.

Hazard and his mercenaries began to advance. They knew if they could control the exit, Chase and his people would not be leaving alive.

"I've had enough of this," Tev yelled. He unclipped one of the grenades from his jacket and hurled it across the pub. Mercenaries rose and tried to dive for cover only to be shot for their efforts. When the grenade went off, it took out a couple more people and brought down a section of the wall. The ceiling drooped, but held.

"Are you insane?" Hazard yelled. He turned to his mercenaries and added, "Kill the moron with the mustache before he brings this place down on us all."

Tendissa crawled into a better position to fire from, but was hit in the leg with a heavy blast from Stone. She cried out in pain and her blaster fell from her hands. Most of her leg below the knee was gone.

Hazard stood to fire again, but Chase was ready and fired first. His shot skimmed Hazard's bicep, leaving a scorched hole in his jacket. "Maybe you should learn how to shoot that thing," Hazard yelled. His men began to advance again, cutting off the only means of egress.

Tev stood up to throw another grenade and Hazard was ready for him. He shot Tev square in the chest sending him flying back almost three meters. The grenade rolled from his lifeless hand and stopped near Chase.

"Tev," Kat screamed, but there was no answer.

Chase dove out of cover to grab the grenade before it went off and shuffle tossed it like a hot potato. It landed right in front of the table Hazard and his mercs were behind. The grenade exploded and the table took some of the brunt of the explosion. Shrapnel flew and some of Hazard's men ran. The odds were fairly even now, and the mercenaries decided this fight was above their pay grade.

Stones friends and the remaining soldiers fired on the mercenaries as they made for the open section of the wall. Chase winced as he stood. All he could feel was the fire in his shoulder. He marched over to where his nemesis lay. Hazard was confused and trying to get his bearings. Chase shot his three injured mercenary friends. He set his blaster to stun and shot Hazard. He wanted the full bounty more than he wanted to kill him. *Prison will be worse for him*, Chase thought. The battle was over and he turned to his people, most of whom he had never even been introduced to.

"Status," Chase yelled.

"I've got one dead and one injured," a soldier replied.

"We're okay. Just a few scrapes," the Boreans answered. Then Chase looked to his friends.

Stone and Kat were kneeling over Tev. Kat cried out, "Tev, no! Stay with me, please, stay with me. Tev?" She was on the verge of tears.

Felicia limped over and put her arms around her distraught cousin and said, "He has already gone from us, Katalla."

"We need to get out of here," Chase said. "Stone, can your friends take Hazard to the *Longshot*?"

"Yeah," he replied. Then he turned to his friends and said, "Josck, Tower, you pick up the trash and Bazz will cover you." He looked to Chase and saw the pain etched on his face. He was sweating and a bit wobbly. "I'll carry Tev, Chase. Maybe you could cover us while Kat helps Felicia."

"Sounds good, Stone."

"We'll take up the rear," the soldier added. "And we'll tell the Vanguard that Hazard has been captured."

"Thanks, and tell the Vanguard that I'll get the information he needs." The soldier nodded and Chase said, "Let's go." The procession left the ruined pub and walked the twenty meters to their speeders. They could see the frightened pub owner emerging from what was left of his establishment after they departed.

Twenty minutes later, they were boarding the ship. Fixer met them at the landing bay of the *Longshot*. "Josck, Tower, could you guys drop off this varker dung in our holding cell?" Chase asked. He tried to point to it and winced at the pain in his shoulder. "Fixer will open it for you."

"No problem," Tower replied, following the mechanic across the landing bay.

Katalla helped her cousin onto the ship, but she was openly crying. It seemed she was leaning on Felicia as much as Felicia leaned on her. Stone's friends were back from locking up Hazard, and a somber silence came over the landing bay when Stone carried the lifeless body of Tev onto the ship. His massive arms were trembling and tears burned down his face, leaving light blue trails.

"He was the best of us. Why did it have to be him?" Stone asked while he gently laid his friend on the deck plating of the landing bay.

"I don't know. I wish I did," Chase replied without meeting his eyes.

Stone's friends each embraced him, they shook hands with Chase, and left in silence. Fixer just stared at Tev. Every once in a while he would look over to Kat, then right back to Tev. After a few minutes, he asked, "Is Tev dead?"

"Yeah, he is, Fixer," Chase replied. He wondered what Fixer thought about it. Fixer just stood and walked back into the ship. Chase tried to close the landing bay, but his injured shoulder refused to cooperate. "Dasnit!" he yelled. Then his body began to tremble and he kicked one of the speeder bikes over and over. Stone laid a gentle hand on his good shoulder and then closed the landing bay hatch. They proceeded in silence to the common room.

+++++

[We have destroyed the Commonwealth Flagship, mighty Battle Conductor,] an officer said.

Garyn's face lit up with excitement. [Did their leaders go down with the ship?]

[Reports suggest their Vanguard made it to a shuttle and into hyperspace, but it would seem their Flag Officer was still onboard when she blew.]

Garyn looked out the viewport. The Commonwealth ships were actually doing better than he thought they would. [Their beam weapons splash uselessly off our xallodium hulls, but their missiles are more powerful than we expected.] He watched one of his warships explode and pounded the console in front of him. [How are they able to destroy our ships?]

[I do not know, My Lord. As predicted, their primary weapons are useless,] the officer replied.

[Why did we not know about the strength of their missiles?]

The officer looked almost embarrassed as he replied, [Those weapons are so outdated, we never even thought to check. Our weapons and our fighters intercept almost sixty percent of them before they can damage our ships, My Lord.]

[Well the ones that do get through are doing significant damage.]

[That is true, oh great Battle Conductor, but at least we know they have a finite supply. We shall overwhelm them in the long run.]

A smile spread across Garyn's face. [True. This cluster will be ours.] He watched in satisfaction as two more Commonwealth ships were destroyed. His satisfaction was short lived.

[Incoming transmission from Q'Tor.]

[Onscreen,] Battle conductor Garyn replied.

The face of Primus Garyn materialized on the bridge and everyone not at a battle station bowed before their leader. [Your gambit worked, brother. A huge Jalindi fleet has just left their homeworld. It is time for you to withdraw from battle and bring your fleet home. Your second fleet awaits in the Daxonna system as you requested. When you arrive, we shall catch them in a cross fire and it will be a long time before the Jalindi have the resources to challenge us again.]

[It will be as you say, Primus, but we may need a few more ships.]

[Why?] Primus Garyn looked surprised at the request.

[The humans put up more of a fight than we anticipated, but we did destroy their Flagship and one of their leaders with it.]

[Another twenty ships will rendezvous with you in the Daxonna system.] The transmission ended and the image disappeared, but Garyn could sense his brother's disappointment.

[Recall all fighters. All ships are to continue the battle until our fighters are onboard, then we jump to Daxonna.]

[Yes, My Lord,] the communications officer replied. If he could sense the agitation of his military leader, he wisely chose not to show it. He sent the message to the fleet and a moment later, could see all of the fighters returning. He was surprised when the human fighters pursued the retreating fighters. [My Lord, the humans are following our retreat.]

Garyn looked out the viewport and watched several fighters, two gunships and another warship blown apart. His anger began to rise and he punched the console again. [When we have taken care of the

Jalindi, we shall return and repay them for attacking our withdrawal!]

Another ship blew up before the officer said, [All fighters are aboard. The fleet will jump to hyperspace in three seconds.]

Three heartbeats later, the Qantaran fleet was gone.

+++++

Bright stars packed tightly provided the backdrop for the largest space battle ever fought in the Luminari Cluster. The black of the expanse stretched out almost infinitely before them, but filling that chasm was an alien armada attacking Commonwealth forces. Light broke up the darkness of the void as the bright white lightning-like weapons of the Qantarah raced across space to impact Commonwealth shields. Hard light, both red and orange, streaked the other way. It was a deadly light show.

Fighters danced around the larger ships, adding their fire to the mayhem and missiles raced toward Qantaran vessels, trailing smoke as they went. The Qantarah seemed to be winning when all of a sudden, they stopped pressing their advantage and recalled their fighters.

"Sir, I think the enemy is retreating. All of their fighters are leaving the theatre," the sensors officer of the *Typhoon* said.

"Give chase and continue firing. Have our fighters launch all remaining missiles at the Qantaran capital ships when they get close enough. We're not giving them a free pass. They took a shot at our leaders. They don't get to walk away from that," Captain Valence replied. With *Commonwealth One* and the Flag gone, along with Fleet Captain Johan, he had the most seniority and had taken command of the fleet.

Several Qantaran ships exploded before their fleet jumped to hyperspace. The crew of the *Typhoon* celebrated while Captain Valence peered out at the debris. "So many lives lost, and for what?" he mumbled. He looked at the expectant faces of his crew and bellowed, "Status report!"

"We've lost fifty-one ships, sir. I imagine it will be some time before we can tally the amount of fighters we've lost and the amount of overall casualties. There are several shuttles full of our people out there waiting for clearance to land on one of our ships," a young female officer replied.

"How did we do, Lieutenant?"

"Sir?"

"How many of them did we take with us, Lieutenant Wen?"

"We managed to destroy forty-two, sir. Five of those were while they retreated. I don't get it. They were winning, why did they leave?"

"We'll have to try and figure that out later. For now, we scan the debris for any active transmitters. Some of our people on those ships may have survived. And if they did, they'll be expecting a rescue. Let's not disappoint them." He turned and marched over to the sensor control station. "Crewman, report."

"All remaining ships are scanning debris. So far we have over two hundred transmitters reporting. Readying rescue teams now, sir."

"Excellent." He patted the young crewman on the back and strode to his chair. He looked out over his weary crew and said, "Put me on fleet-wide."

When his communications officer gave him the signal, he said, "I know you're tired, and I know many of you are injured. We've all lost friends today and we'll be trying to make sense of that for a long time. We're not finished yet, and the aliens might return, but it is important that you realize what we've accomplished here today. We drove off a superior force. We protected our cluster, our planets, our loved ones, and everyone that was depending on us to be great today. I don't know what tomorrow will bring, but today the Commonwealth lives free because of you."

The bridge crew of the *Typhoon* stood and cheered for their captain. He could hear cheering coming over the comms from other ships as well. He let it continue for a moment before adding, "We've got over two hundred brothers and sisters that may still be alive in that debris. Let's bring them home."

Soon, reinforcements began to arrive. Damaged ships were allowed to return to the ship building facilities for repairs, while barges arrived to collect debris to be recycled and tow the disabled ships to Kephri. Captain Valence was sure some of the ships would have to be scrapped and hoped there were still usable parts on those ships. He snapped out of his reverie and called out, "What is the status report on those transmitters?"

"We've rescued one hundred thirty-four of our people," Lieutenant Wen replied. "There are still one hundred forty-seven, sir. As the debris is cleared, we are continuing to discover additional transmitters."

"Very good. Keep me informed, Lieutenant."

"Yes, sir," she replied.

Three hours later, Captain Valence was in the mess pouring himself a steaming hot cup of jav. He was running on fumes and so was his crew. All but his ship and three others had been relieved and he was to remain until all of the rescue missions had been completed. He marched back onto the bridge, jav in hand, and took inventory of which crew members needed a break. A moment later, Lieutenant Wen approached him at nearly a run. A smile was plastered on her tired face.

"Sir, sir, you have to see this."

"See what, Lieutenant? Calm down."

"Sir, we've just discovered nine more transmitters in close proximity to one another, and one of them belongs to Flag Officer Victor."

Captain Valence snatched the datapad out of her hand, spilling his jav on the deck in the process and looked at the tablet in disbelief. "It looks like they're in a damaged shuttle. We're only five minutes out, let's go rescue the Flag."

Chapter ten

The *Longshot* sped toward Avalon. The first stop was to drop off Felicia at her abbey. The second stop would be considerably more difficult.

Chase lay on one of the common room couches. Kat and Stone had managed to get his jacket and shirt off to treat his wound. Sweat poured off his body while Stone held him down. Chase cried out and squirmed, then cried out again. He was delirious.

"Hold him still, Stone," Kat yelled while Fixer watched from a corner where he rocked back and forth, mumbling incoherently. "Fixer, it's going to be okay. Chase is going to be okay," she called out in a gentle voice. She returned her attention to Chase and poured a green liquid into his wound. "This should stem the tide of the infection. Let's bandage him up and get him to bed."

"You're really good at this, Kat," Stone said. Then he nodded his head toward Fixer and added, "And you're really good with him."

"Thanks, Stone. I just hope we can get Chase to a med-center soon."

"Chase will be okay. Avalon will protect him," Felicia said. She was resting comfortably.

"I wish I had your faith, cousin," she replied. "How are you feeling?"

"I am well enough. Avalon will heal me once I return to the abbey." Her countenance dropped and she averted her eyes. "I'm sorry all of this happened to your friends because of me, Katalla. You had accomplished your mission and you were all safe. Now Tev is dead and Chase is injured and you are all in pain. Please forgive me."

"There is nothing to forgive, Felicia," Stone replied. "You didn't plan for this, and you had no control over our response. This is in no way your fault."

"Thank you for such kind words, Stone. I know Tev was like a brother to you and I know you must be hurting. I pray that one day I can return your kindness."

"When is Chase going to wake up?" Fixer asked. "I want to talk to Chase. When is Chase waking up?"

"Fixer, come here," Kat said. "Come sit and keep me company. I'm really sad and I could use a friend."

"I want Chase to be okay, Katalla Swift. You said he would be okay." He plopped down next to Kat and stared out the side viewport. Kat studied him, wondering what was going on in his mind. She wondered how someone with Taklinsen's disorder dealt with loss.

She put her arm around him and said in a soothing voice, "Chase is going to be fine. He'll wake up before we're even out of hyperspace."

"Do you promise, Katalla Swift?"

"Yes, Fixer Faraday. I promise. Would you like a green fizzy?"

"Can Stone have one, too?"

"Of course." In spite of the sadness she felt, she smiled for her childlike friend.

Soon after drinking his beverage, Fixer went to his room to sleep. Felicia was also asleep and Kat was alone on the bridge. Stone had gone to stand guard outside Hazard's cell and every time the criminal woke, Stone would stun him to quiet his bellowing while his friends were sleeping. She wondered if she should treat Hazard's wounds, but decided against it. She knew it was unlikely she would be able to refrain from hurting him and she knew Chase was going to want to do that.

Chase finally woke up and trudged out of his room and onto the bridge. He was still shirtless, with bandages covering almost half his chest. He looked around and spotted Kat, deep in thought.

"Hey, Kat. Where is everyone," he asked in a weak scratchy voice.

His query startled her, but she composed herself and replied, "Stone is in the back, he keeps stunning Hazard to keep him quiet. Fixer and Felicia are sleeping."

"I hope not together," he said and smiled at her shocked expression.

"Not funny, Chase," she said, but her lip twitched upward for a millisecond before she looked back to him. "How are you feeling?"

"I'm in a ton of pain, but at least I'm not carrying on like I was before."

"You remember that?"

"Unfortunately."

"You really scared Fixer. He kept making me promise that you would wake up."

"That reminds me. I have something to ask you."

"Of course I'll take care of Fixer if anything ever happens to you." She stood and put her hand on his arm and said, "But nothing is ever going to happen to you."

Chase smiled and sat down in his chair. He looked out over the bridge and turned back to face Kat. "I've put away a good amount of heskars for him. And, unlike me, he never touches his account."

"Don't even worry about that, Chase. You know I'd take care of him even if he didn't have anything."

"Thanks, Kat," he said with a sigh. He stood and shut off the vid feed and recording functions of the ship. He started off the bridge, but turned and added, "I'm going to find out who Hazard was working for. Maybe you could keep Felicia on the bridge if she wakes. She's not going to want to hear his screaming and carrying on."

"What are you going to do, Chase?"

"He killed Tev, Kat. I'm gonna do whatever it takes to get the info I need."

"I doubt Felicia will stay here. She'll want to be a voice of reason in your head."

"That's fine, as long as she doesn't interfere." Chase turned and left the bridge. He stopped in his room and put on a shirt. He was unable to button it more than halfway, so he gave up trying and grabbed his blaster. He took it off the stun setting and turned it to low. Laboring down the stairs to the landing bay, he put aside his pain and trudged over to the holding cell, where he waited for Hazard to rouse. Kat was already there and the worried look in her eyes meant she thought he might go too far.

In an effort to avoid eye contact with her, Chase inspected the cell. It was some of his finest construction. The back wall was actually the ship's hull and the right wall was one of the bulkheads. Both were made of pentallium. The left side of the cell and the front were old fashioned pentallium bars. The walls were painted white and there was a bench against the back wall and a toilet against the right wall. A light force field covered the bars to prevent the occupant from reaching out to grab anything. The inside of the cell was approximately two and a half meters by three meters and could hold up to four prisoners for transport.

Fifteen minutes later, Hazard let out a groggy growl. "You can't hold me here, Cadogan," he said. "I have rights."

"Shut up, Hazard. You have no rights, and even if you did, they would have died with Tev, murderer."

"That doesn't mean you can deny me medical attention. I demand to have my wounds treated." He stood and glared through the bars at Chase.

"Still trying to intimidate me, huh Hazard? When are you going to realize that I don't care what you think your rights are. You're about to get some more injuries that I won't treat." Stone turned off the force field and Chase pulled his blaster.

Hazard took a slight step back. There was less of an edge to his voice when he answered, "What are you talking about?"

"I need some information and you're going to provide it for me."

"You must have hit your head when I shot you. I'm not telling you anything."

Chase fixed a steely gaze at his nemesis and replied. "Oh, you'll talk! And, if you don't, at least I get to have some fun. Now, who are you working for?"

"What are you talking about? I don't work for anyone except me."

Chase felt his face flush. He glared at Hazard and said, "I'm going to ask you again, and every time you give me an answer I don't like, I'm going to shoot you. Do you understand?"

"You can't—"

"Who sent you to steal the alien from us?"

"No one."

Chase lifted his blaster and shot Hazard in the leg. He fell against the bars on the other side of the cell and cried out in pain. "That was the lowest setting on my blaster, it only goes up from here." He smiled and asked again. "Who sent you after the alien?"

"I'm going to kill you, Cadogan," he shouted through grit teeth.

"Wrong answer." Chase shot him again in the same spot. "A couple more shots like that and you'll have a limp forever. I'm sure that'll be helpful when you're trying to defend yourself in prison."

"Cadogan, you son of a Jalindi whore."

"Who sent you?"

"No one."

Chase raised his blaster again and Kat put her hand on his arm and asked, "Are you sure you want to do this?"

He shrugged her hand off and said, "He killed Tev! Of course I want to do this." He looked back to Hazard and yelled, "Who?"

"You'll have to kill me," he replied while he stumbled to remain on his feet.

Chase shot him in the same spot again and Hazard roared in pain. Chase then made a show of turning up the power on the blaster. "Next shot and you'll never walk again under your own power. Still want to play games? Who sent you?"

"I'm gonna kill you. I'm gonna kill your blue bodyguard, that stupid mechanic, and your dancing whore. I'm gonna kill all of you, Cadogan, but you'll be last. What do you think of that?" He leaned into the bars to get as close to Chase as he could. Sweat began to stream from his hairline down the sides of his dirty face. His jaw was set, almost challenging Chase to shoot him again. The smell of charred ozone already filled the air, and burning flesh was about to join it.

Chase looked at his defiant prisoner and his blood boiled. Bounty hunting had never been about a personal grudge for him, but this man had made it personal. Without hesitation, he shot Hazard again, and this time a large hole burned through half his knee. He fell to the deck crying out, clutching his leg and screaming.

"Chase!" Kat yelled. "I think you've gone too far."

"This isn't far enough!" Chase yelled. "He still has another leg and two arms." He opened the cell and stepped inside. He seized Hazard by the collar and hoisted him into a sitting position. Then he raised his blaster and pressed it into Hazard's shoulder. The recently fired muzzle burned on contact. "Who sent you?" He put his finger on the trigger and Hazard could hear the faint whine of the charge building inside the weapon. Chase waited for an answer that Hazard refused to give, so he shouted, "Fine! Have it your way!"

Hazard could tell by the look in Chase's eye that this was no bluff. He leaned away and yelled, "Wait, wait. It was a Commonwealth captain. He hates you for some reason." Hazard grunted in pain and continued, "He's been helping me stay one step ahead of you. I can't give you his name. Please." He clutched at his leg again while he writhed back and forth in his cell.

Chase lowered his blaster and left the holding cell.

"Chase, what's he talking about?" Stone asked. He locked the cell, re-engaged the force field, and left Hazard alone with his pain.

Chase walked onto the bridge with Stone and Kat on his heels. When the bridge door slid shut, Chase turned and said, "Seraphaz!"

A slight gasp escaped Kat's lips and she brought her hand up to her mouth. "Why? Why is that man always against you?"

"I don't know, Kat, but Vanguard Tobias and the Flag are going to find this information useful."

"Who's Seraphaz?" Stone asked.

"Seraphaz is the one who discharged me from the military. He hated me from the start and it looks like he's not done messing with me yet."

"Why? It doesn't make any sense."

"I know, Stone. It doesn't, but it's time I found out why."

Felicia limped onto the bridge, followed by Fixer. They both had a beverage in their hand and Fixer's eyes lit up when he saw Chase.

"Chase, you woke up. Katalla Swift promised you would."

"Well, we both know that Kat is never wrong, Fixer." He winked at Kat who feigned insult, but Fixer missed the sarcasm.

"We will exit hyperspace in eleven minutes, Chase," Fixer said.

"Sounds good, buddy." Chase sat down heavy in his chair. He slumped against the chair back and brought his hand up to rub his temple. Pain was etched on his face and Kat wondered if it was the injury or the loss of Tev. She decided it was probably both.

"I'm going to bring you some water, Chase," Kat said, "and you're going to drink it." She left the bridge and returned a few moments later with a cup of water. Chase took a long drought, savoring the cool sensation on the back of his throat as the water went down.

"Thanks, Kat." He sat a little straighter in his seat, but he still rubbed at his head.

The *Longshot* exited hyperspace over Avalon. Kat brought the ship in for a smooth landing just outside the abbey. When the hatch opened, they were greeted by the wary expressions of the clergy. Their spirits lifted when they saw Felicia, being helped by Kat, appear at the landing bay of the *Longshot*. They started to make their way off the ship when Kat turned and said, "Come on, Chase. Let's get you healed."

Chase stood frozen in place. Felicia stopped, limped back to the silent bounty hunter and, with a gentle touch, placed her hand on his chest. After a moment, she looked back to Kat and said, "I'm sorry, but Avalon won't heal him."

"Why? He saved you. Why won't Avalon heal him?"

"Avalon won't heal Chase because he wishes to hold on to his pain." Kat looked at the hurt in his eyes and he put his head down and walked away.

"But—"

"Katalla, you know I would if I could. I love you and I would be happy to show kindness to Chase, but part of the healing process is that you have to want to be healed."

"What about me," Hazard growled from his cell. "Your oh so honorable friend tortured me. Look at my leg," he yelled. "Make Avalon heal me!"

Felicia turned her intense gaze on the injured criminal and said in a dispassionate voice, "Avalon has rejected you." Her dark hair swung with her abrupt turn toward the exit. Two of the priestesses boarded to help her off the ship. She wrapped her cousin in a long embrace and said, "Please, come visit me soon, Cousin."

"I will, Felicia." She leaned back in the embrace and brushed a stray lock of Felicia's hair aside. Then she kissed her cheek and released her grip. "I'll come back as soon as I can and I'll bring Talia and Lynx with me."

"I look forward to it." The priestesses nodded to Kat, as they helped Felicia from the ship. When they were clear, the *Longshot* lifted off the ground in a gentle assent. At a safe distance from the abbey, Kat hit the thrusters and the ship shot into the stratosphere. A few moments later, they were in space.

"Where to next, Chase," Kat asked while they orbited Avalon.

"Olorun on Norumbega. That's where Tev's family lives."

"I didn't know Tev was religious," Stone said with a puzzled look on his face.

"He wasn't, but his family is," Chase replied.

"Do they worship Avalon or the old gods?" Kat asked.

"Old gods. Most of Olorun worship the old gods."

Kat started to tear up. "I never knew that about Tev. How could I spend so much time teasing him and not know something so important?" Her voice cracked and she turned away from Chase and Stone. Her hands played over the controls.

"Kat, you know he loved when you teased him. He was just private about his family. I don't even know how many brothers and sisters he had, and he and Chase are my best friends," Stone said.

"He told me he had a big family and that's it," Chase added. "None of that matters now. We just need to get him home where he can be laid to rest by his family."

"I have a course," Kat said, sniffing back more tears.

"Let's go," Chase replied.

+++++

The Jalindi armada arrived over Q'Tor and opened fire on the Qantaran fleet. Space ignited as the Qantarah fired back.

[They were ready for our attack, My King,] the Fleet Commander said to the image floating in front of him.

[That is of little concern. Press the attack, break their lines, and raze their planet. Do you understand?]

[Understood, My King!] The image dissolved and the Commander strode to the command console. [Press the attack!] he yelled. [We do not leave until Q'Tor is in flames! Launch all fighters.] The Jalindi formation continued to press forward, closing the distance between fleets to under fifty kilometers. All weapons were firing as the all-out assault continued.

Jalindi weapons were almost as powerful as the Qantaran energy, but their hulls were not as strong as the xallodium laced hulls of the Qantarah. Still, the sheer size of the Jalindi flotilla and the aggressive nature of the attack had the Qantarah back on their heels. Purple light shot out at Qantaran warships while Jalindi fighters buzzed around the gunships like angry insects. Soon, Qantaran vessels began to explode while the Fleet Commander watched from the bridge of his Flagship in satisfaction.

[Crewman, send the rear guard to the port side of the formation. We will collapse their flank and attack their planet.] The Fleet Commander leaned on the viewport in anticipation of his orders being carried out.

[It will be as you say, sir,] the crewman replied. Almost a hundred ships veered off from the rear of the fleet to port. The Qantaran flank began to collapse under the relentless barrage of the

Jalindi attack. The losses were just about even, but the Jalindi had a much larger fleet.

White energy streaked out from Qantaran warships and splashed off Jalindi shields while dogfights carried on throughout the space above Q'Tor. The Qantarah tried to hold the line and force the attackers back. Jalindi cruisers continued to push towards the fleet with the goal of destroying the planet. Qantaran ships began to explode in the center of their defensive formation, and a mad dash ensued to get more ships into the gap. They may have anticipated the attack, but they had not anticipated the intensity.

Without the Battle Conductor to lead them, the Qantarah were at a tactical disadvantage. Still, they were not to be taken lightly. The Jalindi flagship continued directing all of its purple fire into the center of the Qantaran line. Several Qantaran fighters began a strafing run on the Jalindi flagship, but the shields turned their efforts into little more than a light show.

[We will have this planet, and it will be the end of the Qantaran threat to our galaxy. We will be the empire civilizations cower before, and they will be nothing but a distant memory,] the Fleet Commander cried out.

The Jalindi rearguard began to hammer the left flank of the Qantaran fleet. Immense heavy cruisers began to shred the Qantarah with purple energy. More ships exploded and the light show continued. The Qantarah were usually on the offensive and it seemed that they were less skilled at playing defense.

A large number of additional fighters launched from the surface of Q'Tor to shore up their fighter corps, but several squadrons of Jalindi fighters broke through the line and destroyed them as they were emerging through the stratosphere. The heavy cruisers destroyed three more Qantaran warships and it looked as though the left flank had completely collapsed.

The Jalindi Fleet Commander tried to contain his excitement until the thought hit him, *this is too easy. Even if we caught them by surprise, the mighty Qantarah would never fold this easily.* He looked again at the left flank and realized the collapse was by design.

They were trying to draw his forces in. He looked over to his comms officer and said, [Crewmen, have the rear guard return to formation, I have a feeling the Qantarah have a trick up their sleeve. Have the rest of the fleet press the advantage!]

[Yes, sir!]

The Fleet Commander continued looking out the viewport. Jalindi battleships and cruisers reversed direction on the port side of the formation. Giant thrusters worked hard to stop the advance and change course. Ships hummed while the thrust energy coursed through them. Soon, they returned to the rear of the Jalindi armada. The reprieve gave Qantaran forces the break they needed to shore up their flank, but the Jalindi continued to pound away.

[We have a fleet dropping out of hyperspace, sir. Left flank,] a crewman yelled.

[How big?] the Fleet Commander replied, thankful he had recognized the trap in time.

[Almost two hundred fifty ships, sir!]

[Send a transmission to the King!] the Fleet Commander ordered.

+++++

"Where am I?" Flag Officer Victor asked, confusion evident in his tired eyes.

"You are on Cibola, sir," a young nurse replied.

The Flag took in his surroundings. The harsh lights and white bedding combined with the antiseptic smell and the rhythmic beeping let him know he was in a med-center. "He's awake," the nurse said into a comm unit on the wall. She walked over to him and began fussing over him. He was too tired to shoo her away.

"What happened?"

"I don't know, sir."

"Can you find me someone who does know?"

"They're on their way, sir." She wiped his head with a palm-sized plastic sheet and looked at it before discarding it. "Your temperature is down." She looked at the source of the incessant beeping and said, "Vitals have returned to normal."

Just then, the door burst open and Vanguard Tobias marched in with a big smile on his face. "Juel, you had us all worried. It is good to see you awake, my friend."

"I'm still a little unclear on what happened."

"Your shuttle was badly damaged when *Commonwealth One* exploded. We thought we had lost you, but several hours later, in the aftermath of the battle, Captain Valence on the *Typhoon* picked up several weak signals emitting from your shuttle. He rescued you just in time. There was a small crack in the hull, and the atmosphere was almost gone. Of the eleven people on the shuttle, only four survived."

"Was Crewman Thomes one of them?"

"No, Juel, I'm sorry. Did you know him?"

"He saved my life. He's the one that got me to the shuttle."

"I'm sorry. We lost many good men and women in that battle."

"What happened? I thought we were losing?" the Flag asked while the background noise of steady beeping filled in the silence.

"The Jalindi invaded Q'Tor and the Qantarah had to pull out of the battle. We were fortunate, Juel. We're going to need to increase production tenfold in case they return, but for now, we're safe."

Flag Officer Victor felt his eyes getting heavy. He forced them open and asked, "Have we gotten anywhere on the xallodium yet?"

"No. We'll probably need Cadogan's mechanic for that." The Vanguard looked at his tired friend and added, "But we can talk about that some more tomorrow. For now, just get some rest." He turned and left the room, and the nurse was back. She adjusted the blanket and dimmed the lights, leaving the room to go check on one of her many other patients.

Vanguard Tobias strode through the med-center, visiting with injured soldiers and consoling grieving families. When he finally returned to his office, he called out to his assistant, "Can you get me Chase Cadogan on a transmission?"

"Right away, sir," came the reply.

+++++

The *Longshot* exited hyperspace several thousand kilometers away from Norumbega. Kat set a course for the spaceport on Olorun and hit the thrusters. The transmission alert beeped and she answered it to see the Vanguard.

"Cadogan," he said with a friendly smile when the transmission flared to life.

"No, sir, it's Katalla."

"Miss Swift, is Chase available?"

"Stone is getting him right now, sir. He took some fire when we rescued my cousin and refused treatment on Avalon."

"Why would he do that?" Vanguard Tobias asked with a hint of concern crossing his eyes.

"Because we lost Tev," Kat replied, her voice cracking. "I'm sure he's punishing himself. We're on our way to Norumbega to drop Tev's body off on Olorun." A tear escaped her eye and she was quick to wipe it away. "Then we're heading back to Cibola to collect the bounty on Hazard."

"I will make sure Mr. Cadogan gets some medical treatment on Cibola, Miss Swift."

"Thank you, sir. Here he comes," she replied and stepped aside.

"Vanguard, sir. To what do we owe the honor?" Chase asked with a tired look in his eyes.

"We need your friend Fixer's help with the xallodium. Miss Swift tells me you will be heading back to Cibola after a brief stop on Olorun. Would I be able to borrow your friend for a few days at that time?"

"Tell him I can help, Chase. I want to help the Vanguard. Tell him yes," Fixer yelled into the conversation from his usual seat on the bridge.

"Well, looks like that's a yes from Fixer, sir," Chase said.

"Thank you, Chase," he replied with a smile. "I'm sorry about your friend."

"Thank you, sir. Tev Gavar was a great man and an even better friend. We never would have been able to rescue Sym on Nibiru without him."

"Was he former military?"

"Yes, sir. He and Stone were both in my unit."

"Please send me his family's information; I would like to send my condolences in person. He will also be buried with full honors if they wish it. I will also be depositing a sizeable reward into his parents account, so please don't worry about paying him out of your bounty."

"Thank you, sir." He averted his eyes and tried to find the words to ask why, but nothing came.

"What is it, Chase? After all of this, you can speak freely."

He hesitated, but then asked, "We failed to stop the war, sir—"

"So why am I rewarding your friend's sacrifice?"

"Yeah? I don't get it."

"Your mission was successful. I tasked you to find the scientist and you did," Vanguard Tobias replied. "And, I believe you did stop the war."

"Sir? When we left, things were pretty hairy. For all we know they could have attacked because I stuck a blaster in Garyn's face, so how did we stop the war?"

"That had nothing to do with it. If anything, you gained his respect. We now have the big picture. The Qantarah withdrew from battle, but not until after they destroyed fifty-one ships. We took over forty of theirs, but I now believe they attacked to draw the Jalindi into a precipitous action."

"The Jalindi, sir?"

"Yes, a massive Jalindi fleet attacked Q'Tor after a second Qantaran fleet jumped into hyperspace. That second fleet never arrived here, so I believe the whole thing was a Qantaran ruse to draw out their enemy. Still, if we didn't return Sym to them, I think we would have a lot more to worry about."

"If we took out over forty of their ships, we might still."

"I agree, but at least we will have some time now to build more ships and outfit them with xallodium enhancements. They'll come eventually, but we will be prepared."

Chase hesitated again, but the look on Vanguard Tobias' face encouraged him to continue. "Sir, I had a conversation with Hazard after we captured him and I, um, persuaded him to tell me who sent him after the alien. After some prodding, he told me it was a Commonwealth captain that sent him, but he didn't give me a name. I believe it to be—"

"Seraphaz," Vanguard Tobias replied. "Yes, Flag Officer Victor's investigation revealed that he had been harboring Hazard."

"Is he being disciplined, sir?"

Vanguard Tobias let out a heavy sigh and said, "Unfortunately, when the Qantarah made their first incursion, Captain Seraphaz stopped them, but he called the press before he did so."

Chase felt his face flush and he bit back a curse. "So you can't drop the hammer on him because the people see him as a hero."

"Unfortunately, yes. Even though it was the sacrifice that Captain Cheston made with the *Trident* that actually won the battle."

"I see." The steel in his voice drew the attention of the rest of the bridge.

"Rest assured, Chase. At the very least, he will know we are on to him, and he will be made to stop his vendetta against you. He will also be demoted in the sense that we have no more ships to give him, so instead of five, he will be back to commanding three. We currently have a lot of captains that are without ships. I may not be able to punish him because of public opinion, but he is not going to get away with this. You have my word."

"Thank you sir, we'll be landing shortly, so I should get going," he tried to hide the disappointment in his voice, but he suspected the Vanguard knew it was there. "We should be back on Cibola at some point in the next two days."

"I look forward to it." The Vanguard ended the transmission and Chase hung his head.

"What happened?" Kat asked.

"They can't go after Seraphaz because he's the hero of the first incursion. He knew the Flag was on to him, so he called the press when the Qantarah first attacked. Now he's a media darling and we can't touch him."

"Chase, I'm so sorry," she replied.

"What am I supposed to tell Tev's family?"

"Tell them that the man who killed Tev will spend the rest of his life in prison. They don't need to know the rest," Stone said, trying to keep the anger from his voice.

Kat brought the *Longshot* in for another smooth landing and Chase said, "We can talk about this some more, later. It's time to bring Tev home."

Chase stood and left the bridge. He walked down the corridor followed by his crew. He descended the stairs to the landing bay and lumbered past the holding cell. He stopped when he noticed that his prisoner was sleeping and his wounds had been tended to. He raised his eyebrow and said, "Kat?"

"Yes, I fed him, gave him some pain meds and bandaged his leg while Stone stood guard. We're not monsters, Chase!" She brushed past him and continued to the speeder. She was still angry he had taken the interrogation as far as he did and had no desire to hear him complain about her taking pity on their enemy.

Chase caught up to her in the landing bay and said, "I'm not mad about it, Kat. I'm just surprised you would show him that kindness after what he did to your cousin."

She wasn't sure how she should reply, so she just hopped in the speeder and waited to leave. Stone loaded the body into the speeder and he and Fixer sat in the second row.

Chase walked over to the passenger side and said, "Kat, scoot over. I don't think I should drive with all these meds in me." She shuffled over and took the yoke without a word while Chase slid into the passenger seat. She was still upset with him. She had seen him kill before, but it was always out of necessity. His treatment of Hazard, however, showed a side of him she was unsure she liked. He was grieving, but she still knew what he did was wrong. She put that out of her mind and pulled out of the spaceport setting off across the dusty terrain.

They arrived at their destination to quite a sight. "Wow, Tev's family is even bigger than I thought," Chase said when he saw the crowd of people out in front of the Gavar ancestral home. The home stood three stories and was built with hard polished xardac wood. A grand white staircase led up to a colonial blue porch that wrapped around the entire dwelling. Their home looked more like a hotel than a house with all of the rooms represented by white trimmed windows. Dozens of grieving people met them when they stepped out of the speeder.

"Wow, Tev's brothers and father look just like him," Kat whispered.

"Where is my son?" A middle aged woman dressed in black asked. It was evident that she had been crying and Chase recognized her as Tev's mother.

"He is right here, Mother Gavar," Chase replied. Stone and Chase carried the wrapped body over to a stone table in front of the home and set it down, taking great care to show respect. "I'm sorry, ma'am. We didn't know your customs."

"It's all right, Chase. Tev never learned them either," Father Gavar replied with a sad smile. Tev's mother had an anguished look in her eyes that Chase was sure would haunt him. She draped herself over Tev and wept while she kissed his face. She took off his helmet and smoothed his hair. Tev's three sisters brought out the traditional burial garb and perfumes for a funeral performed in the old religion. The scent of the sojja flower filled the air when the women sprayed the body. They went about putting the beige robe on Tev while his six brothers surrounded the body and offered traditional prayers. Tev's nieces and nephews, aunts and uncles, and cousins all milled about while his sisters prepared his body.

Father Gavar approached Chase and Stone and said, "Tev considered you two to be brothers. There's nothing he wouldn't have done for either of you."

Chase looked at the ground and replied, "That is kind of you to say, sir, but I let him down. I asked for his help and now he's gone." He was barely keeping it together and needed to leave before he became a sobbing mess.

"Nonsense. I know you would have done the same for him. This is not your fault, Chase. Tev made his own decisions. He would not have gone with you if he did not want to." He pointed to the heavily bandaged shoulder and added, "From the look of it, you took your fair share of the punishment, as well." He paused a moment before asking, "How did he die? Did he die well?"

"Your son died the way he lived, Father Gavar; protecting his friends. Tev was a hero," Chase replied, tears were now streaming down his face and Kat laid a hand on his arm and leaned her head into his good shoulder. He could see the bright pink steaks down her face as well.

"Tev was shot while rescuing my cousin, one of the priestesses of Avalon. You should be proud," Kat managed to squeak out.

A gasp escaped Mother Gavar's lips and she said, "Thank you, Katalla. That means a lot to us."

"Tev died quickly, he didn't suffer, sir," Stone said in a voice that quivered. "I'm—"

"Thank you, Stone. Thank you all. My son spoke highly of all four of you, and you will all be forever welcome among the Gavar clan." He nodded to each of them and Chase realized that Fixer had been strangely quiet since they left the *Longshot*. He made a note to talk with him when they were back on the ship.

"Thank you, sir," Kat replied. "Now, if you'll excuse us, we won't be able to attend the burial because we have to get back to Cibola. Your son was doing important work for the Commonwealth, and we have to finish the mission."

"Yes, of course. The Vanguard contacted us to offer his condolences, so we figured the job was important," Mother Gavar said.

"Take solace in the fact that your son was a hero," Chase added.

"We know he was. As are the rest of you. Remember that! Now, we must take our leave. May the gods bless your journey," Father Gavar said. The whole family turned and began a slow procession down a path through the yard and past the back of the house. The scent of the sojja flowers still filled the air. Tev's brothers carried the body while the parents followed and the rest of the family was out in front. Tev's sisters spread flower petals on the ground before Tev's body as they walked. Soon, they disappeared into the trees, but the sobbing, wailing and a ceremonial horn could still be heard. Chase turned away and trudged back to the speeder. He felt he lacked the strength to stand, and when he sat down in the speeder, he wiped the sweat from his brow and closed his eyes.

Kat sat down next to him and said, "You look feverish. I think your shoulder is infected. When we get to Cibola, you are going to a med-center if I have to stun you and drag you there. Do you understand me?" When there was no reply, she looked at him again, but he was already asleep.

"I don't think he's gonna fight you on that one, Kat," Stone said. They drove back to the ship in silence.

Chapter eleven

Captain Seraphaz walked with a spring in his step toward the Capitol Palace. The massive structure had been the center of Commonwealth operations for several centuries, but it was still an imposing building. The palace stood only seventy-two stories high, but the girth of the building was immense. It was three kilometers long and a kilometer and a half deep, which made the Palace one of the most massive structures in the entire cluster. The polished silver appearance made the building gleam in the sunlight. Throngs of media lined his path, hoping to catch a glimpse of the first Captain in over a century to win a battle for the Commonwealth. Reporters shouted out questions while he walked.

"Captain Seraphaz, how does it feel to be the hero of the Commonwealth?"

"Captain, are you married?"

"Captain, when will your ship be ready for action again?"

Seraphaz walked with a polite smile firmly in place. He loved the accolades. A shapely young reporter with dark hair and a red jacket caught his eye. She knew when he glanced at her that she had him, so she asked, "Captain, is the Vanguard going to be promoting you today? Is that why you are here?" A content smile spread across her face when he slowed his march and stopped.

He looked at the beautiful young lady and replied in theatrical fashion, "Anything is possible. I mean, why wouldn't he? We lost one of our most beloved fleet captains at the cluster's mouth, and I am one of the most experienced captains in the fleet." He smiled for the vid cams and waited for the next question.

"Do you think Vanguard Tobias would give you the position left vacant by the death of Fleet Captain Johan?"

"I would hate to speculate. Now, if you'll excuse me. I would not want to keep Vanguard Tobias waiting." He bowed just enough to be seen as magnanimous and then paraded into the Capitol Palace. He took in the cavernous foyer and spotted the information hologram that would direct him to where he needed to go. This was his first time inside the Capitol Palace, and he wanted to savor every second.

The hologram directed him to a row of lift tubes almost forty meters to his left. He strutted to the lift and the door slid open. He stepped into the tube which took him up to the seventieth floor. Stepping out of the lift, he saw a middle-aged woman behind an elaborate counter, flanked by two guards. The counter reached his chest and was overlaid with a silver marble composite that caused it to sparkle.

"May I help you?" she asked when he stepped up to the counter.

"Yes. Captain Seraphaz here to see Vanguard Tobias," he replied. He held his head up, refusing to even look at the woman while he awaited a reply. After a few moments of silence, an annoyed look crossed his face and he looked at the woman.

"Have a seat and he'll be with you shortly." She motioned to a row of three chairs lined up against the wall across from the counter.

"I don't think you understand, Miss, I have an appointment," he said, maintaining his superior tone.

"I understand very well, but my understanding is not going to make Vanguard Tobias finish his earlier appointment any sooner. Now, have a seat."

Seraphaz had to control himself to keep his face from turning a bright shade of red. *Who does this woman think she is, speaking to me in such a manner?* He walked over to the chairs, composed himself, turned around, and sat down to wait.

An hour and ten minutes later, the receptionist called out, "Captain Seraphaz, Vanguard Tobias will see you now."

He stood and the two guards escorted him in to the executive meeting chamber where Vanguard Tobias sat at a large conference table. The Vanguard stood and motioned him to sit in one of the high-backed chalsen leather seats around the table. He walked over to the closest seat to Vanguard Tobias' right and shook hands with the Vanguard before sitting.

"Captain Seraphaz, do you know why I've called you in today?"

"No, sir."

"But that didn't stop you from speculating for the media outside. Did it?"

"Sir?" Seraphaz asked.

"Really, Tol? Publicly campaigning for fleet captain? We haven't even had a memorial service for Fleet Captain Johan yet, and you're out there in front of the cameras hinting that you might be getting the position."

Seraphaz knew this meeting was going to be far different in tone than he had hoped, but he still knew the Vanguard would not publicly punish him. "Sir, that's not what I was—"

"You were and you know it. Now, stop acting as if I'm a fool. That was a nice little trick you pulled off, inviting the media out to the battle, so you could look like a hero. We both know it was actually Captain Cheston who was the hero of that battle."

"Sir, I—"

"When it is your turn to speak I will let you know." Vanguard Tobias said in a loud voice. He stood, put his hands on the table and leaned forward. "Let me put your mind at ease. You will not be filling the vacant fleet captain position. In fact, as long as I am Vanguard, you will never be a fleet captain. Now, I do have some questions about your recent behavior. Let's begin with Jay Lee Hazard." He paused to let the name sink in and at this point Seraphaz was just hoping to leave the room with his job intact.

"Why would a captain in the Commonwealth Cluster Patrol be harboring a wanted murderer?"

"I wasn't harboring him, sir."

"Save it, Captain. I know all about your arrangement. I know you were warning him whenever Chase Cadogan got too close. I know he spent time aboard your ship, and I know you sent him after Cadogan to steal the alien from him before he could bring her to me. I'm sure you are aware that during this mission that you sent him on, he murdered one of the priests of Avalon, kidnapped a priestess, and killed Tev Gavar. You are responsible for all of that. Now, explain yourself."

"Sir, you have it all wrong. I wasn't harboring Hazard. I was working him. He's been an asset of mine for some time. I was just protecting an asset. I sent him after Cadogan because I was unsure the bounty hunter would complete the job. Hazard was just the motivation. If at any time, Cadogan strayed, Hazard was to take the alien off his hands and bring her to me. This way I could make sure she was brought to you in time to avoid war. Hazard is the one that went outside the assignment parameters."

"And who tasked you with this assignment?" Vanguard Tobias asked. He had started pacing now. "I personally tasked Captain Bander of the *Legendary* with the assignment of helping Cadogan with the search, and the Flag was with me when I did it, so it is doubtful he gave you the order."

"I took the initiative, sir. I was protecting the Commonwealth."

"Enough," Vanguard Tobias yelled. "I will not have you sit here and lie to my face. I don't know what you were doing, but it wasn't protecting the Commonwealth. I don't know what your problem with Cadogan is, but it ends now. I know you've been causing him trouble for years. You unceremoniously dumped him after he had saved my daughter's life, and you've been hassling him ever since. Then you send that monster Hazard after him? The only reason you are not sitting in prison right now is because of that little stunt you pulled with the press. We need to look strong and united right now. I'm sure you realized that our sending you to prison wouldn't accomplish that, but rest assured, there is no promotion in your future."

Sweat started to trickle down Captain Seraphaz's face. He shifted in his seat and tried hard to keep a neutral look in place. He was listening to his dream go up in smoke and there was nothing he could do about it. His hope of a public promotion was gone. His only hope now was that he would not be deemed useless to his other employer.

"Now, here is what's going to happen, Captain. You will receive a new XO who will report directly to the Flag. He will have orders to report anything unorthodox, suspicious or even annoying immediately. All of your communications will be monitored by him. You will no longer command five ships, you will command three. If the press asks, I will tell them you would have gotten five, but there were not enough ships available. You will retain command of the *Elysian Pride* and the *Borean Spear* and you will also be given a gunship. Your new assignment will be to patrol near the smugglers entrance. I will spin it to the press that this is of vital importance to the war effort."

A beep indicted that the Vanguard had an incoming message. He motioned for quiet and tapped the intercom.

"Chase Cadogan will be arriving in two hours, sir."

"Thank you. Please clear my schedule and prepare my hovercade."

"Yes, sir."

"Thank you. Please hold all other transmissions until I am finished with this meeting."

"Yes sir."

Seraphaz burned with anger. Not only was he being demoted, but the Vanguard had actually stopped their meeting to take a message about Chase Cadogan. And he was clearing his day for the kid.

"Now, where were we, Captain?" Vanguard Tobias asked. "Oh yes, your posting. You will be on leave until your ship is repaired; then your new assignment will begin immediately. Cluster Command will clear any intelligence assets or criminal informants you have, and if we find out about any you haven't reported, you will be going straight to prison. I'm sure my PR people could still spin that into a positive. Do you understand?"

This meeting had been as close to a worst case scenario as Seraphaz could have imagined. All that was left was to reply, "Yes, sir."

"Good, now if you'll excuse me." The Vanguard motioned for him to stand and walked him to the exit. Before he opened the door he added, "And whatever your fixation is with Chase Cadogan, it ends now. If I hear of you sabotaging any more of his bounties or if you bother him in any other fashion, I will put you in prison. Do you understand?" He opened the door to the waiting area before Seraphaz could reply. The guards in the corridor and the receptionist at her desk did their best to focus on their duties.

Seraphaz was not aware that his face was quite so red. He could barely bite out a polite, "Yes, sir," in front of the audience he now had. To make matters worse, the Vanguard had his practiced politician's smile plastered to his face, as if this had been a friendly meeting with an amicable ending.

+++++

[Take Sym Triot to the surface of Q'Tann and put her under guard. She is no longer worthy to set foot on Q'Tor. There is more to her story that she has yet to tell us, but she will,] Battle conductor Garyn said to his security chief.

[Yes, My Lord. May I request an escort to help my shuttle through the battle?]

[Of course, Chief. She has some valuable information she will share with us. Now, retrieve her from her quarters and go. Tell her you are bringing her to safety and that the guards are for her protection.]

[It will be as you say,] the chief replied. He marched off the bridge of the Qantaran Flagship. He called the scientist to report to the hangar and when she arrived said, [Our wise Battle Conductor has tasked me with getting you to safety. Please join me on the shuttle. We will have a fighter escort all the way to the surface of Q'Tann.]

Sym looked at the armed guard, and the look the chief gave her suggested it was not a request. She knew they did not believe her, and that her life was about to become much more difficult. She forced a smile and replied, [Thank you for showing me this kindness.] She boarded the ship and began thinking of a way she could escape her people.

Space was lighting up around the shuttle. Giant vessels, built for war, continued to pummel each other. The white lightning of the Qantarah was being met by the purple light of the Jalindi. Ships were exploding all over space around Q'Tor and Sym wondered if the fleet would still be large enough to attack the Luminari Cluster by the time this battle was over.

[How does the battle go, Chief?] Sym asked, continuing to act as if she suspected nothing.

[We will be victorious over these Jalindi dogs,] he replied.

She shifted in her seat and said, [They have a much larger fleet than I thought they had. Still, there are none that can defeat us.]

[Indeed you are correct, Sym Triot. Even though these Jalindi have attacked with a larger fleet than we thought, they will fall.]

Sym smiled. She had just gotten the Chief to admit that they were unprepared for the size of the Jalindi armada. That information could be useful if she could escape and get back to the cluster.

[We will arrive shortly, Sym Triot. My personal guards will stay with you until the battle is over and Battle Conductor Garyn can come and retrieve any information you have gathered concerning the Luminari Cluster.]

[I look forward to it, Chief. Thank you.] She had to say the right things now. She had to make them believe she was on board, so that perhaps she could find a way to escape. She knew she would be branded a traitor, but she had no family anyway, thanks to Battle Conductor Garyn. The scientific core was very competitive, so there was no one she would even consider a close friend. The first people to show her any kindness since the death of her family resided in the Luminari Cluster. That was where she wanted to go. Although, it seemed unlikely she would ever be able to find a way back there, especially with a four-man detail tasked with watching her. *Maybe if I can contact Chase Cadogan somehow...*

+++++

Chase could feel the infection in his wounded shoulder sapping his strength. Kat was right, as usual. He needed to get to a doctor soon. For now, he was collecting the sizable bounty on Jay Lee Hazard.

"Well done, Mr. Cadogan," the prison official said while his guards took custody of Hazard. "I heard he murdered a priest on Avalon a couple days ago. He will never see the light of day as a free man again."

"You don't know how happy it makes me to hear you say that, sir," Chase replied.

Hazard whirled on his good leg and shouted, "You'll pay for this, Cadogan. I will kill you and every person you care about. Mark my words."

One of the guards punched him in the mouth and said, "Shut up, murderer." He spun Hazard back around, causing him to stumble and fall. Hazard shouted a curse on the way down.

Chase smiled and said loudly enough for Hazard to hear, "I think he hurt his leg during the capture. You might want to have someone check it out."

"We'll get to it eventually," the official replied. "You should be receiving your bounty any moment now." A beep on his wrist unit let Chase know the funds had been delivered.

"Just came through, now." He checked his account and said, "Whoa, this is a lot more than I thought it would be."

"Vanguard Tobias tripled the bounty after Hazard killed the priest."

"Looks like drinks are on me tonight," Chase said.

The official shot him a dubious look and said, "Son, you can barely stand. I think you should spend some time in the med-center before you start buying rounds."

"Okay, okay, drinks are on me after I get my shoulder taken care of. Jeez, you sound like Kat."

"She sounds like a smart girl," the official replied as Chase was walking out of the law center.

"How'd we do, Chase?" Kat asked when he reached the speeder.

"Really well," he replied. He leaned against the speeder and transferred heskars into Kat, Stone and Fixer's accounts. He heard each of their wrist units ping and they all checked.

"That's a lot of heskars," Stone said in a reverent whisper.

"Chase always splits it evenly after expenses are covered," Fixer said. "Usually he splits it in thirds, but today he split it four ways because you're here, Stone."

"Wow, that sounds like a good gig," he replied. "Let me know if you ever have steady work, Chase."

"Will do, buddy."

"Okay, let's get Chase to the med-center. The Vanguard is meeting us there. He's going to personally make Chase get his shoulder operated on, and Fixer is going to figure out why the Commonwealth eggheads can't process the xallodium correctly." Kat sat in the speeder waiting for Stone and Chase to get in.

"And Katalla Swift is going to join me, so I won't be lonely," Fixer said with a smile.

Kat turned to face the back seat before replying, "That's right, Fixer. And, Stone is going to join us to make sure no one messes with you."

"I am," Stone said while getting into the speeder.

"Unless you've got something better to do. Vanguard Tobias is going to pay us."

"Then I don't have anything better to do," Stone said with a laugh.

Chase fell heavily into the passenger seat and Kat pulled away from the law center. The drive to the med-center was short, but by the time they arrived, Chase was asleep.

"Chase, wake up. We're here," Kat said while giving his good shoulder a gentle shake.

"Where?"

"The med-center. Let's get you checked in."

"Chase, you look terrible," Vanguard Tobias said as he approached the speeder with a beautiful young woman in tow. A dozen body guards formed up around him. "You remember my daughter, Delaina, right?"

"Yes, sir," he mumbled in a groggy voice.

"Delaina, this is Katalla Swift, Fixer Faraday, and Stone... I'm sorry, Stone, I haven't been told your surname."

"No problem, sir. My last name is Ejarus. It is a pleasure to meet both you and Delaina."

"No, son. The pleasure is all ours. Please, let us get Chase settled, and then I'll get the rest of you acquainted with our science center and the people in charge of the xallodium project."

"I will stay with Chase, Father," Delaina said and walked into the med-center, leaving no room for discussion.

Stone looked at Kat and could swear her light pink skin had just gotten redder. Not noticing, the Vanguard replied, "That's fine. I will see you this evening, my dear."

Two medics pushed a hover gurney out to the speeder and Stone helped Chase onto it. "See you when it's done, buddy," Stone said.

"Wait," Chase said, looking at the Vanguard. "Sir, I do have a favor to ask."

"Go ahead."

"My father is very sick, terminal in fact and I was supposed to go home today. It would mean a lot to him to know I'm doing something important. Do you think you could send a transmission telling him I was on a mission for you and that I'll be there tomorrow?"

"Consider it done. Now, you need to let these men get you inside."

"Yes, sir. Thank you, sir." He waved to his crew and the techs pushed him into the med-center.

Kat watched him disappear into the building and Vanguard Tobias put his hand on her shoulder. "He will be fine, Katalla. Please, come with me. One of my men will bring your speeder." She turned and followed him into a waiting speeder with Fixer and Stone.

An hour later, they were walking into the research facility where the Commonwealth scientists were testing the xallodium. After a brief conversation with the head of the facility, the Vanguard left, and Fixer was anxious to get started.

A tall man in a white lab coat approached Kat, Stone, and Fixer. He was focused on some numbers on a datapad while he walked and he almost walked into Stone before he stopped short and looked up. "Which one of you is Fixer Faraday?" he asked.

Fixer shoved his hands in his pockets and did not meet the man's eyes. "I am. I m Fixer Faraday and this is my friend Katalla Swift and my other friend Stone Ejarus. My friend Chase is in the med-center and my friend Tev died."

That last line seemed to jar the scientist out of his calculations. He looked at Fixer, then back to Kat and said, "Is this some kind of joke? Where's the man that wrote out these calculations?"

Kat glared at the man and asked, "And you are?"

"I am Dr. Kendall. I am in charge of this project, and there are some things here I don't understand. I need someone that knows what they're doing, not... him." He pointed at Fixer with a look of disappointment on his face.

"Well, too bad. He's what you've got," she replied in an icy tone. "And it's a good thing, too. He's the one that talked to the Qantaran scientist. He's the one she trusted enough to give the information to, and he's the one that translated it."

"Well his translation was wrong."

"No it wasn't. My translation was not wrong, Katalla Swift. Don't believe him." Fixer was as animated as she had ever seen him.

"No one thinks you were wrong, Fixer."

"I do—"

"Doctor, a word please," Kat said in an icy tone. She walked several steps away and the doctor followed. When they were out of earshot, she said, "Fixer is a genius, but he has Taklinsen's Disorder. If you speak to him the right way you will find he's capable of more than you can imagine. If you continue to speak to him as if he were inferior, two things will happen. One, you will be wasting your best resource and, two, you will wake up in a med-center. Am I clear?"

"You can't speak to me —"

"I just did. You'll find I'm very protective of the people I care about. Stone and I are here to help Fixer interact with everyone. If you have a problem with him, bring it to me and I'll take care of it. That's what I'm here for." She paused and waited for a reply. When none came, she said, "Good, now let's go see if Fixer can help you understand all of this." She took the datapad out of Dr. Kendall's hand and started walking back toward Fixer.

"Can I see the datapad, Katalla Swift," he asked.

"Of course, Fixer. Here it is." She handed the tablet to him and his focus was drawn to it.

Doctor Kendall stood silent, waiting while Fixer reviewed the notes on the datapad. Suddenly, Fixer asked, "Are you having trouble converting the xallodium back to a solid state once you have it in a liquid state?"

The doctor was taken aback. "Yes, that's exactly the problem. Why?"

"Someone misunderstood my notes. Sometimes it happens because I don't do calculations very neat. The third calculation on page seventeen is incorrect."

"What do you mean, "Incorrect?"' the doctor asked, suddenly very interested in what the awkward young man had to say.

"Whoever translated my notes, whichever person it was, they forgot to add in the chemical compound quasic-actride, which acts as a solidifying agent when the xallodium is in liquid form. It should be three parts quasic, ten parts actride for every kilogram of liquid xallodium. Add that and the xallodium will solidify." He handed the datapad back to Dr. Kendall and the doctor poured over Fixer's adjustments.

"Fixer, I think this will work. Follow me and we'll test it right now."

"Katalla Swift, we are going to test the xallodium now. Do you and Stone want to come with us?"

"Stone will join you, Fixer. I am going to check on Chase. I'll comm you as soon as I know how he's doing. Okay?"

"Okay, but I know he's fine because Vanguard Tobias said he would be fine."

"That's true, but I'm going to check anyway. I'll be back later."

"Okay, Katalla. I'm going to go with Dr. Kendall to test xallodium." He turned and followed the doctor while Stone walked beside him.

+++++

Chase woke up and the first thing he saw was a beautiful woman looking down at him, just not the one he had hoped for. "Delaina?" he said, confusion etched on his face.

"Chase, you're awake. How are you feeling?" She took hold of his hand and smiled at him.

He shifted in his bed and said, "Better, just tired."

"That's to be expected."

"What are you doing here, Delaina?"

"Just wanted to make sure you were taken care of. I can't stay long."

"Neither can I. I have to go to Kephri tomorrow," he said, and tried to sit up.

"Let me help you with that," she said and adjusted the bed. "And I don't think you should be leaving for anywhere tomorrow."

"I have to. I have no choice."

"What's so important on Kephri that it can't wait an extra day?"

"Family stuff."

"Family stuff? That's it? You don't give up much information, do you?"

"I have been told I need to share more," he replied and cracked a smile.

Delaina sat down on the edge of the bed and began to fuss with Chase's pillow. She leaned in and kissed his forehead.

"What was that for?"

"I never got to say thank you when you saved my life a few years back. By the time my father let me take a detail to see you at the hospital, you were already gone."

"Yeah, I'm still trying to figure out what happened."

"Anyway, I thought I should finally say thanks."

"Well, you're welcome," Chase replied. She chuckled and started fussing with his pillow again.

Kat was walking toward Chase's room when she saw Delaina lean over and kiss him. She stopped in her tracks, not knowing whether to be angry or disappointed. She had hoped she could use this time to get closer to Chase again, but now he looked plenty happy with Delaina. Suddenly, someone was calling her name.

"Miss Swift? What are you doing here?"

She looked away from Chase and Delaina and laid her eyes on a pleasant distraction. "Captain Bander. How good to see you again," she purred. "I was just checking on Chase. What brings you here?"

"I was visiting some of my men that were injured in the battle. You know, keeping morale up."

"That's very kind of you."

He paused for a moment to get up his nerve before asking, "Katalla, would you like to go to dinner with me?"

"I would love to," she replied. She intertwined her arm with his and they began to walk. "After all, someone should help keep your morale up, Captain." She flashed a seductive smile and it seemed the captain had a little more bounce in his step. They walked past Chase's room and out of the med-center.

While Delaina was adjusting his blanket, Chase saw Kat walk past his room arm in arm with Captain Bander. Seeing her with Bander bothered him.

"What's wrong, Chase?" Delaina asked.

"Nothing, just a little pain, that's all," he replied.

"Well let me see if I can help with that." She stood up and closed the door to the room, dimmed the lights and sat back down on the bed. She leaned in and kissed him on the lips. She lingered there for a moment and he kissed her back.

+++++

Sym was now under house arrest on Q'Tann, and her personal detail had stopped with even the pretense of her being an asset. Now she was trapped and alone in a small dwelling with four guards always outside her door. She had taken to trying to make the guards believe she still thought she was an asset to the Qantarah.

She walked to the door and asked, [How is the battle over Q'Tor going?]

No answer.

[When will the Battle Conductor be here to debrief me? I know many of the secrets of the Luminari Cluster.] She waited for an answer to that one while a smile spread across her face.

No answer.

[I believe I am pregnant with a human child. What should I do?] Now a grin replaced her smile and the door flung open. [It is about time one of you opened the door to answer my questions,] she said.

[You are not pregnant?]

[No I am not. When is lunch?] The door slammed in her face and she started to chuckle. Still, in spite of her attempted games with the guards, she knew she was in trouble. She had been exploring the small dwelling for any way she might evade her captors. The habitat consisted of a common room, with a small kitchen area in the corner, a sleeping chamber only an arm's length bigger than the bed inside of it, and a small toilet closet. There was not very much to work with, no hiding places and no way to leave the domicile.

She lay down on the bed to read, and started to become weary. She dozed off and the datapad slipped from her hand and hit the floor, bouncing under the bed. The sound woke her and she began to look around for her datapad. She knelt down and looked under the bed. The light from the datapad drew her attention immediately. Her arms proved too short to reach the tablet, so she stood, pulled the mattress off the bed, and stood it up against the wall. She repeated the process with the bed frame, and she finally picked up her datapad.

She noticed that something seemed off with the flooring, so she pulled the carpet up from the corner and saw a trapdoor. Her interest was piqued and she started to work the latch. It took almost forty minutes for her to open the trapdoor. By then it was close to lunch, so she put the bed back in place and sat out in the common room, pretending to read. The door opened at the exact time it had the previous day and a guard walked in and placed a tray of food with a beverage on the table. Without a word, he left.

Sym ate just enough of her meal to keep from looking suspicious. She went back into the sleeping chamber and uncovered the trapdoor. She opened it and climbed down into the darkness. When she reached the bottom, she took out her datapad and turned it on. The tablet lit up and she moved it from side to side, lighting her way. On the floor near the opening she found an illumination sphere. She turned it on and it rose slowly from her palm, stopping a few inches from the ceiling.

Thanks to the light, Sym could see she was in a tunnel. [Now this is interesting,] she mumbled. She followed the tunnel almost twenty meters before it turned. Ten meters of tunnel later, she was entering a chamber. The illumination sphere entered the room with her. The chamber was filled with old equipment. [What is this place?] she asked in a low voice. She shook her head when she realized there would be no one to answer.

She continued looking around the room and began to realize that at one point, this had been a transmission room. The equipment looked like it dated back to the failed rebellion Q'Tann staged a century earlier. *I wonder if this equipment still works.* She found the power, flipped the switch, and the console flared to life. After studying the equipment for an hour, she figured out that it would still send a coded transmission. Now, she only needed to determine what to say.

She left the console and searched the room for a means of egress other than back to her guarded habitat. She found a false wall with a ladder behind it. Approaching it, she opened the hatch and climbed up. She saw dim lavender light shining through windows mounted high in the room. Standing on a table, she looked out the windows and her needed a moment to figure out where she was. *I'm in the basement of the old village house of meeting.*

She returned to the underground room and sent a transmission. Praying the message would reach Chase, she navigated her way back through the tunnels and up into her sleeping chamber. She arranged everything exactly as it had been and waited. Now it was a race. Would Chase reach her first or would it be Battle Conductor Garyn?

Chapter twelve

Chase knocked on the door to his ancestral home. His sister answered and yelled, "Chase! I'm so happy to see you! We weren't sure you would make it." Her enthusiasm was replaced with caution when she noticed his injured shoulder, but she still managed a long hug.

"I wasn't sure I'd make it either. It's good to see you, too, Laney."

His mother arrived at the door and wrapped her arms around her son. "I'm so sorry I didn't believe you, Chase. Please forgive me."

"There's nothing to forgive, Mom. Mind if I come in?"

She noticed that he was still standing outside and smiled. "Of course. Please, come in." She called out to Laney's husband, "Sol, please take Chase's bag. He hurt his shoulder on a mission for the Commonwealth."

He could hear the pride in her voice. The last time he had heard that was when he saved Delaina's life. *The beautiful Delaina, I won't be forgetting last night any time soon.* "How's dad doing? Is he awake?" Chase asked, walking with his mother into the common room. When they entered the room, Chase could see his dad lying on a couch. He looked to be in a lot of pain, but he still smiled when he saw his son.

"Chase, come here, son."

"Dad, how are you feeling?"

"Terrible, but I've got something to say to you that I should have told you a long time ago. I know I'm going to die soon, so there's no point waiting." He started coughing, and Laney brought him a drink. When the coughing fit died down, he looked at Chase and said, "I'm sorry, son."

"Dad, it's okay—"

"No, it's not. When you were forced out of the military, I thought it was your fault and I was disappointed. I said some things that I wish I could take back, but I was too stubborn to admit it to you."

Tears started to stream down his face which unnerved Chase more than the apology. "I gave up the last few years I would have with the son I love over stupid stubborn pride. No matter what happened in that hospital, I should have supported you. For that I was wrong and I'm sorry."

Chase had never been the type that needed outward validation, but this conversation was good for his soul. "That means a lot, dad, but you weren't the only one being stubborn and prideful. I forgive you. Can you forgive me?"

"Of course, Chase." Chase knelt down and embraced his father. He never could have imagined this moment. He could see the tears streaming down his mother and sister's cheeks, and not long after, he felt them on his own. His family was whole.

"Chase. Vanguard Tobias had a lot of nice things to say about you. I felt so stupid for not believing you," Mom said.

"Don't worry about it mom, it's in the past. Let's just enjoy these next couple days together."

"Couple days?" Laney asked.

"There's a lot going on I can't talk about, and I may only have a couple days to stay."

"Surely it'll take your shoulder longer to recover than that?" Chase's mother said.

"No, the surgery Chase had is fairly common. Three to four days recovery time," Sol replied. Laney elbowed him in the gut, so he added, "But I could be wrong about that."

Two and a half days later, Chase received a transmission routed through the *Longshot*. Sym's face appeared on his terminal and she looked scared.

"Chase, time is... not long. Sym is under arrest and have been taken to a small village on Q'Tann. When the battle with the Jalindi ...ends, it will not be long... Battle Conductor Garyn comes to interrogate Sym and end Sym's life. Sym is blamed for all the ships Qantarah lose at cluster. You are Sym's only hope for... survive. Please to rescue Sym one more time. Battle Conductor Garyn means to annihilate all people of cluster ... so he can have for self. Sym can help stop him. Please rescue Sym."

Sym outlined a rescue plan which she hoped would fool the Qantarah into thinking she was dead. When the message ended, Chase was alone with his thoughts. Any incursion into Qantaran territory would be dangerous, and he refused to put his crew in that kind of jeopardy so soon after all they had been through. They were all on Cibola anyway. He had no desire to see Sym be interrogated and killed either. She had not been in the cluster long, but she probably had some damaging information, not to mention that she could personally advance the cluster's xallodium research a long way in a short time.

Chase walked through the common room with his bag slung over his good shoulder. "I just received an urgent message, I have to go. I will be back as soon as I can. I promise."

"Chase, please. It's been such a short visit," his mom replied.

Chase hugged his mother, knelt down next to his father, and said, "Dad, I'll get back as soon as I can. I wouldn't even go, but this is really important."

"Be safe, son." Chase hugged him then stood and hugged Laney and Sol. Then he was off to Avalon.

While he was in hyperspace, he recorded a message for Felicia to give Kat in five days if he had not yet returned. It may not have been everything he needed to say, but he hoped it was enough. When he landed outside the abbey, Felicia was waiting for him. He walked down the landing bay ramp and picked her up in an embrace.

"It's good to see you feeling better, Felicia."

"I was about to say the same to you, Chase. Now, what is so important that you pull me from my supplications?"

"I'm going on a mission and I might not make it back. If I don't, please give this to Kat." He handed her a datapad.

"If it is so dangerous, why not bring your crew? You might have a better chance to succeed." As soon as she verbalized the question, she knew the answer. She took Chase by the hand and with all the seriousness she could muster, said, "Tev's death was not your fault."

He averted his eyes and said, "Just give this to Kat if I'm not back in five days. Okay?"

"Of course I will. You take care of yourself, Chase Cadogan." She kissed his cheek before turning and disappearing back into the abbey.

Chase closed the landing bay hatch and walked back to the bridge. A moment later, the *Longshot* was heading for Q'Tann.

+++++

Flag Officer Victor sat behind his desk for the first time since the battle. In front of him sat an apprehensive Agent Ponta Black. "Agent Black, when you were placed with Captain Seraphaz, what was your mandate?" the Flag asked.

"To make sure he was following Commonwealth Cluster Patrol regulations and acting in the best interest of the Commonwealth."

"Very good, agent Black. At least you remember what your reason for being assigned to him was. Now, would you please tell me why you failed so miserably in your duties?"

That comment felt like a slap in the face, but the Flag was right. He had dropped the ball and now he was getting called on the carpet. "I have no excuse for my failure, Flag Officer Victor."

"Don't give me the squared away routine, son. I invented that routine. You not only failed in your duty, you profited from it as well. You are in serious trouble here, so here's how it's going to work. I ask you questions, you give me answers. If you lie, hold anything back, leave anything out, or refuse to answer, I have a prison cell reserved for you right next to your pal Jay Lee Hazard. Do you understand?"

"Yes, sir."

"Why was Seraphaz after the alien?"

"He received a coded transmission with the instructions."

"From who?"

"I don't know. He never shared that with me, sir."

"Why does he hate Chase Cadogan so much?"

"I've asked myself that same question many times. According to the captain, he only met Cadogan the one time when he reported injured, but Seraphaz already held a grudge toward him."

"Why?"

"He would never say, but during the search for the alien, I heard him mumble that Cadogan wouldn't ruin his plans again."

"What does that mean?" The Flag was interested now.

"I don't know, he thought the transmission had ended, so he didn't know I heard him. If I were to guess, Cadogan must have inadvertently interfered or ruined something Captain Seraphaz was working on. I don't know how that would be possible. Maybe Chase scored the winning point in a game he was betting on, I really have no idea."

"This grudge he has against Cadogan just doesn't make any sense." The Flag stood and began pacing behind his desk. He leaned over the desk and fixed Agent Black with a look that made him shiver. He said in a low voice, "You are going to tell me everything Captain Seraphaz has ever had you do and why, and then I am going to send you back to his ship and you will send me weekly reports about him."

"Sir, are you sure this is necessary?"

"I think something bigger is at play here, and it's the only way you get to stay out of prison, so he is never to find out that you are reporting directly to me. Do you understand?"

"Yes, sir."

For the next two hours, Agent Black answered the Flag's question, and when he was given thirty minutes for a lunch break, he knew the inquisition was just getting started.

+++++

Chase exited hyperspace above Q'Tann. He checked all of his sensors to make sure his arrival had gone undetected. The ship was close enough that he could see the battle raging, but far enough away that it had not yet been seen. He saw debris everywhere. "I can't believe the size of this battle," he mumbled.

There must be hundreds of destroyed ships out there. This battle has been going on for twelve days. While Chase flew toward Q'Tann, what was left of the Jalindi armada jumped into hyperspace. Chase thought it would be a good idea to set the *Longshot* transmitters to intercept and record as many transmissions as it could while he was in the system. If nothing else, at least he would leave with some valuable information.

Chase pinged the location Sym had left on the transmission and waited. He hoped she was ready, because even in stealth mode, the *Longshot* would not remain unseen for long. He felt exposed and time seemed to stand still with every second he had to wait. After what seemed like an eternity, the *Longshot* received a ping and Chase put the plan into action.

He landed the ship just outside the small settlement. He gathered all of his usual weapons for a hunt, put them in their proper holsters, and prepared to leave. The last item he grabbed was the remote Fixer built. He knew his friend had put the finishing touches on it before they reached Cibola and it was the key to the entire plan. He exited the ship and sealed it up. He crinkled his nose and thought, *This planet smells like dead zarack.* Then he took off at a run toward where Sym was being held.

Chase felt the cool night air breeze past his head while he ran. He went over the phrase that Sym had assured him was a terrible insult to the Qantarah while he ran. [*Hey, ugly. There is no honor in your family.*] He only hoped he could say it right. He stopped when he was in position behind a small dwelling across from where he thought Sym was located. He leaned over, put his hands on his knees and took several deep breaths. *That was only three kilometers. I need to start exercising again.*

He peered around the corner and saw a lone guard out in front of the door. *Sym's message said six guards. Where are the others?* He wiped the sweat from his neck, pushed down that lump in his gut that was telling him he was about to die, steadied himself, and yelled, [Hey, ugly. Your mother is a drunken noodle.]

The guards started laughing and replied, [Who is out there? Is that you, Nevtah? How much ale have you had to drink?]

Laughter was not the response he expected. *Dasnit, I knew I was gonna mess up that line.* He yelled out again, [Hey, ugly.] When the guard took a few steps his way, he rolled out of the cover and fired off two shots. The guard dropped and now he had the attention of the other five. Three arrived from the other side of the domicile while two had been on patrol and were now running toward his location from the other direction. *Great, I'm in a crossfire. At lease I'm wearing black.*

He took off running away from where Sym would be exiting the meeting chamber. His blaster was ready in his hand. Sweat was now rolling down his face and his collar was starting to feel damp. He stopped running, dove behind another habitat, peeked out and fired on the Qantarah that were chasing him. He hit one in the leg and watched him tumble to the ground. He took off running again. He could hear the shouts in the harsh language of his enemy and even though he had no understanding of the Qantaran language, he was pretty sure he got the gist.

[Come out and fight like a Qantarah, you coward,] the first pursuer yelled.

[We are under attack. Someone is trying to kill scientist Sym Triot!] another guard snarled into his comms.

[The assassin ran that way,] a third guard yelled. Then he turned to the fourth and said, [Nevtah, stand outside the dwelling. Make sure no one goes inside. If anyone is to kill the scientist, it will be our mighty Battle Conductor.]

[Yes, sir,] Nevtah replied, breaking off the chase and returning to guard duty, alert for more intruders.

Chase continued to run and he knew that time was not his ally. Soon, there would be too many Qantarah to run from. He holstered his weapon and pulled the remote from his pocket. He took cover behind a stone outcropping and hit the thrusters. He heard the

Longshot flare to life. The Qantarah stopped and looked around for the sound of the noise. Chase flew the ship right toward them and pressed the button to fire. The *Longshot* strafed the ground, hitting one of the Qantarah. The other two retreated.

[Where are those reinforcements?] one of the guards shouted while he ran.

Chase looped the ship around and flew it behind the meeting chamber. He brought it in for a less than smooth landing, destroying three of the small habitats. He pressed the button that would unlock the landing bay hatch and Sym emerged from the Meeting chamber. She ran the ten meters to the ship, quickly boarded, and closed the hatch. Chase fired up the thrusters and the *Longshot* took off again. He looped the ship around again and fired on Sym's habitat until it was a smoking crater in the ground.

[He's over here,] a harsh voice called out, and a moment later, blasterfire was whizzing by Chase's ear. He unholstered his blaster and returned fire, then ran for the nearest open space. Several Qantarah followed, and the *Longshot* now had a fighter tailing it. He thumbed the shields to life and made another pass, firing on the aliens chasing him.

"Sym," he said into his comms. "You're going to have to take the helm and you are going to have to engage the fighter on your tail. Can you do that?" He could hear the Qantarah closing in. He was going to run out of space to run soon.

"Sym is not sure," she replied.

"Just do your best. I can't run and fly the ship at the same time. As soon as you take care of the fighter, drop into the clearing and I'll meet you there." Before Sym could reply, Chase was tackled. He hit the gritty dirt hard, but used the momentum to roll over onto his attacker. He pressed his blaster into the alien's stomach and pulled the trigger. Charred fur and flesh filled his nostrils and more blasterfire erupted around him.

He dove over an old fence and came up firing with two blasters. The unexpected barrage slowed his pursuers and he sprinted for the *Longshot*. "Sym, is the fighter gone?" he wheezed while he ran.

"Sym did not engage. Sym could not find the fighter."

"Dasnit," he yelled, then took another deep breath while he ran. "Let's just hope he's not bringing any friends to the party."

"What is a party?"

"Never mind." Chase tripped and fell when a blaster bolt hit him in the leg. His boot took most of the hit, but he caught enough that he knew he would be limping for a while. He rolled onto his back and fired wildly. His gambit worked as two Qantaran bodies dropped before they reached him. He was still almost fifty meters from the ship and the aliens were gaining on him fast. He forced himself off the ground and holstered his blasters to run.

He took out the remote and began firing on the Qantarah with *Longshot*'s weapons. He was limping more than running at this point, and sweat mixed with blood trickled into his eye. He was not sure where the blood was coming from, so he pushed the question from his mind. He had other priorities to worry about until he was safely away from this planet.

"Open the landing bay," he said into his comms. He was trying not to use Sym's name because she was supposed to be dead. He was gasping for air, but he thought he just might make it until he heard the guttural language right behind him.

[Not so fast, human.] Chase felt a clawed hand grab his collar and the next thing he knew, he was on the ground. The Qantaran warrior hit him in the face three times before he got his leg around the alien's head and knocked him off. Chase tried to stand, but the injury to his leg and the head shots he had just taken caused him to stumble back to the ground.

The warrior growled a curse and drew his blade. He charged at the stumbling human. Chase rose to his feet in time to catch the warrior's knife hand. He fell back and held on to the alien's arm, sending the warrior sprawling to the ground behind him. He drew his own knife and slowly rose to his feet.

+++++

"Fixer, how is the test going?" Kat asked. She handed him a green fizzy and handed Stone a cup of jav. She walked over and put another cup of jav down in front of Dr. Kendall and took a sip of her own.

"We have coated the test shuttle. The bonding should be complete in two hours, Katalla Swift. Are you going to stay here this time or are you going back to Captain Bander's house to sleep over again."

Stone cracked up laughing and Dr. Kendall raised his head from his work in time to see Kat failing to hide the deep shade of red that covered her lovely face. "No, Fixer, the Captain has been redeployed, so I'll be here. Besides, it's Stone's turn to have some fun."

"Stone is having fun, Katalla Swift. He told me."

"True, buddy, but now it's time for some fun that involves loads of alcohol," Stone replied.

"How are the other tests going, Fixer?" Kat asked. She sat down on the edge of Dr. Kendall's desk and smiled when she noticed the Doctor staring at her posterior. "See anything you like, Doc?" she asked in a teasing tone.

"What? No, could you please not sit on my desk, Miss Swift." He busied himself in a datapad to try and hide his embarrassment.

"The xallodium wiring has not yet been finished, Katalla Swift. We need more information."

"We need a lot more information," Dr. Kendall added.

A young soldier hurried into the lab and said, "I have an urgent message for Katalla Swift."

Kat looked over to Stone and he shrugged his shoulders. She looked at the soldier and said, "I'm Katalla. What's this about?"

"One of the priestesses of Avalon said she had to speak to you. She said it was urgent."

She knew it was either Felicia or it was about Felicia, so she strode over to the soldier and asked, "Where can I take the transmission?"

"In the next room, ma'am. Please follow me." He spun on his heel and marched out of the lab with Kat right behind him. He led her to a transmission terminal and she was relieved to see Felicia's face waiting for her. "Here you go, ma'am," the soldier said before marching away.

"Felicia, hi. What's going on? What's so urgent?" Kat asked. She saw the look in the eyes of her cousin and asked, "Felicia, what's wrong?"

"He told me to wait five days before I contacted you, but I just couldn't wait any longer. I fear he's in great danger."

"Who?"

"I feel like I'm betraying him just talking to you now."

"Felicia, who?"

A frown unfolded and she said, "Chase. He told me to give you this message if he wasn't back in five days." She played the message for her cousin and when it was finished, she said, "And that was three days ago."

"Felicia, he went to Q'Tann alone? Why would he do that? Why would he not pick us up?"

"He said that you needed to finish a secret project, but I think it's because he didn't want to lose any of you."

"That's so selfish!" she yelled. A few heads rose from their work, but her glare sent them right back down. "He doesn't want to feel the pain of our loss, but it's okay for us to lose him? What was he thinking?"

"I do not know, Katalla, but I do know it is not quite as simple as you make it out to be. You and Fixer and even Stone mean everything to him."

"I know it's not that simple, but I'm furious," she growled. "And now, I have to try to see the Vanguard to let him know my friend may have just started the very war we had hoped to avoid."

"I will leave you to it, then. I will see you soon, cousin."

"Yes, I'm looking forward to it. Bye, Felicia." The screen went blank and Kat rushed back into the lab. She asked Dr. Kendall to get the Vanguard to come down and was told he was already on the way because it was time to see if the xallodium had bonded to the shuttle.

Vanguard Tobias entered the lab with Flag Officer Victor and they were flanked by a dozen men. Without preamble he asked, "Did it work, Dr. Kendall?"

A big smile filled the Doctor's face and he replied, "Yes, sir. Even better than we had hoped." He ran the gamut of tests for the Vanguard and the shuttle passed each one.

"Very good, Dr. Kendall. Well done to you and to Fixer. We'll start coating our ships right away."

"Are you sure, sir? It may be a little early for that," Dr. Kendall replied.

"We really have no choice, Doctor. Anyway, I trust you and Fixer."

"Thank you, sir. We'll begin at once. Miss Swift has something to share that she thinks you will find important."

Vanguard Tobias' eyebrow raised and he shot an expectant look at Kat. "Yes, Miss Swift?"

"Sir, Chase has gone to rescue Sym on Q'Tann."

"He what?" Vanguard Tobias could barely keep the shock out of his voice. He looked to the Flag and asked, "Did you know anything about this, Juel?"

"No, sir."

"No one did, Sir. I wasn't even supposed to know until he was back, but my cousin Felicia could not keep the secret from me any longer. Sym contacted him begging to be rescued. She used all the types of phrases that someone like Chase could never turn away from, including a threat to all life in the cluster."

"Do you think she was playing him?" Flag Officer Victor asked.

"I don't know, sir. It is possible she just doesn't want to die," Kat replied.

"If he gets caught, we're going to have big problems with the Qantarah," Vanguard Tobias said.

"We already have big problems with them. If he does retrieve the scientist, she may be of great use to us."

"Sym Triot will be able to make the xallodium wires. I cannot make the xallodium wires," Fixer said. "If we want better weapons, we need Sym Triot."

"Thank you, Fixer," Vanguard Tobias said with a kind smile. "Miss Swift, I would like to see the entire message he left you and hear more about this alleged threat. Please come with Juel and me." He asked politely, but she knew it was not a request. "As soon as Chase Cadogan is back in the Luminari Cluster I want him brought to me for debriefing, Juel."

"Yes, sir," the Flag replied. He spoke into his comms and returned his attention to the Vanguard. "It will be taken care of."

"Good. Let's go hear that message." He turned and left the room with Flag Officer Victor and Kat in step right behind him and his personal guard surrounding them.

+++++

The angry warrior charged while the *Longshot*'s weapons continued to spray the field and village with blaster bolts. By this point it was apparent that the only living beings in this area were Qantaran warriors. The village looked like a war zone. Several domiciles, including Sym's, had been destroyed. Fences and trees burned and there were over twenty Qantaran warriors dead. Still, Chase knew there would soon be more opposition than he and his ship could handle. Right now, however, Chase had to handle this one.

[I will kill you, human. Then my people will destroy your home.] The warrior brought the knife down in a tight arc.

Chase stumbled backwards. "I can't understand a word you're saying, but you're in my way." He brought his knife around and the alien jumped back. Chase pressed his advantage and kicked the warrior in the chest, knocking him back further.

[I will kill you like the honorless vermin you are!]The warrior threw his knife at Chase's midsection. Chase tried to dodge, but not before the knife ripped through his jacket and into his side. He cried out and the warrior charged.

Chase stumbled, but drew his blaster in time to shoot the warrior in the leg. Then a strong hand knocked the blaster from Chase's grip while they both tumbled to the ground. Chase pulled the knife out of his side and plunged it into the chest of the warrior while they rolled. Chase stood and kicked the dead warrior. He picked up his blaster and stumbled to the ship. The moment he was aboard, the hatch closed and the shields were activated.

Chase lumbered onto the bridge, sweaty, dirty, and bloody.

"Chase, you are injured," Sym cried.

"Yeah, but we need to get out of here before I can worry about it." He took the helm, smearing blood across the console and hit the thrusters. This was no gentle ascent like on Avalon. The *Longshot* raced into the stratosphere, leaving a patch of scorched earth in its wake. When the ship reached orbit, Chase noticed several Qantaran vessels heading his way. The battle with the Jalindi was over, but all of the defending vessels were still in orbit. He flew full speed at the enemy hoping to be able to make the jump to hyperspace before they could get a target lock on him.

"Sym, I need you on shields and sensors," Chase grunted. His vision was going dark around the edges and pain was threatening to take consciousness from him.

"Sym is here, Chase."

"When I give the signal, I want full power to the forward shields, then—" he was interrupted by a warning klaxon. Two fighters were on their tail and closing in. Chase fired two missiles at them. The first one hit, leaving nothing but a spreading debris cloud where the fighter had been. The second one missed and the fighter began to fire on the *Longshot*.

"Shields are holding," Sym called. Chase looped the *Longshot* and followed the maneuver with a tight spiral. The force of the move almost pushed him into unconsciousness. Fighting off the blackout he knew was coming, he banked hard to port and came around to see the fighter right before him. He fired another missile and was satisfied to see the fighter explode. The dogfight had cost them precious seconds.

Chase was no longer sure they could beat the Qantaran vessels to the hyperspace coordinates. He looked at Sym and yelled, "Strap yourself in. This is going to be close."

She did as instructed and checked the sensors. "Eight seconds to hyperspace," she said.

"Six seconds to weapons lock. Full power to forward shields, Sym," Chase replied.

Two seconds later, the lightning-like energy of the Qantaran weapons was streaking toward them. Chase juked and the first barrage missed. The second shot hit them dead on. Sparks flew across the bridge. "Main thrusters have been damaged and our sensor array is no more. Shields holding at nineteen percent," Sym said.

More lightning raced toward them, but Chase evaded the next salvo. A hyperspace window opened and they were gone. When the stars began to stretch out before them, he let out a weary sigh and slumped in his seat.

"Come. Let Sym look at your wounds."

He stood and Sym could see the blood smeared on the chair and the console. She laid a blanket out on the common room couch and Chase staggered over and fell into the couch. "The worst ones are on my leg and my side," he grunted.

"Well your head and neck also have deep... gash." She started to say something else, but stopped when his eyes slid shut [This human has bled for me twice now,] she said to herself.

She undressed him and cleaned all of his wounds. She used the extensive medical kit to the best of her ability and an hour later, all of Chase's wounds had been stitched or glued. She disposed of the medical waste and cleaned the blood left on the bridge. When that was finished, she allowed herself some sleep.

Two days later, the *Longshot* came out of hyperspace around Cibola. Chase flew toward the planet on maneuvering thrusters. "We should be there soon, Sym. I'm sure Vanguard Tobias and Flag Officer Victor will want to speak with you."

"Of this Sym has no doubt. How does Chase feel today? You slept... long."

"I'm hungry and I feel weak, but I've been hurt worse." He watched Cibola grow in the viewport and prepared for reentry.

"Does Chase have anything Sym should do?"

"You know what? Yeah. I intercepted a ton of communication around Q'Tor and Q'Tann. Do you think you can translate any of it? They might be encrypted. Just see what you can do."

"Sym will try."

Twenty minutes later Sym said, "Sym has broken the Qantaran encryption."

"Great. We can go over it later. Prepare for landing." His fingers flew over the controls and the ship touched down smoothly on the reinforced plating of the Cibola spaceport. "Now remember, it is imperative that the Qantarah not know you are here." He tossed her one of Kat's hooded jackets and a pair of mechanic's goggles. "Put these on," he said.

When the hatch opened, they were greeted by the Vanguard's honor guard. A lieutenant stepped forward and said, "Chase Cadogan, you and your friend are to come with us."

"What is happening, Chase?" Sym asked while he closed the landing bay hatch.

"Felicia gave Kat the vid too early and she overreacted," he replied. Sym cast a quizzical look at him, but there was no elaboration on the statement. He just trudged along with the soldiers next to him and she filed in right behind him. The soldiers ushered Chase and Sym into a waiting aircar.

"I'm not sure what's going on here, but I haven't done anything wrong," Chase said to the lieutenant.

He looked at Chase and said, "Vanguard Tobias disagrees. Flag Officer Victor has instructed us to quietly bring the two of you before the Vanguard the moment you were spotted inside the Cluster." He faced forward and the aircar continued toward the Capitol. By the time they arrived, Chase was fatigued. Every muscle in his body felt like they were on fire. *I really am out of shape*, he mused. They exited the aircar and were led through the nearly empty atrium of the Capitol Palace.

"Where is everyone?" Chase asked while they approached the lift tubes.

"The Flag thought it would be better if as few people as possible knew your friend was here," the lieutenant replied as they all stepped into the tube. The tube shot upward, but the passengers felt no acceleration.

When they stepped out of the lift tube, Flag officer Victor met them. "That will be all, Lieutenant," he said.

"Yes, sir," the lieutenant replied. He turned and got back on the lift tube with his men. When the door closed, Flag Officer Victor motioned for them to follow him.

"Been a busy man, haven't you, Chase?"

"You could say that," he replied.

"Vanguard Tobias would like a word with you." The Flag stepped past the two guards. Chase and Sym followed him into the executive meeting chamber. Chase was surprised when he saw Vanguard Tobias sitting at a table, speaking with Kat.

"Kat? What are you doing here?"

"Chase, thank Avalon you're okay." She rushed over to him, wrapped her arms around him and kissed him hard on the lips. Then she released him and slapped him hard across the face.

"Dasnit, Kat. What the—?"

"Don't you ever do that again. We're partners. You don't leave me behind. I make my own decision on what's too dangerous for me. Do you understand?"

"As entertaining as this is," Vanguard Tobias said. "We do have a lot of questions for Chase. You can get back to whatever that was when we are finished, Miss Swift."

Kat blushed and avoided the Vanguard's eyes. "Yes, sir," she said in almost a whisper, sitting down at the table.

Chase and Sym took their seats as well and Flag Officer Victor began to ask his questions. "First of all, we're glad you're back safely, but if you ever fly into enemy territory again without my authorization, even if you live through it, you'll spend the rest of your life in prison. Am I clear, Mr. Cadogan?"

"Yes, sir."

"Will Miss Triot be able to help us on the xallodium wiring project?"

Chase shrugged his shoulders and looked at Sym. She looked uncomfortable at the sudden attention, but she said, "Sym can do it. Will Fixer be there?"

The Vanguard looked to Chase and said, "Did you not ask her about this on the way back from Q'Tann?"

"I'm sorry, sir. I got beat up pretty good during the rescue, and after we entered hyperspace I was out cold until about an hour before we arrived."

"Chase was hurt bad saving Sym. Sym have to stitch and glue several injuries... and one deep stab wound Sym didn't fix all the way."

"Okay, we'll discuss Miss Triot's role in the Commonwealth with her while Chase gets checked out at the med-center. Should we start reserving a bed for you there, Chase?" Vanguard Tobias asked.

"Maybe, sir, but before I go, I have hours of stray transmissions that the *Longshot* picked up around Q'Tor and Q'Tann. I saw the end of the battle. The Jalindi withdrew with less than a hundred ships, and, by the looks of it, the Qantarah had less than two hundred left."

"Two hundred is still quite a bit, son," Vanguard Tobias said.

"Agreed, but is it enough to protect Q'Tor and invade the Cluster?"

"That's a good question, Cadogan," Flag Officer Victor replied.

"Maybe the answer is somewhere in those transmissions, sir. Sym has already broken the Qantaran encryption. Kat can lead a team to retrieve the communications and maybe we'll have some solid intelligence," Chase said.

"Agreed. Well done, Chase. Keep this up and I might have to put you on the payroll," Vanguard Tobias said.

"That might be a pay cut for me, sir," Chase said with a wry grin.

"It just may," he replied. "For now, you go get checked out. We'll make sure Sym gets vetted and reunited with Fixer. Kat can get the intel off the *Longshot* for us."

+++++

Two weeks later, Stone and Fixer were sitting in a crowded pub by the Cibola spaceport waiting for Chase and Kat to arrive. Music blared and the lights were dim. Patrons crowded around the long rectangular bar while wait staff weaved in between thirsty parties, navigating their way to the proper tables. A pretty Elysian girl wearing a top emblazoned with a rising sun placed a beer in front of Stone and a green fizzy in front of Fixer.

"We don't sell many of these," she said pointing to the soft drink.

"You will tonight," Stone replied. He flashed his most winning smile and asked, "Could you run us a tab, sweetheart?"

"I suppose," she said and then vanished into the crowd.

"Why is Chase late? Chase is never late. Katalla Swift is late sometimes, but not Chase," Fixer said, looking nervous.

Stone shrugged his shoulders and replied, "But who is Chase with right now?"

"Chase is with Katalla Swift and he's late," Fixer replied, not getting the point of Stone's question.

"That's right. Maybe Kat is making him late for some reason. Don't worry, Fixer. They'll be here soon."

"I hope so. I don't like to be outside at the spaceport without Chase."

"Don't worry, buddy. No one will bother you with me around," Stone replied. Fixer looked at his large friend and decided he was right. He relaxed a little and popped open his green fizzy.

"Starting without us, guys?" Chase said as he approached the table with Kat.

"Chase, you're late," Fixer said with a frown pasted on his face. "You said seven and now it's seven-forty. You are forty minutes late."

"I'm sorry, pal. I was busy getting something for you," he replied.

"Stone thought Katalla Swift made you late," he said. Then he realized Chase had something for him. His eyes lit up and he asked, "What did you get for me?"

"It's a gift from me and Kat."

Kat stepped forward and handed Fixer a small bag. He swiped it from her and tore the bag open. A grin spread across his face and he held the gift high in the air. "You found my screwdriver." He turned to Stone and said, "Chase promised he would find my screwdriver and he did." He hugged Kat and smiled at Chase.

"Kat helped me. I never would have gotten it if not for her," Chase said.

"What's so important about that old screwdriver?" Stone asked.

"My dad gave it to me with my wrench," Fixer replied, pulling the wrench from his pocket and still grinning ear to ear.

"Well I'm happy you finally have it, Fixer," Kat said, taking her seat at the table. The waitress returned and Chase ordered a beer for himself and an ale for Kat.

"So where was this screwdriver? Why was it so hard to get?"

"Because Mags Bishop stole it from him."

"Mags is one mean son of a jocawolf. How did you get that back from him?"

"I offered to buy it along with all of Fixer's other belongings that he stole, but he laughed at me and walked away. I tried a few times, but he wouldn't budge."

"So?"

"So, I had Kat distract him while I broke into his ship and took it along with an interesting book that also belonged to Fixer."

"What's so interesting about it?" Stone asked. The waitress returned and placed the ale in front of Kat and handed the beer to Chase with a seductive smile. She looked back over her shoulder when she walked away. Kat lifted her glass and with a soft clink, touched it to Chase's beer bottle. Then she brought her glass to her lips and took a long sip.

Fixer had gone silent. He was completely engrossed with his screwdriver. He had taken it apart, revealing three pieces, and his wrench was also in pieces on the table. "What are you doing Fixer?" Kat asked.

"I'm getting ready to see my dad. He will talk to me, but I can't talk back." He continued laying out the pieces and then began to put them back together. "They're a set. The wrench and the screwdriver are a set. When they are together, my dad can talk to me."

A commotion by the door took Chase's eye off Fixer's project. A large angry man was pushing his way through the crowd. "Where is it?" He yelled. "Where is it?" He stopped in front of Chase and yelled above the music, "You stole something from me, Cadogan. Did you think I wouldn't find out?"

Chase looked up at Mags and said, "If I were you, I'd leave now." Most of the crowded bar had stopped what they were doing to watch the brewing showdown. The lively music continued to play, but the atmosphere was suddenly tense.

"Not until you give me back what you stole from me." Three men fanned out behind him and Chase imagined they thought they were intimidating.

"I didn't steal anything from you, Mags. Now get out of here. You're killing my buzz."

"Not until you return my property," he said in a voice that sounded like a growl.

Chase was up so fast that Mags along with several onlookers flinched. "Your property?" he yelled and got in Mags' face. "Your property?" Just then Fixer finished putting the pieces of the two tools together, and a small holographic face flared to life just above the table.

"Hello Fixer," the floating head said. The face looked similar to Fixer's and the man had a kind smile. "Your mother hates it when I call you Fixer. She's always telling me to call you Freddy, but she doesn't realize what a genius you are." Fixer touched what used to be the screwdriver's handle and the recording stopped.

"That's my dad, Katalla Swift," he said, grinning from ear to ear, unaware of the tension building around him.

"I saw that, Fixer. Let's watch the rest later. Can you put that away for me?"

"Okay, Katalla Swift."

Chase took a step forward and bumped Mags. "Please, tell me again how that's your property." When there was no response Chase said, "That's what I thought, now get out of here."

"Get out of my face," Mags yelled and shoved Chase back. Chase retaliated by punching Mags in the face. He stumbled into the next table, spilling all the drinks. Kat and Stone were on their feet, while Mags' three friends moved forward.

The scene threatened to spiral out of control when a lawman stepped in between the two parties and asked in not quite a yell, "What's going on here?"

"Yeah, Mags! What's going on here?" Chase repeated with an edge to his voice.

"This isn't over, Cadogan," Mags replied. He pushed through the crowd and out of the pub. The lawman, convinced a brawl had been averted, left the premises as well.

Chase looked over to the patrons whose drinks he spilled and said, "I'm sorry about that, guys." He called the Elysian waitress over, handed her a hundred heskar chip and said, "Next three rounds for this table are on me." She smiled and took their drink orders, and Chase leaned over and said, "Again, I'm sorry, guys. I hope this makes up for it." They nodded their thanks and Chase sat back down.

"Now, Fixer, let's see what your dad has to say," Kat said with a curious look in her eyes.

Fixer fished the device out of his pocket and put it back on the table. "Here it is, Katalla Swift. You are about to see my dad."

The image flared to life again and picked up where it left off. Fixer was enthralled by the image as it spoke. "If you're seeing this message, it means I'm dead and you've gotten smart enough to figure out how to put this playback device together. Fixer, what happened to your mother and me was no accident. We were murdered."

"No!" Fixer yelled out, drawing puzzled looks from some of the inebriated customers of the pub. Fixer paused it and a tear rolled down his cheek.

"It's okay, Fixer," Kat said with a sympathetic frown and put her arm around him.

"It's not okay, Katalla Swift. Someone killed my parents," he replied.

"Keep playing the message, Fixer. Maybe your dad will leave a clue, so we can help you find whoever did this," Chase said.

"Okay, Chase. I'll keep playing it," he replied and turned it back on.

"You have to understand, Fixer, I owned a very successful company, P&D Designs, and there were powerful people who wanted what we had."

"Fixer, pause that," Stone said. He looked over to Chase and Kat and said, "P&D? As in the hyperdrive manufacturers?"

"That's them," Chase replied. "I'm starting to get a bad feeling about this. Some of this is mentioned in the book we found as well." A somber look crossed his face and he said, "Fixer, hit play."

The image flared to life again when Fixer hit the button. "Governor Giovani will stop at nothing to take our company, which is why we're sending you away, to keep you safe." The face disappeared and a holographic document floated above the table. "This document shows you to be the sole owner of P&D Designs if your mother and I should be killed. There is also a physical copy hidden in the lining of your book. Tell no one about this, Fixer. This information could get you killed. If you have friends you trust, see if they will help you get back what belongs to you. Your mother and I love you very much, son. Goodbye."

"Wow, that was intense," Kat said and downed the last of her Ale. The waitress was by with another a few moments later, and Kat picked it up and brought it to her lips.

"Right now, P&D is run by a man named Arman Satrap. I always assumed he owned it," Chase said.

"Mags is known to receive a lot of work from P&D," Stone said. "He was probably paid to keep this info from Fixer."

"Well paid if he was willing to cause a scene like that to get it back," Chase added with a nod.

"But why keep it. Why not destroy it?" Kat asked.

"Maybe there will be some more answers in the book," Chase replied. "Come on, let's get out of here. Looks like we've got our next job."